LEFT ON MAIN STREET

A NOVEL

BY

STEVEN JAY GRIFFEL

Copyright © Steven Jay Griffel 2022
All Rights Reserved

This is a work of fiction. Names, characters, places, and incidents either are the product of the author's imagination or are used fictitiously, and any resemblance to actual persons, living or dead, businesses, companies, events, or locales is entirely coincidental.

For permission to reproduce selections from this book, write to: info@staythirstymedia.com – Atten: Permissions

ISBN: 979-8-218-08853-8

STAY THIRSTY PRESS

An Imprint of Stay Thirsty Publishing

A Division of

STAY THIRSTY MEDIA, INC.

staythirstypublishing.com

Books by Steven Jay Griffel

The Ishi Affair
Grossman's Castle
Grand View
The Deadline
Forty Years Later

LEFT ON MAIN STREET

A NOVEL

BY

STEVEN JAY GRIFFEL

Dare of a Lifetime

Lainey Roth

Though Lainey had once loved her husband, she favored their current arrangement: him, six feet below ground; her, way up above, in sole dominion of their top-floor, three-bedroom, East Seventy-Third Street co-op.

Twelve years a widow, Lainey adored her quietly impressive domain, daily relishing its beamed ceilings and crown moldings, its polished wooden floors and perfectly faded Persian carpets. She also loved its wide, wraparound terrace that provided a glorious panorama of Central Park and its tall windows that measured each day with perfectly captured sunrises and sunsets. More, her home was near the best East Side boutiques and cafés and only a short walk to the magnificent Park East Synagogue, where her best friends congregated. Despite its manifold advantages and charms, she'd proposed to gift her son the multi-million-dollar apartment as soon as he married and made her a grandmother.

Lainey did not see her proposal as manipulative. She knew her son (the unmarried novelist) was onboard with her desire for grandchildren, differing only in terms of timeline. Lainey wanted results *soon;* thirty-two-year-old Barry was okay with *sooner than later.* This did not sit well with Lainey, who already trailed by fourteen on the Upper East Side Grandma leaderboard. And while Lainey had no reasonable hope of overtaking first place (the leader was an orthodox Jew with no time for Malthusian Theory), at fifty-two she'd be the youngest and most svelte grandmother in her set if she had a grandchild in the next few years, which, for Lainey, would be a victory of sorts.

Barry Roth

In the ensuing years (and despite his mother's best-laid plans), Barry produced only books, not babies. His first novel, *The Secret Loves of Baron Rothschild*, was the splashiest debut of the year and earned him a six-figure advance on his next book. Unfortunately, Barry's reprise of the Baron's exploits (set in America, where the Baron traveled under the pseudonym "Barry Roth") was a critical disappointment; so much so, Barry wondered if his meteoric rise had spent his allotment of literary fuel.

Barry took his reversal personally, and it wasn't certain he would recover. For a long while he did a lot more talking than writing, telling anyone who would listen that his early acclaim had been an impossible standard to bear. Some friends appreciated his honesty, but those who were yet unpublished thought he was full of shit and told him so.

"Your first book got published by one of the Big Five. You got an advance large enough to be deposited. GRANTA included you in their hallowed list of Thirty Under Forty—and you're complaining? Man, you either have brass balls or no feelings for the rest of us peons still beating on the door."

Barry thought his high school buddy Chris was mostly right. He knew he could be brassy and ballsy but had no idea how to excuse his behavior without referring to the residual influence of his overbearing father and the continual harping of his interfering mother. And really, who gave a shit about any of that? Everyone was in the same boat. Everyone was emotionally bootstrapped to some degree of dysfunction.

Could he really blame his double-stranded helix from hell for his limitations? He couldn't. It was a trap. For as soon as he started to confess the lingering effects of his father's crippling criticisms, or his frustration with his mother's procreational goals, someone would point out his silver platter of advantages: his good looks, his private education, the thousand and one ways he'd always been praised and indulged. In fact, his friends would get so worked up in their response to his pathetic "woe is me," Barry decided to lay low and suck it up.

Lainey Roth

Sometimes I just want to slap him. Thirty-six and world weary! Give me a break.... My dead husband Bert could be a difficult bastard, but the man had some serious spine. I wish Barry had more of his dad's backbone.

Still, it kills me to see him so unhappy. I really think he needs to be married. He needs to care for someone other than himself ... focus his energies outward. I've tried to set him up with my friends' daughters or nieces—all beautiful girls—but he doesn't seem to care. It's like the rules of life don't apply to him.

Maybe it's my fault. Maybe I went too far with all that "Follow your own star" and "Be your own man" crap. I mean, we're social animals. We're meant to live together and procreate. If we lived in a tiny shtetl, like my great-grandmother, I'd pay a *shadchan* to find him a nice girl. But we don't. Fact is, I live in New York City and have only one living link in my chain.

Do I focus on Barry too much? My friends think so. They say I focus on him as a way of avoiding my own growth.

Some say (behind my back) that I live my life through Barry because my own life doesn't amount to much. What a bitchy thing to say! I have a rich life—and not because Bert left me loaded. I'm rich because I have great hopes and an exquisite fantasy life. And, just between us girls, my hopes are not so hopelessly fantastical that they can't come true. In fact, I can achieve almost anything I want—and all by myself—though I could really use Barry's help in some cases.

There you go, wailing away about my focus on Barry! ... Look, I'm not the first mother to take an active interest in her son's life. Besides, cut me some slack. I have one child and he's a little needy. I mean, he's perfectly healthy and brilliant, as everyone knows, but he could use a little seasoning, if you ask me.... Yes, I know, maturing is part of the natural process, but it's taking him much longer than I expected.... I get it, I shouldn't compare him to my friends' sons—but they're all happily married with children! Besides, I have a mother's eyes. I can see that he isn't happy, and I know he'll be happy when he finds his true love.... Yes, I know, I proclaimed perfect happiness when I married Bert. But I was so young! How could I know what a controlling asshole he'd be? ... Barry's different. He's old enough to know what he wants in a woman. God knows, he's dated half the eligible women in Manhattan.

"How can they all be wrong? You must have liked one of them."

"I like them all," he said with a straight face. "I have a hundred girlfriends. What are you so worried about?"

I hate when he's flippant. It makes me feel stupid and unimportant.

"A hundred is not as good as one."

"Actually, it's a hundred times better."

"Oh yeah? Name one girlfriend. Name one woman you care about."

He paused, spluttered, then gave up.

"So, I don't have a special girlfriend. It's not the end of the world."

There was something in his eyes that told me I'd broken through. That he'd finally heard me.

"Honey, you shouldn't be alone."

"You're alone, and you love it. You're the queen of your castle and couldn't be happier."

"Actually, I could—and so could you."

I hadn't planned what I'd say next … but it would change our lives, though not exactly as we might have guessed.

"Trust me, when you find love, you'll find your passion for writing again. And then you'll have your next book—and many more after that. Mark my words. It will begin with love."

Barry Roth

I couldn't tell my mother the truth. That I'd revealed myself to the world and had been rejected. That I was damaged goods. That love, marriage, babies might not be in my future. How could I say that to my hopeful mother?

But it was the truth. And I had only myself to blame.

You see, I didn't start out fearlessly as some writers do. I was knock-kneed with self-doubt. Eventually, I overcame my fears by creating an illusion of myself, a fictional uber me: Barry Roth inflated to Baron Rothschild. With that conceit in place, I let 'er rip: empowering the boundlessly uninhibited Baron with my every desperate yearning, my every fantasy, my every dark-diving perversion.

It worked! Readers lapped it up. Success was mine! ... I had it all—so long as I lived large in my imagination. But I couldn't leave well enough alone. I needed to know that I was as lovable as the Baron. My answer came with the public response to my second novel ... for when I shaped the disguised Baron as a character more like my real self, my wax-wings melted and my sales and fragile ego plummeted. I had my answer: America loved the Baron; but Barry, the Jewish Mini-Me? Not so much.

I should have left bad enough alone. I should have listened to my ancient agent, Lois Saperstein.

"How many times do I have to tell you? Forget the critics and the peanut gallery. You can't win a public pissing contest. Even if you think you've won, all anyone will remember is you standing alone, shaking your dick."

Lainey Roth

Barry wasn't doing much of anything. As far as I knew, he wasn't even dating. When my suspicion was confirmed, I knew he needed a break. Time to get out of Dodge, as Bert used to say. My first thought was to suggest a trip abroad, my treat. I knew he liked castles, so I looked into several European river cruises that specialized in tours of the kind of ancient castles he liked to draw as a boy. But all the marketing for those trips showed older couples holding hands, so I thought he might feel out of place and bored. I considered exotic destinations like China and Russia, but I knew that for all his facility with English, Barry isn't a language person and would struggle by himself. I thought I had the perfect answer when I thought of Israel: exotic, historic, and filled with unmarried Jewish women who spoke English.

Almost immediately I began fantasizing about Barry and a beautiful, young Israeli woman: shopping in Old Jerusalem ... sitting at a beachside café in Eilat ... climbing the steps to the top of Masada.... I was loving this romantic reverie until the young couple in my mind's eye married and moved into a concrete settlement in the West Bank and began raising a brood of olive-skinned kids, largely unaware of my existence. I imagined visiting every six months or so, bringing presents to remind my grandchildren who I was, my well-meaning daughter-in-law directing the little ones: "Children, this is your Grandma Lainey. Don't you remember her? Give her a kiss."

With a scream and a shudder, I banished the idea of Barry living seven time zones beyond my grandmotherly reach. I wanted my son to stretch his wings, not fly the coop.

***

Don't ask how I found out that Barry had stopped seeing his therapist. Suffice to say, if my cousin's daughter's girlfriend wasn't Dr. Shapiro's receptionist, I'd still be in the dark. But thank God I have my sources, for as soon as I'd guessed Barry's darkening mood, I threw my plan into high gear.

Okay, perhaps I didn't have a plan, per se, at least not a fully articulated one, but I had a basic idea along these lines: I had to convince Barry that he needed a change ... not just a vacation, but a temporary relocation (somewhere in the continental USA), where he could reset his compass, find his confidence, and ready himself for the adult world of marriage and fatherhood. That's it. It was vague, I know, but it came together so quickly, it was hard not to see God's hand in the affair.

Here's what happened: I work at the Manhattan Landlords Association and for this I have dearly departed Bert to thank. You see, Bert fancied himself a real-estate mogul, which he wasn't, I assure you. His portfolio was worth several mil, but it represented a dozen, low-income housing projects—all profitable because Bert's superintendents worked extremely hard to make substandard repairs or to avoid them altogether. Bert paid one fine in ten and ignored the others.

My Bert loved playing the role of the bigshot, the big *macher*, as we say in Yiddish. When asked what he did for a living, he'd say, "Nothin'. I'm in real estate," implying that New York real estate was easy pickings for a clever guy like himself.

Way deep down, Bert was clinically superficial. But below that, if you kept digging, you'd find a conscience, a shiny little thing buried in the bog of his shady experience.

One day, during a rare rising of his conscience, Bert visited the office of the Manhattan Landlords Association, where he was a disreputable member of long standing. But on this day, he was something new and better. Feeling the chastening effects of his ascending angels, he stood proudly before a gathered audience and announced his pledge to work every Friday afternoon in whatever capacity was deemed helpful, requesting only the symbolic salary of one dollar per annum.

Color me dubious, but I saw Bert's pro bono generosity as just another ruse to disguise his scofflaw stink. As it turned out, I was half right. Bert's higher lights were genuine, but low-wattage benefactions. In this case, he was hedging his bets, hoping a few hours of Friday philanthropy would en-

courage God to whitewash his many transgressions.
And then he was gone, and it was quiet. Bert's sudden death shocked everyone. Like many men, he'd been on a regimen of cholesterol and blood pressure meds, but his doctors hadn't issued any dire warnings. Barry and I dealt with his loss in our separate ways.

With Bert gone, I had a lot of time and quiet space to myself. I also had a lot of money. Not oodles, but more than enough. Bert left me the apartment, his retirement fund, the stocks, and the housing projects. I kept everything, except for the projects, which I sold as soon as I could. One day, two months after the final papers had been signed, I ran into Mildred Graber, the main receptionist at the Manhattan Landlords Association. We had met several times before and she asked how I was doing. When I confessed that I was looking for ways to fill my long hours, she suggested I take Bert's place as the organization's Gal Friday. She said I could work however long and hard as I liked. There were plenty advocacy groups and even a tenants' rights committee. It sounded perfect, and it was, though I committed to Wednesdays as a way of breaking up my long week.

Over the years, I developed a special expertise in sub-leasing arrangements. Many people wrote to our organization from all over the world, inquiring about apartments to lease for months, or even years, at a time. In some cases, they offered their own residence as a swap. I received one such email from a woman in the Midwest who wanted a year's lease on a nice Manhattan apartment in a reasonably quiet neighborhood. As quid pro quo, she offered her own home, a half-acre, late-Victorian beauty, with white picket fence, flowering bushes, and a shady wraparound veranda, based on the dozen photographs she included. She also added a personal note that struck me: "To really know a place, you have to live there long enough to vote, at least once."

Barry Roth

My mother handed me an envelope filled with photographs. I looked at each one and then shrugged my shoulders to conceal my excitement. The house was beautiful, purty as a postcard. I pictured myself sitting on the front veranda, sipping something sweet and strong, nodding to all the passersby as if I were already one of their own. Of course, I was jumping the gun. All I could see in the photos was a house and its green, well-tended property. I knew nothing about the town and little about the state, other than it was in the Midwest. But thank God for Google. There was only one town in the state called Three Corners. Surprisingly, small as it was, it had some notable attributes and even one claim to fame, which was a sort of scary claim, from my point of view, but I think that's what attracted me. You see, I'm not naturally brave or adventuresome. I won't cross Central Park alone after dark. I could not have written about my lusts and fears without the Baron as a fictional mask. But where had my real-life timidity got me? Thirty-six years old. Tapped out of ideas. No woman in my life—other than my mother. And then Three Corners came out of nowhere. Well, not exactly nowhere. It came from the place where my father had worked, and now my mother ... as if they were conspiring to send their brilliant but slightly nebishy son an opportunity, the dare of a lifetime.

America's Most Conservative Town

Alice Bouchet

Some people know instinctively to say *Boo-SHAY,* but most who visit Three Corners Americanize the pronunciation of my family name in the crudest way: *BUTCH-it.* However unintentional, the slight has always rankled me. Now on the cusp of sixty, I've decided to own my real feelings and to make consequent changes, which is why I wrote to the Manhattan Landlords Association about sub-leasing an apartment.

I was born in Three Corners and have lived there all my life. I'd like to be buried there, in the plot that has been readied for me, near my parents and dead ancestors. But before that first spadeful of dirt plops on my coffin, I want to see a little more of the world. I've been as far as St. Louis and Kansas City, and while they are both impressive, compared with Three Corners, they struck me as much the same pie, just larger slices. I want to see the greater world, in all its exotic and strange glory. I've read that New York City is the whole world in a concentrate form. Given my limited resources and tentative health, I think living there awhile is my best option.

Barry Roth

I looked at the situation every which way. *What do I have to lose?* Worst-case scenario: I'd return to New York and live with Lainey until I could return to my own apartment.

"What's the woman's name?"

"Which woman?"

"The woman who owns the house. The woman who wants to swap with me."

"Alice Bouchet."

"*Boo-SHAY*. I didn't expect that."

My mother let it slide.

"She knows I live on the Lower East Side?" I asked.

"She does."

"She knows it's funky town?"

"She knows you live on the top floor of a nice, five-story building in a colorful neighborhood."

"Colorful."

"That's how I described it."

"Lainey, Charleston is colorful. The Lower East Side is something altogether different."

"She seems like an educated woman—and sharp too. She knows what's what. She has the internet."

"If you say so."

Lainey turned to face me, a movement meant to convey full-disclosure. "I'm not putting anything over on her. I like her. I want this to work for both of you."

I was definitely interested. I needed a change.

"So, if I'm interested, what are the next steps?"

"In another day or so, I'll send each of you two copies of the contract. You'll each sign both, return one, keep the other for your records."

"That's it?"

"That's it. Easy-peasy. I have the written pre-approval from the owner of your building. Alice is the sole proprietor of her home, so no other approval is needed there."

"Simple enough."

"It is, if all the paperwork is handled correctly."

"But it's weird," I said, looking away. "It's like I'm moving into her life and she's moving into mine."

"For god's sake, you're not switching bodies. You're just exchanging where you hang your hat and go to sleep."

I turned hard to face her. "Oh, Lainey, it's so much more than that."

Alice Bouchet

Other than Emily Schnyder, no one really understands my French soul. My great-great-grandfather was François Bouchet, an army colonel born in France. I don't recall the story, but I know he met and married an English army nurse from Devonshire, where they lived for several years before coming to America.

I'm the great-great-granddaughter of our town's greatest man. I'm also the owner and director of Freedom Hall: the amber of our town's memory and also its living heart. There is a letter in the Hall's archives from General George Long, West Point graduate and silent architect of the Vicksburg siege, expressing his fervent hope that my great-great-grandfather (then living in Devonshire with his wife) would accept the post of Commander at the military college Long was building in his own name to preserve his legacy. How General Long knew my great-great-grandfather is lost to history, but the letter expressed his desire that my great-great-grandfather and his wife Mary would be present to welcome the school's freshman class in the Fall. The letter, dated February 1869, offered specific terms of compensation, which were impressive for the day, even accounting for my great-great-grandmother's expected service as the college's nurse. The archives do not include my great-great-grandfather's acceptance of Long's offer. What we do know is that by the time my great-great-grandparents arrived, François was known as Frank and Mary was unhappy, already longing for the graces of European life they'd left behind.

Three Corners did not yet exist. Long Military Institute was conceived as a model of self-sufficiency: commissary, barracks, classrooms, mess and cafeteria, infirmary, small auditorium, arsenal, muster grounds, recreation green, gardens and farm lands, officer house, and the comparatively grand, offsite residence for the Commander and his family.

As a thwart against the noise and unvarnished manners of the military college, Mary named her new home Haven House and assumed an air of European superiority, a combination of Franco and Anglo affectations that were immediately met with complaints and sneers from the junior officers. As her Frenchiness was the more obvious of her airs, it was derided more emphatically. Eventually, the Colonel (who appreciated the situation) offered his wife a compromise:

"Mary, you are my best soldier because you sacrifice the most. Let us embrace our old habits, but just us two ... and behind drawn blinds."

And so, there was born in Haven House a tradition of covert cultural piety. Behind closed doors, my great-great-grandmother practiced her French language skills until her speech and comprehension excelled. In time she also became a competent French cook. According to her journal, the Colonel liked his beef, bourguignon and his coq, au vin. When winter winds shivered the windows of Haven House, husband and wife read the untranslated novels of Balzac and Hugo before a blazing fire. In romantic moods, they sometimes danced the gavotte to a remembered tune. But in public, Mary never muttered so much as a "Oui."

Over the years the George Long Military Institute grew in scope and enrollment until it could no longer function efficiently as an isolated, self-dependent community. As its needs became known, a collier, smithy, butcher and baker were the first of a dozen skilled artisans to set up their shops on the wide path that ran south from Haven House to the area's only main road, a mile away. Not surprisingly, the street was named Washington, after the president whose portrait hung in the main lobby of the school. Eventually, two other streets angled off the main boulevard like a pair of wings: Adams and Jefferson. (Eventually, *Washington* would be referred to as *Main* by the locals.) A grassy common developed at the confluence of the three streets, and it was there that the Courthouse was built when the town was incorporated and officially named Three Corners. The town's military history and staunch patriotic airs are still its greatest defining characteristics.

Barry Roth

"Lainey, you do know that you're sending me to Crazytown, USA."

"I'm not sending you anywhere. You googled the place. You found out all you needed to know. You signed the contract."

"I did, and I don't regret it. I'm just saying that Three Corners sounds certifiable."

"Then why are you going?"

"I need a change."

"I agree."

"I need something to shake up my life."

"I know. I hope Three Corners does the trick."

"But it feels like a trap. Like I'm walking into the lion's den."

"Why would you say that?"

"Did you read the article I sent you? *Three Corners: Nation's Most Conservative Town.*"

"Oh that. That's just local politics."

"Lainey, people show their most honest selves in politics."

"You going to declare yourself a flaming lefty?"

"I'm not a flaming lefty. I'm a progressive democratic socialist."

"Oh, you'll fit right in," she said laughing. "You going to change your name?"

"No. I don't want to lie. Anyway, my name is not a label."

"I'd guess Jew."

"You're a New Yorker. If you lived in Osh-Kosh and never met a Jew, you would not automatically assume that a person named *Roth* is Jewish."

"So, you're going to lie."

"No. I'll just be as anonymous and evasive as I can."

"But why?"

"I want to fit in, at least on the periphery, so I can get to know the place. I don't want to be an outsider."

"Don't kid yourself. It's a small town. And you're moving into its grandest and most famous home. You'll arouse curiosity—and suspicion—as soon as you arrive."

Alice Bouchet

Though Three Corners' history is largely marked by the reigns of its college's Commanders, I prefer to think of my inheritance in matrilineal terms: link by link, each Commander's wife teaching her daughter the importance of self-reliance, critical thinking, and French culture. Of course, generational context is always changing and mothers are individuals; as a result, women's progress throughout my family's history (and in general) is hardly a straight line. It zigzags and backtracks, depending way too much on the fathers and brothers in charge, especially when their authority was unquestioned.

***

For a while, a black man was our President and I thought the country was headed in a positive direction. And then we almost had a woman President and I was excited beyond expression. But then the worst kind of man—venal and stupid and aggressive—won instead, much to the joy of almost everyone in Three Corners, men and women alike. Things got worse from there. That's when I knew I needed a change and decided on New York City.

There are many things on my New York bucket list but trying new foods is near the top. I may be a decent French cook, but my palate is essentially parochial. There are many well-known foods I've never tasted, exotic delicacies by Three Corners' standards. For example, I've never had soul food. I'm not even sure what it is, besides fried chicken. I have a sense of what *kosher* means, but I have no idea what Jewish people eat. And this new trend I've read about—*fusions*. How exciting! Like smashing culinary atoms! Korean-Spanish, Portuguese-Chinese, Mexican-Indian ... my lord, the possibilities are endless ... and I can enjoy them all in New

York—like an international gourmand!

Of course, I want to take my time; live and learn at a leisurely pace. That's why I took the new apartment for a year. A wise person once told me, "To really know a place, you have to live there long enough to vote, at least once." I think that's brilliant. I want to learn about New York politics. I want to see American politics from a New York point of view. And, if I'm being entirely honest, I want to stick a black fly in Three Corners' perfectly white ointment.

Barry Roth

Am I running from the fire or towards it? Really, I don't know. For sure, I'm leaving the cultural capital of the world for a tiny bastion of conservative belief. Some might say I'm going from the godless to the god-fearing. Damned if I know which is worse.

For sure, things will be different. Three Corners has fewer than a thousand souls scattered over three main streets and maybe one square mile. I'll probably meet half of them in the first few weeks. Try doing that in New York, which has nearly nine million people, six thousand miles of road, a thousand bridges, six hundred miles of coastline, and a dozen rivers. I know all this because I just looked it up. But I also know that most New Yorkers feel happy and secure within the familiar precincts of their own neighborhood, surrounded by a dozen other, less-familiar neighborhoods. This special combination of familiarity and anonymity has always appealed to me. Which is why I'm concerned about living in Haven House, at the top of Main Street, which is not only the town's northern terminus but also its highest point. Alice Bouchet's bedroom—soon to be mine—is on the top floor.

People will feel me looking down on them. And, for better or worse, they will be looking up at me, suspiciously.

Raison d'être

Allen Briggs

I'm not sure which hurt worse, Alice saying she was going to New York or the casual way she said it—as if it didn't affect me personally. But that's on me, I suppose. For all the conversations we've had in fifty years, I never told her how I really feel about her. Of course, she knows she can trust me. I'm her closest friend, besides Emily Schnyder (the young girl she raised), so if Alice wants me and Emily to pick up the slack at Freedom Hall while she's gone, then that's the way it will be.

I don't think New York will be too big for Alice, even if she is a small-town girl. I never once saw her flustered, though she came mighty close six years ago when her father and brothers died and the future of the college seemed uncertain, to put it kindly. I asked her then what she thought would happen to Three Corners. She said she didn't know (even though we both knew she was already working on her plan to save our town). She said the college had been the town's *raison d'être* for a hundred and forty years. I asked what the French-sounding words meant and she told me: *reason for being*. I liked the phase, so I asked her to write the words on a piece of paper. Not long after, I had the phrase elegantly tattooed on my chest, right above my heart: my own secret reason for being. I figured I'd eventually declare my feelings for Alice and if I got tongue-tied, I could lift my shirt and use my only French as a conversation starter.

I've had these thoughts about Alice since we were kids.

We grew up together in Three Corners and remain close in age—which, I just realized, is a dumb thing to say. But I never was the smart one, not like Alice. She was always tops in class and, for my money, the prettiest girl. I had a crush on her since kindergarten. I used to tease her—toss pebbles, call her funny names—but my courtship went unrequited. It seems she liked me well enough, but like a pal.

I never pushed it. I should have, but I always pretended she wasn't special to me.

But some hearts need only one good spark to beat hotly. For me, that spark came the day she asked me to go to the prom. I hadn't asked anyone else and I might have skipped it altogether if she hadn't stopped me one day after school and said matter-of-factly, "Allen, you and I are the only unpaired seniors left. Maybe we should be each other's date—for the sake of convenience."

I've spent a lifetime believing she meant to convey more to me than those mere words. But nothing ever changed between us ... and here we are, both of us nearing sixty.

Come to think of it, she's not even here. She's somewhere in New York, where I can't protect her, should she happen to need me, which isn't likely. Afterall, she's the one who preserved the legacy of our military college. She's the one who singlehandedly saved Three Corners.

You see, only Alice understood that the college had been slowly dying ... that while other military schools were marching in step to the new digital age, Long Military Institute remained stuck in yesteryear's protocols and traditions: a giant, sluggish anachronism. Only Alice saw that the college's outdated curriculum and refusal to admit female cadets would prove costly. And she was right on all counts. In our part of the country, more modern and inclusive military colleges had been attracting most of the cadet business for years. So, it was no real surprise when we learned that the college's budget and bottom line were hopelessly out of whack. We both hoped something might be done by way of alumni fundraising or revamping the college's curriculum and admission policy ... but tragedy struck unexpectedly, forcing Alice herself to make the necessary changes.

Within the same calendar year, fifty-year-old Alice lost her elderly father, Colonel Karl Bouchet, former commanding officer of Long Military Institute, who died at his desk of a stroke; his son, Colonel Daniel Bouchet, Long Institute's commanding officer, died in what was officially labeled a local traffic accident; Major Joseph Bouchet, the younger son (and Alice's favorite brother), died a particularly tragic death from friendly fire in Syria. The old colonel's wife, Kate Michelle, had died four years earlier; neither of their sons, Daniel and Joseph, ever married.

The sudden loss of all her family was a terrible blow for Alice. Still, she did not wallow in misery for she understood the great responsibility placed on her shoulders as the sole Bouchet heir and executor. She explained to me and Emily that even though the college was the town's *raison d'être*, it would have to close as there was no other male Bouchet to take command. And even if the tradition of Bouchet leadership could be overlooked for the sake of the school's survival, no one would take command of a bankrupt military college with a dwindling student base.

Alice spoke to the Town Council, explaining how the situation was an existential crisis for the college and town, and that she was working on a plan to keep alive Long Military

Institute's spirit, if not its actual doors.

It took her three months to initiate her strategy. Her first self-appointed task was to sell the college's extensive lands, along with its buildings, most of which were in good shape, not only habitable but architecturally impressive—if you like ivied brick and ornately mullioned windows. Anyway, the land was primo: beautiful meadows tucked among soft rolling hills, bordered by a freshwater stream to the north and a babbling brook to the west. Having worked with a real estate developer to divide the property into attractive parcels, she made a small bundle.

Having kept the parcel with the largest single building, Alice partnered with a creative team from St. Louis to conceptualize Freedom Hall, a tribute museum to celebrate America's hard-won freedoms, emphasizing the role played by the brave and protective American soldier. Combining the former college's great wealth of military artifacts with two surprisingly slick videos, Freedom Hall is a Yankee doodle dandy of a museum and Three Corners' new calling card.

Alice didn't stop there. Like I said, she's the smart one. She knew that "build it and they will come" would be no guarantee of success. Having seen the slow ruin of Long Institute, she understood the importance of targeted advertising and catchy messaging. So, following two consecutive election cycles in which every voter in Three Corners cast ballots for conservative Republican candidates, she came up with a pair of effective slogans:

Three Corners
America's Most Conservative Town

Visit Freedom Hall.
Do Your Duty!

I take credit (or blame, depending on your view) for suggesting to Alice that a highway billboard might literally drive business to Freedom Hall.

"Allen, you're a genius!" she said, planting a quick kiss on my cheek (the first since prom night) and hurrying away, apparently anxious to put my advice into action. Three weeks later I saw the fruit of my genius: a two-sided billboard on the highway that runs east-west, a mile south of our town. Impossible to miss.

A Hug for a Lifetime

Emily Schnyder

Alice Bouchet was the daughter of Colonel Karl Bouchet (then commander of Long Military Institute), the most powerful man in our town, looming over our mayor, sheriff, pastor, reverend, priest, and even Clyde Lissome, Three Corners' richest citizen, who owned the gas station and the general store, along with the gas station and egg farm in nearby Marion.

I have a memory of twenty-something Alice coming into my father's tailor shop on Main Street. She looked tall and pretty to my young self, sitting on the floor, dressing my dolls in the cloth scraps tossed aside by my father. My mother sat behind him at her own work table. I loved the shadowy space between them, where I could watch the street traffic unnoticed. Sometimes, if I remained quiet, my parents forgot I was there.

Even then I knew my father did important work. The gray uniforms he made and repaired—silk stripes, brass buttons, braided epaulettes—looked like royal costumes. My mother handled the town's other tailoring jobs, but her work did not garner the cachet, or the cash, recompensed to my father.

Though my father was business-like with all the women who entered his shop, he treated Alice deferentially. And while I appreciated, even then, that she dressed well and walked with a regal posture (as if the world were not a threat, as it had always seemed to me), it would be several years before I understood why Alice was responsible for the care and repair of the Institute's uniforms and not her military brothers.

Over the years I'd learn of other examples of gender bias she'd had to bear, but I can say truly that I never saw her shirk or flinch or do anything else that betrayed any hard or negative feelings. She was always the most stalwart and loyal supporter of the college and our town, and unfailingly kind to me.

Whenever she saw me in the shadows, she'd ask what I was doing and, on one occasion, sat beside me on the floor to help dress my dolls! I thought my parents would be furious with me for drawing Miss Bouchet down to my level, but they never said so. Anyway, though Alice never again sat on the floor with me, she'd always ask how I was, taking a probing interest in what I liked to read. One Christmas day (I must have been around ten), my family and I were home alone when Alice brought me a wrapped package, attached with an open card for all the world to see: *To my friend, Emily Schnyder, Happy Holidays!* It was a beautifully illustrated edition of *Bridge to Terabithia* and remains one of my most cherished possessions.

By the time I was eleven, Alice visited me quite often, at least once a week. My parents were continually surprised, but not me. I knew we saw a kindred soul in each other's heart, despite the generational difference in our ages.

Our relationship intensified when, just before my twelfth birthday, both my parents died very suddenly. I distinctly remember it was a Sunday. My mother made great Sunday omelets but on that day I'd just wanted some fruit salad, left over from a previous day's barbecue at First Baptist Church, where I sometimes socialized but never went to be sermonized, as my father liked to call it. Anyway, my parents fell sick within an hour of eating their breakfast: my father hugging the upstairs toilet bowl, retching and groaning; my mother, kneeling before the downstairs toilet (right outside the kitchen), rocking back and forth as if she were praying, swallowing her roiling pains so as not to trouble me with her agony.

I ran up and down the stairs between them. My father screamed I should go away; my mother begged me to leave her alone. I didn't know what to do. It never occurred to me to call the doctor or to run for help. At some point I climbed halfway up the staircase and sat down, clamping my ears against my parents' howls and the occasional flushing away of their heavings.

I must have fallen asleep. When I awoke, it was quiet. I walked slowly to the kitchen, hoping to find my father reading the newspaper and my mother washing the dishes, but I saw an empty kitchen and my heart sank. I knew I should check the bathroom (only a few feet away), but I seemed unable to move. Eventually, my resolve exceeding my trepidation, I peeked into the bathroom to find my mother collapsed on a vomit-sodden rug, rigidly still. I stared for several seconds but did not come to her aid. I did not even cross the threshold. I simply left and, with even greater fright, slowly ascended the stairs. At the landing I drew a deep breath, then forced myself to peer into the upstairs bathroom. My father was on his knees, his arms still crossed over the rim of the toilet bowl, his lifeless head lolling to the side. Without touching the banister, I raced down the stairs and out the front door.

***

Alice took care of everything, and I do mean everything. She held a small service for my parents in the backyard of her home, having asked the college's chaplain to give a plain, non-denominational speech that honored the quiet goodness of Jack and Carol Schnyder, who had outfitted the college and many of Three Corners' citizens for many years, just as my grandfather and great-grandfather had done for nearly as long as the Bouchets had commanded the Institute.

Perhaps some other people attended other than the chaplain, Alice, and me, but for a long while I didn't remember. At the time, Alice commented on the conspicuous absence of our town's supposed moral lights: "I thought they'd show some decency and pay their respects."

After the funeral, standing just outside her front porch, in the great shade of the town's largest elm, Alice told me that my parents had left her instructions in the case of their untimely death.

"They asked me to ship their bodies to Saddle Brook, New Jersey, not all that far from New York City. That's where they will be buried."

"Why there? Why so far away?"

"I'm not sure. I think your grandparents are buried there."

Orphaned and abandoned, I started to cry. "But how can I visit them?"

Alice put her arm around my shoulders and drew me close. I buried my face in her bosom and sobbed hard, aware that I was wetting her blouse. When my sobs subsided, I pulled back and asked, "What do I do now?"

Alice firmly explained that my parents had filed a proper will with the Town Hall registrar that named her my legal guardian and executor until I reached the age of twenty-one.

"What does that mean?" I asked.

"It means you will live with me and I'll do everything I can for you."

"Can I go back to my house?"

"Of course. It's yours. You own it. And you can visit there whenever you like. I just need to have it cleaned before you go back. I'll pick up your clothes and personal things and bring them here. Don't worry, you'll be okay."

My eyes filled with tears of loss and gratitude. Alice opened her arms and gave me a hug meant to last a lifetime.

Play It By Ear

Barry Roth

Like most New Yorkers, I don't own a car, and even if I did, I wouldn't keep it in Manhattan. What with our subways and taxis, Ubers and Lyfts, it's an unnecessary expense.

"But I'll need a car when I'm out in the sticks."

"Don't say *sticks*," said Lainey. "It's offensive."

"To whom?"

"To the people who live in the sticks."

"They must know where they live."

"Well, don't say it when you're there."

"Duly noted."

"I mean it. You don't want to piss off your new neighbors before they get to know you."

"You think they'll be pissed off when they do get to know me?"

"Depends."

"On what?"

"On whether you come across as a commie-kissing socialist who wants to denounce God and steal their guns."

"Wow, Lainey. That's pretty good. What if I just say, 'Hi neighbor. Nice to meet you. I'm a Jewish writer from New York'"?

"You're toast."

I chewed that for a few seconds.

"I could pretend to be one of them ... or I could just lurk in the shadows."

Lainey shook her head. "Maybe you should just play it by ear."

***

With a week to go, almost everything I knew about Three Corners I'd learned from the internet and my mother, who'd become quite chummy with Alice Bouchet, soon to assume my apartment on the Lower East Side.

"Normally, I wouldn't connect two swapping lessors," Lainey said to me, "but Alice suggested the two of you should talk directly. Here's her email and cell number."

I spoke with Alice the following day. After a prolonged exchange of pleasantries, I warned her about my apartment's strange sounds: the clanging pipes in the early winter (the radiator clearing its throat) and its midnight death rattles (the fridge's wheezing attempts at self-defrosting).

"You sound like a writer."

I wondered how much Lainey had told her about me. I was tempted to self-promote, but I let it go with a cheery "Thanks."

"Anything I need to know about Haven House that wasn't in the brochure?"

I heard her charming laugh.

"Since you ask, if you hear skittering claws or fluttering wings, it's probably a bat."

"A bat?"

"Don't worry. Unless rabid, they're generally harmless. But do set the garbage containers tightly. Hungry bears have powerful snouts."

"Bears?"

"Browns and grizzlies. Their huge claws can rip off the top of unsecured receptacles."

"You have bears?"

"You'll be fine ... just don't provoke them."

"I'll remember that," I said, suddenly more scaredy-cat than city slicker. "By the way, if you need any help with the apartment, call Rolando, the building superintendent. Lainey can give you the number."

"Many thanks. In my kitchen, next to the wall phone, I posted the number of my friend, Allen Briggs. He'll gave you the town's ten-cent tour."

"What if I want the long tour?"

"That is the long tour. Ciao!"

Once more, her charming laugh.

Ms. Dowdy Midwest

Alice Bouchet

I did not overpack. I did not want to arrive with a wardrobe of inappropriate and unstylish clothing. There was no reason to announce myself as Ms. Dowdy Midwest, nearly sixty. I figured I'd ask Lainey, a few years younger, where she liked to shop.

A few days earlier, we'd arranged to meet outside Barry's apartment building on Essex Street. She'd generously offered to personally hand me the keys and help me carry my luggage up the five flights of stairs.

"What the apartment lacks in lift, it makes up for in charm!"

We'd both laughed the laugh of aging seniors. For me it was all a great adventure. I had never lived in an apartment building, much less one in New York City.

***

The flight to LaGuardia Airport went smoothly, and though the airport was in the midst of a massive reconstruction, I easily found the baggage terminal and the taxi stand to Manhattan. Determined not to be the rube who is taken for a ride (so to speak), I carried a printout of the approximate fare to my new address on Essex Street.

The taxi driver was actually very nice. He asked me where I was from and when I told him I was fresh from the Midwest, he recommended some small gems I must see, citing (among others) the High Line in Manhattan and the Cloisters in the Bronx.

All the while he spoke (politely snatching glances at me in his rearview mirror), I stared (not so politely) at his silk turban. I thought he must be Hindi or Muslim (or something like that) and determined to discover the fact. At the same time, I noted we were driving on an expressway called *Van Wyck,* which I assumed was Dutch, which also excited me, as I had never seen anything Dutch, other than my friend Becky's Delft trivet. Immersed in so much that was new, I hazarded a personal question.

"Excuse me," I said, tapping what I thought must be a panel of bullet-proof glass. "I mean no offense, but what are you wearing on your head? And what does it signify?"

In the rearview mirror I could see his happy expression.

"No offense, madam. None at all! I am a Sikh. It is a little like Islam, a little like Hinduism, and a little like Buddhism. It originated in northern India and it is our own unique faith."

"I see," I said, though I didn't quite. "Can you please tell me a little more?"

"Of course, madam. The word *sikh* means 'disciple' or 'learner.' We believe in one God, equality, and community service. As part of our observance, we do not cut our hair. The turban protects our hair and helps keep it clean. There are many reasons for wearing the turban, but, mainly, it shows our love, obedience, and piety."

I reached for my tote, where I kept my journal, so I could capture the moment to share with Allen—but my tote was locked in the trunk. Disappointed (for Allen's sake, as much as mine), I stared out the window at the passing novelty of my new world.

Very soon I was struck by how slowly we were moving. I understood it was New York, but it was only eleven a.m. I was about to ask the driver about it, but then it occurred to me that I should just shush and go with the flow. After all, I'd have another story to tell: *I was stuck in New York traffic!*

After ten more of minutes of highway crawling, I asked the driver what time he thought we would arrive. When he told me that we'd be there in about thirty minutes, I called Lainey.

"Hi, Lainey! Can you hear me?"

"I hear you loud and clear. Did you land yet?"

"Oh my, yes! I landed, got my luggage, and found a taxi. We're on the highway! I should be there in about thirty minutes!"

"Okay. Good thing you got me. I have to hurry. I'll meet you downstairs, as planned. After you get settled, I'll take you out to lunch—New York style."

I was so excited. I wasn't sure whether to expect *Breakfast at Tiffany's* or *When Harry Met Sally* … and really, I didn't care! It was an adventure!

Lainey Roth

She was unmistakable. Who else would wear an unflattering sack and a hat pinned with plastic fruit? The poor thing looked like a schoolmarm on holiday.

"Alice!"

"Lainey, is that you?"

I took her extended hand and drew her towards me for a quick hug, which seemed to surprise her.

"Oh my!" she said, stepping backward. "You're not how I pictured you."

"How's that?" I said, smiling.

"You're so pretty. I mean, you have an adult son.... I pictured you much older."

I thought: *I love her. She's my new best friend.*

"Is that all the luggage you brought?"

"I was hoping you could suggest some stores where I might ... re-style myself."

I tapped her shoulder and grabbed the larger of the two suitcases. "Come on, let's get you settled."

The Honor Stone

Barry Roth

I had no idea what stores or services would be available in Three Corners, so I came fully prepared with three over-packed suitcases, a stuffed duffel bag, and my laptop case, which never left my sight.

***

I was walking down a wide and bright corridor in this nice Midwest airport when I saw a series of startling signs: *Jesus Loves You … Jesus Welcomes You … Fly High With Jesus …*

Now, I'm a sophisticated traveler, but I'd never seen such signage in an airport. I continued walking, but the messages stayed with me. By the time I found the car rental kiosk, my mood was unsettled.

"Good afternoon, sir. How can I help you?"

I told the neatly suited, middle-aged man where I was headed and that I wanted to rent a sedan for a year.

"Okay, sir. I can help you with that. But for such a lengthy term, you might want to consider a lease arrangement. It might prove less expensive."

"What's the difference?" I asked. I'm sure I knew, but the words just slipped out.

"Well, sir, you can rent a car by the day, week, or month. But in a lease arrangement, you sign a contract to maintain the car for an extended time, say thirty-six months, paying it off in monthly installments."

"And that's the cheapest way to go?"

"Actually, the cheapest way is to buy a car outright."

"But then I'd still own it after a year or so."

"That's true, sir. But if you maintain the car well, we would make a fair offer to buy it back from you."

"Hmmm. That sounds reasonable. Do you have used cars for sale?"

"Indeed, we do. We have thirteen used cars in our inventory. Twelve are Chevrolet Impalas, and one is a sporty, two-door, red Fiat."

"Wow. I thought the Impala was extinct."

"It's the most popular car in the Midwest, sir."

"Really?"

"Yes, sir. Impala has an iron-grip on seven contiguous states: Iowa, Missouri, Nebraska, Minnesota, Wisconsin, North and South Dakota."

"Hmmm," I said, digging through my memory. "I think my Uncle Izzy drove a lime green Impala."

"Very nice, sir."

That was all I could remember about Uncle Izzy. He died many years before my father.

"So," I said, getting down to business, "what's the Fiat cost?"

"Actually, sir, it's our least expensive car. It runs perfectly well, but it's sat on our lot for fourteen months. I can offer you a very good price."

The neatly suited gentleman led me outside to a nearby lot, where all twelve Impalas were tightly herded. The red Fiat grazed some distance away, as if ostracized. My heart went out to the little guy.

***

Did I mention it was a convertible? That me, Barry Roth—the guy who'd painted his apartment seven shades of beige—was driving a red Fiat convertible? *Cool!*

***

The drive to Three Corners took two hours and I enjoyed every minute. I'm a confident and capable driver when I know where I'm going, and thanks to the car's dashboard GPS, all I really had to do was steer and mind the posted speed limits. *Sweet!*

***

I was cruising the country highway, enthralled by the shimmering sunlight and dappled greenery. (When I was little, Lainey had read me the tales of City Mouse and Country Mouse. I'd loved them both—was torn between the two—though I lived in the City and the only Country I knew was Central Park.) Driving to Three Corners, I experienced a deep, visceral wave of nostalgia.

Eventually, the Interstate put me on a two-lane road, which my GPS identified as Marion Pike. In stretches, the road was sinuous and shadowy, the high branches of leafy trees intermingling above the road, creating a series of light-dappled tunnels.

Coming out of one such tunnel, I was gobsmacked by a large billboard:

Three Corners
America's Most Conservative Town

Having slowed to a crawl, I saw the sign's obverse in my

rearview mirror:
Visit Freedom Hall
Do Your Duty!
Alice had told me about the billboard but she hadn't done it justice. For all its patriotic stars and stripes, it was a daring piece of guerilla marketing—implying that all who disobeyed were ethically derelict.

***

Driving up Washington Street, I saw all manner of pickups and flatbeds, several SUV's and a couple Impalas, but not a single Fiat, much less another red convertible.

I drove slowly, not exactly like Patton through the streets of cheering Palermo, though I did feel rather brazen and conspicuous. At the top of the street, I pulled into the wide driveway of the town's largest and most conspicuously grand home.

I exited the car, stretched, and looked all about. Facing west I could see Freedom Hall and, beyond that, the hazy suggestion of large stone homes and the crosshatch white fencing that separated the properties in soft, undulating meadow grasses. North appeared to be woods, maybe even a forest. I had no idea how far it extended but judging from the size of its tallest trees, I imagined they might have witnessed the arrival of Col. François Bouchet, George Long Military Institute's first commander, who'd arrived after the Civil War with his English wife Mary in tow.

Attracted by singing voices carried on the breeze, I turned east and saw—about one hundred yards away—the impressive white steeple of First Baptist, the town's largest and oldest church. I didn't know whether Alice belonged to that church or one of the others: a small Lutheran church on Jefferson or an even smaller Catholic church on Adams.

The voices on the breeze were the first human sounds I'd heard since arriving at Three Corners. I thought: *Sunday—everyone is in church.*

Feeling the first pangs of my outsider status, I was suddenly anxious to take shelter in my new home. For the moment, leaving all my luggage in the car, I opened the gate in the white picket fence and approached the stairs that led to a wide verandah. Just as I was taking my first step, I noticed a large, crescent-shaped bush to my right. In its center space was an impressive boulder, the word HONOR deeply engraved into its shaved façade. Sticking out from the top of the boulder was the hilt of a great sword.

I wasn't sure if I should take it seriously. I mean, I knew about the succession of Bouchet commanders who had resided in Haven House—but who has a sword in a stone on their front lawn?

Staring at its silver shaft and golden handle, I fantasized what might happen if I were able to draw it free. I assumed everyone in Three Corners had already tried and failed. I was sure Alice expected me to try (otherwise she would have forewarned me against it) and that Lainey, my greatest admirer, would be crushed if she found out I hadn't. I imagined my dead father groaning sarcastically: *Jeez Louise, just pull the damn thing!*

For a full minute I stared at the sword in the stone, stoking my courage ... and then, catching myself by surprise, I closed my eyes and yanked the sword's golden grip with all my strength.

It didn't move. My head pounding, my face flushed, I pulled again and again until my arms ached. Still, the sword didn't move. I thought I would have better success if I changed position, so I threw one leg over the boulder and climbed on top. Astride the boulder (my eyes still tightly shuttered), I pulled so hard I bucked myself over the side, managing to hold onto the sword's hilt as if it were a bronco's pommel. Hanging off the side of the stone, I opened my eyes for a split second to regain my balance—and that's when I saw a large crowd of Three Corners' finest staring at me, dumbstruck and horrified.

Allen Briggs
I helped him off the Honor stone and led him inside, directly into the kitchen.

"What were you thinking?"

He seemed shell-shocked and I didn't press him to respond.

I pulled back a kitchen chair and directed him to sit. He was a young man, mid-thirties, nice looking, brown hair, button-down shirt, slacks, sunglasses. I figured the red convertible was his.

"Tea?"

"Yes…. Please."

He sat down, his elbows propped on the kitchen table, his hands supporting his head. From the double-wide window above the sink came a strong, early afternoon sunlight.

I filled Alice's kettle, a porcelain cow, purchased years ago from the Sears catalog. While it boiled, I laid out a neat presentation of napkins, brown and white sugars, biscuits and butter, just as Alice would have done.

At that moment, thinking of Alice was bittersweet. I already missed her, but I was still sore that she'd bolted for New York in such a happy mood. I'm not sure what that said about me, but it sure didn't feel good.

Hurt as I was, I was grateful that Alice had provided her replacement, for that's how I thought of the young man seated at the kitchen table—*Alice's temporary replacement.* Before she left, she told me that she'd temporarily swapped homes with a young man from New York City. "But why are you going?" I asked. "It's on my bucket-list," she said. I asked about the young man. She said, "His name is Barry. Get to know him on your own terms. That way, no prejudgments." I accepted her advice, as always, but her words struck me as strangely ominous.

Barry seemed a little better after a few sips of tea.

"You okay?"

He smiled wryly. "What do they say about first impressions?"

"I'm not sure. But yours was—unforgettable."

"I'm so sorry."

"You should be. You thoroughly disrespected Alice and the very soul of our town. You're damn lucky I came along when I did."

He rubbed his head, as if trying to remember. "Thank you. Who are you?"

"Allen Briggs."

"Allen Briggs," he repeated, as if trying to place the name. "Alice mentioned you. She said you were her special friend and I could count on your kindness."

"Really? She said that?"

"She did."

"She say anything else?"

"She said I should call you. She said she wrote your phone number next to her kitchen phone."

I sidled over to the phone and saw her note.

"So she did."

"She said you would give me the town's ten-cent tour."

I laughed. "Yeah, that's just what she would have said."

"So," Barry said, rising to his feet, "can we start over?"

"You owe me an apology. You owe everyone in town an apology."

"I am truly sorry," he said, appearing honestly contrite. "I meant no disrespect. I was just trying to pull the sword—you know, like Arthur and Excalibur. I guess I got carried away. I'm really sorry."

I knew Alice would give him a second chance, so that's what I decided to do. The problem was everyone else in Three Corners. By tomorrow, they'd all have an opinion, thanks to Squirrel.

Squirrel Evans

I came by my nickname as a quick and nimble shortstop and not because I look like a damn squirrel. But never mind, I like my nickname. Not everyone has one, and most who do, bear a heavier cross. Besides, Jacqueline likes it. She says it is *distinguished*, and while I'm pretty sure she means *distinctive*, I no longer correct her because she doesn't take correction well, especially from me. One time, to settle an argument, I pointed out that my high-school degree trumped her tenth-grade education ... and she taught me that her right-cross was quicker than my bob and weave. That was the day I ceased to clarify and elucidate for her benefit. But I do like to keep up my own education. I read lots of different kinds of books and I'm not too proud to check the dictionary or online encyclopedia when there is something I don't understand. Jacqueline is very proud of me, but doesn't say so aloud. She believes there is a direct correlation between complimenting me and swelling my head, and she just hates the look of my swelled head.

Another surefire way to anger Jacqueline is to call her Mrs. Squirrel. It's not the nickname she objects to but the *Mrs.* part. You see, we've been together ten years but haven't yet married. The *yet* is key. Without the *yet*—my sworn promise to marry her—she likely would have hooked up with someone else from Three Corners, or maybe someone from as far away as Marion, and that's twenty minutes by car.

I do hope to make good on my promise. The problem is that Jacqueline doesn't like the nature of my employment. It's not that I don't work hard or steadily. I work all the time. I have three different jobs, sort of rolled into one. But Jacqueline doesn't see it that way. "I ain't marrying no peddler" is how she puts it. She doesn't like that I go door to door, selling and delivering. She says it's not *respectful*. I know she means *respectable*, but I'm not going there.

Truth is, I make a good living—much better than Jacqueline knows. If she knew how much I made, she might overlook my peddler status and we could marry. But before that happens, I want to hear from her own lips that she respects my work ... and promises not to hit me anymore.

A Boy Named Allen

Alice Bouchet

I wasn't sure I was going to make it. By the first landing I huffed. By the second landing I puffed. At the third landing I might have keeled had Lainey's strong hands not steadied me. I took a breather. Hunched over, my sweaty hands clamped on my chubby knees, I felt weak and ashamed.

Over many years I'd learned to rely on the wisdom of military strategist and philosopher Sun Tzu for my survival. In this case, gasping for breath on the third floor of a five-story walk-up, feeling too weak to retreat and too spent to push forward, I recalled these ideas:

If it is to your advantage, make a forward move. If not, stay where you are.

I thought: *Yes! I need to move forward!*

If the mind is willing, the flesh could go on.

I thought: *Yes! My mind is strong. I will go on!*

"Give me the luggage."

"All of it?" asked Lainey.

"Yes, all three. Slip the tote over my shoulder, please."

Like a determined pack mule, I stubbornly persevered. Lainey (she of little faith) followed behind me, ready to prop my hefty load if I threatened to totter backwards.

But I needed no help. Imagining the two flights of stairs in my home, the steps I had climbed ten thousand times, I pressed forward with every ounce of my strength, determined not to falter—or even to slacken—until I had reached my goal!

Lainey Roth

As soon as I opened the apartment door, Alice tumbled inside and collapsed on the living room couch.

"You okay?"

"Water. Please."

The kitchen was only three steps away. I filled two large tumblers with ice water and handed her one, all the while thinking: *It's all my fault. The five flights were a death sentence. If she doesn't die here and now, she'll never leave the apartment. If she does leave, she'll never come back.*

She took two tentative sips ... paused, then threw back her head and quaffed the rest in a single draught.

"Another, please."

I handed her the second tumbler and she downed it just as quickly.

"Perfect!" she said, smacking her lips. "Thank you."

Color me impressed. "Anything else? Bathroom?"

"Not right now. Come sit," she said, patting the space beside her on the couch.

When I sat, she laid her hand on top of mine. "Thank you, Lainey. Thank you for everything."

"I thought I killed you."

She laughed a good one. "No, no. Not at all." And then she started to cry.

"I'm so happy."

Alice Bouchet

I told Lainey that I never cry from physical pain, but when a loving hand stirs my emotional wellspring—well, just watch while I cry me a river.

"It doesn't happen often," I said, both of us settling in for a good talk.

"You remember your first?" Lainey asked.

"I do. It happened prom night. I was president of the high school graduating class and didn't have a date, which was embarrassing, but not surprising. You see, I was smart—but not pretty—and my father was Commander of the town's military college. Most of the smarter boys would be attending in the Fall and they all wanted to have some fun and let off some steam before they enrolled ... but not a one of them had the guts to date the Commander's daughter, which is just as well, as I didn't want any of them either.

"But there was a boy named Allen. I've always liked him and I think he's always liked me. We'd played together when we were small but were rarely together and never alone as teenagers. I waited a long time for him to ask me to the prom, but he never did. I don't know why. To this day, we've never discussed it. Anyway, as class president I had to go and I wanted him to go with me. So, I did what I thought my Commander daddy would do: I took matters into my own hands. I caught him one day after school and asked him—in my most matter-of-fact, businesslike manner—if he would be my date, and he said yes. Really, that was the whole conversation. Next day, without any prompt from me, he went to see my father and asked his permission to take his daughter to the prom. The formality wasn't necessary, as I'd already extended the invitation, but I was so impressed with his style and maturity.

"On the night of the prom he looked so handsome in his new suit and he presented me with the prettiest rose corsage I ever saw. I knew he'd plucked the rose from a bush near my father's office and entwined it himself with baby's breath and silk ribbon. I loved it so much…. I still have it. It's in my trousseau."

My eyes started tearing and I had to pause before I could continue.

"I was a young girl while my mother lay dying. One day, she called me into her bedroom and pointed to the large, handsomely carved wooden crate, set parallel to the foot of her bed. 'That's my trousseau,' she said. 'Open it.' I remember struggling with the heavy lid and being surprised by the scent of cedar chips and all what lay inside: her finest linens, special silk underthings, and her satin wedding dress. 'This now belongs to you,' she said. 'Keep what you want. When you are preparing to marry, put your own fine things inside this box.'"

I paused again because I'd started crying again, even harder. When I recovered, I said, "I never did get married. Never did have children." I thought of Emily but that story would have to wait.

"Never too late," said Lainey, "if that's what you want."

"Too old for children, but marriage is still on my bucket list."

We both laughed tenderly and then I continued my story of prom night.

"He danced reasonably well, without standing too close and without stepping on my toes. After the prom, we drove all the way to the ice cream parlor in Marion, where we shared a huge sundae. At the end of the night, but well before midnight (as he had promised my father), he saw me to my lighted door and thanked me for inviting him. He said it was the best night of his life. He then paused a few seconds, looking down at his new shoes. When he looked up, he told me I was the most beautiful girl who ever lived. He then quickly kissed my cheek and nearly ran back to his car.... I swear, that night I soaked my pillow in tears."

I paused, as Lainey and I both needed a moment.

"I didn't cry like that again for many years, not until my father and two brothers were buried in the same year. The three funerals were mostly private affairs, but a few months later the town organized a memorial service to acknowledge the selfless leadership rendered by the Bouchets for one hundred forty years. The Governor, who had received his degree from Long Military Institute, was the main speaker, but there were quite a few others, including the mayor, a couple journalists, and a well-known country singer who'd gone to Three Corners High. I cried hard that day, but so did a lot of other people.

"Since then I hadn't cried hard until I told Allen I was going to New York City for a year. He nodded and said he was going to miss me. Stupid me, I asked how much. He muttered 'more than a little' and then turned around so I couldn't see his face. Well, I walked away pretty stoically—but when I'd put some distance between us, I let loose a caterwaul to shake my family crypt."

Lainey Roth

I hugged her and then we sat quietly on the couch another minute or so. I figured I'd heard enough dramatic confession for one afternoon. For sure, there'd be more sharing from us both.

"Would you like to see the apartment?"

"I'd love to," she said, and we both got to our feet a little creakily.

"Here we go!" I said. "We have the East Wing, West Wing, and Lower Forty. Where would you like to start?"

She laughed. She was a good sport.

"I love to cook," she said. "How about the kitchen?"

She followed me three steps across the living room.

"Voilà!" I said, with a sweeping gesture of my right arm.

The kitchen showed especially well. The back wall was glazed brickface. The countertops, a polished black granite flecked with gold. The appliances were the red of Dorothy's ruby slippers. On the back wall were display plates and long-handled utensils in matching aquamarine that made one think *Caribbean*.... All had been purchased and arranged by yours truly, a housewarming gift to my son Barry, following the success of his first book, *The Secret Loves of Baron Rothschild*, which I utterly adored.

"Oh my," said Alice. "No one in Three Corners has a kitchen like this. They wouldn't dare!"

"But do you like it?"

"I love it!" she said with gusto.

The bathroom was close by, but as it was only slightly larger than an airplane commode, I decided to save it for last.

"Let's take another look at the living room and then I'll show you the bedroom."

Barry shares my philosophy of interior design. We both love to mix and match styles, so long as each piece is interesting and beautiful. In the living room, Barry had paired an Andy Warhol print with a Louis Quatorze chair, illuminating both with a Tiffany torch lamp. Trés cool ... with my help, of course.

Alice took it all in. "It's beautiful, and now that I see it, the couch is stunning,"

"It's vintage Danish velour," I said. "Pearl-gray and tufted, as you can see."

"I can't believe I plopped my sweaty body on it."

"Don't you worry. A living room is meant to be lived in."

"Still, I will be more careful."

I was about to suggest we look at the bedroom when she said, looking all about, "I just love all the little knickknacks and gimcracks."

"The what?"

"All these beautiful little things."

"Oh, the tchotchkes."

"The what?"

"*Tchotchkes*. Yiddish for knickknacks. Come, check out the bedroom."

Entering Barry's bedroom was a catch-your-breath moment. Above his king-size bed was a full-size, *giclée* reproduction of Van Gogh's *The Starry Night*. Directly below, the bed was covered with an Aztec-inspired, blue-and-white comforter, bright and fluffy. On the wide bureau were more tchotchkes, mostly Mexican figurines, garishly colored, and a couple candomblé gods, carved from Brazilian black onyx.

"You like?" I asked.

"What planet am I on? Really, Earth to Alice, don't wake up! It's a beautiful dream."

"I'll take that as a *yes*."

Alice Bouchet

Before we left the apartment, I saw the bathroom. Lainey did not save the best for last. It was a tiny stall of bamboo and black lacquer—beautiful, but I didn't think I could fit and was embarrassed to say so.

I think she read my mind: "Barry's friend, a big boy who played football for Columbia, didn't think he could fit. But he did. Angled himself just so … and slipped right in."

I left that alone.

Lainey Roth

As we'd were preparing to leave, I looked at her meaningfully and said, "I don't think you'll need your straw hat."

"Not quite right?" she'd asked, intuiting my meaning.

"It was all the rage last year."

She laughed.

"Hard to keep up with changing trends," I said. "Lucky you, I know just where to shop."

She made a show of leaving her hat on the couch and then said with a smile, "Whither thou goest, I follow right behindest."

I thought: *I'm really starting to like this woman.*

Alice Bouchet

Lainey gave me two sets of keys and showed me how to secure all three door locks. "The neighborhood is very good. But better safe than sorry."

As we began walking down the five flights of stairs, Lainey added, "Big upside to the top floor. You probably won't hear any street noise. I mean, you might hear a Haitian street fair or a Gay Pride march … otherwise, it should be as quiet as Three Corners."

If I didn't love Lainey so, I would have burst out laughing.

New Neighborhoods

Barry Roth

"Let's wait a bit on the ten-cent tour," said Allen. "I need to do some damage control before I show you around. I'd like to be able to introduce you with a clean slate."

"Everyone knows what happened?"

"They will by morning … unless I head this off at the pass."

"What does that mean?"

"It means I have to talk with Squirrel Evans to see if we can make this right."

"Can't I just apologize?"

"That would be reasonable—or even unnecessary—if you weren't intending to live here for the next year or so. But *here* happens to be Haven House, the most grand and historic home in Three Corners. This house is filled with history. This house is history. So, like it or not, people expect impeccable conduct from anyone visiting, much less living here."

I liked Allen. He was a straight shooter, fair and honest. "Okay, so what do we do?"

"Squirrel Evans is one of our more popular and colorful citizens. He lives in a small house at the end of Adams Street with a woman named Jacqueline. Now, if you don't want her to punch you in the mouth, don't ever call her 'Jackie' and don't ever call her 'Mrs. Evans,' because she isn't either."

I repeated his injunctions to show I wouldn't forget.

"Squirrel is our town crier. He delivers the mail, which arrives at a General Delivery box at City Hall, which is the same building as our Courthouse and police station. Along with the mail, he delivers the *Three Corners Courier,* our town newsletter, which he writes and produces on his computer."

"Busy guy."

"There's more. He buys interesting and useful things on eBay, mostly from China, and then repackages them for resale here. He advertises them in the *Courier* and delivers door to door when he brings the mail and newsletter."

"What's he sell?"

"Perfumes, print cartridges, magnetic tape … almost anything you can think of. Squirrel is our chief purveyor of hard-to-find goods and gossip. And we never had a newspaper of any kind until Squirrel thought of it."

"What kind of news does he publish?"

"Mostly he summarizes stories he's heard on Fox News and adds opinions from everyone he talks to. He's lived here all his life and knows how to stir the pot. But he also writes local stories, like who was born … who has died—"

"Who has just arrived?"

"Exactly. And before everyone sets a hard opinion of you, I'd like Squirrel to write a nice welcome piece for tomorrow's edition."

"How do you plan to sugarcoat what happened?"

"Not sure. I'll figure something. Luckily, tomorrow is Monday. Squirrel always has a Monday edition. If all goes well, the town will have a better opinion of you by noon."

"I'm sorry to put you through this."

"I'm not doing this for you."

I think he realized how harsh his words sounded. "Listen," he quickly added, "why don't you bring in your luggage and get yourself settled. We'll have dinner here tonight. Anything you don't like to eat?"

"Fresh sushi."

"Good thing you told me," he said, chuckling. "See you around seven."

Alice Bouchet

What kind of food do you like?" Lainey asked when we had reached the street.

"What do you have around here?"

"Everything."

"Tough choice," I said, smiling. "Surprise me."

"Okay," she said, linking my arm with hers. "Come with me to zee Kasbah."

The Kasbah. What an adventure!

I followed Lainey about the neighborhood, squealing each time we crossed a famous street—Delancey, Canal, Essex, Ludlow, Grand … (Only twice before had I seen a famous landmark in person—once, when I visited the St. Louis Arch, and once when I went to a baseball game at Busch Stadium. But this was a whole new level of excitement. This felt like *world* history.)

On Orchard Street, Lainey paused outside an old brick building with a large sign: *Tenement Museum.*

"Put this on your bucket list," she said.

"It's already on my list! It's famous! You recommend?"

"It's supposed to be great. You should see it."

"You haven't gone?"

Lainey shook her head. "Nah, I grew up around here. These were my streets. My grandparents lived two blocks away. Hell, I could give the damn tour!"

"Oh my!"

"That's why I haven't seen the museum. I wouldn't appreciate it as you will."

"How do you think you'd see it now?"

Lainey came to a complete halt in the shadow of the museum.

"Hmmm. Let me put it this way: I married a man named Bert when I was quite young. On our first date he asked, 'What do you want in life?' And I said, 'I want out of these tenements.' He swore he'd take me away, so I married him."

"He keep his promise?"

"He did. He took me uptown and gave me a good life. But, funny thing, he got into real estate and started buying tenement buildings around the city. Crazy bastard made a fortune as a slumlord."

"Did he buy around here?"

"No, but some years later, the older buildings around here started attracting serious investor dollars. Now they're all pricy hipster homes."

"Still mostly Jewish?" I didn't want to pry, but I was dying to know.

"Not like the old Lower East Side, when the place was teeming with Jews. But yeah, there are some, like Barry and his friends."

I was right! I was so excited. Lainey was my first Jewish friend! Three hours in New York and my new horizons were already bursting at the seams!

"Come," she said, leading me away from the tenement's classic stoop. "You must be hungry. The Kasbah calls!"

Making Amends

Barry Roth

I had just finished arranging my things in my upstairs bedroom when the phone jingled like it had a pair of bells inside, which it did, as I later discovered. The small pink rotary (made for a bedside table) rang insistently, but as I was sitting on Alice's pretty bed for the first time, I was hesitant to answer. Still, I couldn't hold out forever. When the ancient device did not go to voicemail after a dozen *briiiinngs*, I had no choice but to lift the plastic handset (attached to a three-foot coiled cord) and ask, "Hello?"

"Barry, is that you?"

"Yes," I said, recognizing Allen's voice. "Doesn't sound like you."

"Well, it's me."

"You in the kitchen?"

"No, upstairs."

A slight pause. And then, "Where upstairs?"

"Alice's room. I mean, my room. My bedroom."

"Oh."

"Something wrong?" I asked.

"No…. Is it nice?"

"It's lovely. You've never seen it?"

"No. Never have."

"Well, c'mon up when you get here."

"Thanks … but … no."

His words seemed oddly spaced, as if he were struggling with his thoughts.

"Listen," he said, suddenly changing the subject, "I spoke with Squirrel. He agrees something has to be done—and fast—but he says it's too late to write an article about you."

"So, what do we do?"

"He said he could email you some questions and if you send back your answers before 6:00, the text would appear in tomorrow morning's newsletter."

"You think that's a good idea?"

"Not sure. An interview is something new. It might be a nice way to introduce you to the community … depending on what you say."

"What do you think he'll ask?"

"Where're you from? … What are you doin' in Haven House? … Where is Alice Bouchet? … Why were you wrestling the sword while everyone else was in church?"

"No getting around that, huh?"

"Not unless you bury the lead … and keep it buried."

"Is that possible?"

"Not a chance in hell."

Squirrel Evans

I resented Allen's request. The *Courier* was my domain. I decided what was newsworthy and wrote my opinions as I saw fit. But I didn't think I could turn him down—him being so close to Alice and all. Anyway, it was easy enough to write the ten questions (I know what Three Corners likes to read and how it thinks), but it rankled, and I worried that Barry's answers might reflect poorly on me, the publisher.

As soon as I finished, I emailed the questions to Barry. Here's what I wrote:

Nice to meet you, Barry. Please answer the following ten questions:

What's your full name?
What brought you to Haven House?
How long do you expect to stay?
Where is Alice Bouchet?
What were you doing on top of the Honor Stone?
What do you do for a living?
What church do you belong to?
Why drive a red Fiat?
What does the Second Amendment mean to you?
Do you want to help make America great again?
Thank you for sharing your answers. Welcome to Three Corners!

Barry Roth

A half hour after I had emailed my responses to Squirrel, Allen used the brass lionhead knocker to announce his presence outside my front door. (There was no doorbell or electric chime. Haven House was old school.)

"Squirrel has your responses," he said, stepping into my wainscoted foyer. "The interview will be in tomorrow's newsletter."

"He say anything?"

"Not really. He just said, 'Well, this should be interesting.'"

"Meaning, the town's response to my responses?"

"That's how I took it."

Allen said nothing more, so I let it go. To my mind, Squirrel's questions had trammeled my privacy. Still, I didn't want to make a bad second impression, so I'd answered honestly, where possible, and with careful ambiguity, where necessary. What else could I do?

Allen led the way to the kitchen, which I thought a tad presumptuous (after all, this was now my home), but I let it go as he was holding a large bag filled with food containers whose mingled scents excited my taste buds.

"You check the fridge for liquid refreshment?" he asked.

I hadn't. I hadn't done anything since his phone call except go to the bathroom, write my responses, and check my email.

"Mind if I look?"

I did mind. "No, go ahead."

He swung open the large door and smiled. "Ah, fully stocked. Thank you, dear Alice!"

"What's in there?"

"Alice favors French wines and tonic water … but she always has sparkling water and ginger ale for guests. What's your pleasure?"

"I'll have seltzer."

"Seltzer?"

"Seltzer … sparkling water. Same thing."

Allen made no further comment. Instead, he arranged the drinks and sandwiches while I sat at the table like a little boy.

"By the way," I said, "what do you mean by *guests*? Alice told me no one had ever rented Haven House before."

"Well, that's true enough. But you're hardly the first guest. Governors and generals have stayed here. And under Alice's command—"

"Command?"

"That's how I think of it. This was a military college that grew into a town. Up until a few years ago, this was the Commander's House, essentially off limits to the public. Now that the college is gone, Haven House is a private residence and Alice is a very warm and welcoming hostess."

"So, she's not actually a commander. She's more like the

town's chief civilian."

"Well, she's more than that. We have an elected mayor ... and we have Gavin Lissome, our town's richest man ... but Alice owns and commands Freedom Hall."

"Which is what, exactly?"

"It's our town's famous museum ... our lifeblood ... our *raison d'être*. You understand?"

I ignored his execrable French.

"I get it. Three Corners' existence depends on Freedom Hall."

Allen made a slight grimace. I think he would have liked some credit for his tiny acquirement of French. I needed to buck him up.

"I'm really looking forward to visiting Freedom Hall," I said. "Really, I'm honored to be here."

Allen looked me dead in the eye. "It didn't look that way when you were humping our town's most sacred monument."

"I get it," I said, honestly contrite. "That's a lot to live down. Hopefully, my interview will personalize me ... make it easier for people to forgive."

"We'll see."

Emily Schnyder

Monday morning, around seven-thirty, Squirrel stepped onto my porch to leave my mail and a copy of the *Courier* in my mailbox. He knew I was awake because my kitchen light was on. I knew he wanted a word with me because he remained dawdling on the porch. I opened the door to get my mail, knowing full well he would pounce.

"Good morning, Miss Emily."

I hated *Miss Emily*. It made me feel like a child or an old maid. He liked *Squirrel,* so I never uttered it within his hearing.

"Good morning," I said coldly.

He said, "I think you'll find today's *Courier* very interesting."

I said, "I'll take a look after I've read the real news."

We left it at that. Our relationship was an endless exchange of slights and gibes as if from a pair of opposed foxholes. Like most conflicts of long duration, neither of us gave much thought to the motivation behind our entrenched positions. Suffice to say, we didn't like each other. Never did and never would.

Inside, I reheated my coffee, then resumed my seat at my breakfast table, pushing aside my laptop so I could peruse what passed for news in the *Courier*.

I expected to read of someone's engagement or someone's new baby. Squirrel liked to call such events to my attention, knowing they were likely to spoil my mood. It has always been this way between us. Even as a young boy, Squirrel intuited my otherness and wished to punish me for it. I don't know why. I suppose some people resent oddities and outsiders, and I was certainly both: a naturally expressive, self-effacing waif, living in the shadows behind curtains and blinds. My parents might have eventually shed some light, had they not died so suddenly, when I was so young.

I cry when I imagine them buried so far away. It makes it harder for me to remember them. My memories are already faint and I worry my past will soon disappear. And then what will I have?

Championing my undefined uniqueness, Alice says "Vive la différence!" But how can I revel in my difference if I don't know what it is? Yes, I have Alice and Allen, Freedom Hall and my snow globes, but I struggle to name the essential things that make me *me*.

With no one else to blame, I blame myself for my sorry state. Accepting my undefined difference as a penance, I look for small ways of making myself happy.

***

That particular issue of the *Courier* was the usual tripe: cherrypicked national news summarized with a conservative bias, followed by notices of garage sales, church teas, and adverts for Squirrel's eBay products. Mercifully, there were no notices of engagements, weddings, or babies. Instead (and to my happy surprise), page four featured something totally unexpected: an interview with Three Corners' newest resident—the first male inhabitant of Haven House not named Bouchet. (Alice hadn't given me much advance warning, but she had told me of her plan to live awhile in New York, swapping residences with a Barry Roth, of whom she'd said almost nothing, other than she thought I'd find him interesting.)

Like everyone else in town, I'd already gotten wind of Mr. Roth's bronco ride on the Honor Stone, which I thought outrageously inappropriate—but also hysterically funny. In any case, I was surprised to see Squirrel's interview with Mr. Roth in the next day's paper. I began reading the interview with an undefined sense of hope and was soon thrilled to see that Mr. Roth hadn't bowed to Squirrel's inquisitorial crap. Instead, ignoring Squirrel's bias and insinuations, he'd managed an adequate apology without compromising his personal integrity and privacy, emerging relatively unscathed—even mysteriously attractive—which I knew would piss off Squirrel. Bravo! I was proud of him. Envious too. I couldn't wait to meet him.

Allen Briggs

Having just read Barry's responses in the *Courier*, I thought: *Oooh weee. What we have here is a failure to communicate.* I mean, did Alice vet this guy? If so, why'd she invite him? Did Barry know what he's getting into? If so, why did he agree to come? I mean, what sane lamb seeks out the lion's den? As to Squirrel's questions, sure they flouted basic standards of privacy, but if a man has the right to protect his home, doesn't a collection of likeminded homeowners—*aka* a tightly knit town—have the right to assess a visiting stranger, especially one who has already behaved so disrespectfully?

… Oh god! What's wrong with me? Alice is gone two days and I'm already thinking like *them!* Thank god she can't hear my thoughts. I mean, I wouldn't want her to know how easily I can backslide. But even if she knew, she'd forgive me. Who knows better than she what it means to be born and raised in Three Corners? And she did it the hard way: for years, the only female in the Commander's house of Bouchet men. That could not have been easy. So, really, I should be strong for her, 'cause I owe her a great deal. I mean, she taught me how to think for myself and I've come a long way. How far? Well, keeping in mind I was raised in our nation's conservative heartland, in a military college town that fostered a cult of crewcut soldiers, I'll just say this: off the top of my head, I can name a dozen progressive ideals … describe the necessity of separating church and state … explain the difference between a democracy and a constitutional republic … highlight the benefits of individualism and inclusiveness … and example differences between free speech and hate speech.

For all that, I still proudly declare myself a Three Corners man. This is my home. This is where I was born and raised. Here I have seen gentle and wise parenting, acts of generosity, and deep fellowship. For sure, we are traditional and slow to change, but that doesn't make us evil—just wary of social norms and ways of thinking that are foreign to us.

Still, whenever I am out and about and hear the worst conservative bias, I think to myself: *There but for the grace of Alice go I.*

Not the Most Refined Lady

Gavin Lissome

A reverend, priest, and pastor walk into a bar ... really, no joke. In fact, those three meet me at the Red, White, and Brew once a month and I always pick up the tab, which I don't mind. Suffice to say, I get what I pay for.

My daddy Clyde (who'd inherited the town's only gas station and general store from his daddy) wanted to be the richest and most powerful man in Three Corners (other than the college's Commander, who had his own fiefdom), so he ran for mayor—and lost badly. His daddy said to him, "Son, you failed to become the most powerful man in town because you tried to win the hearts and minds of the people. That is a noble endeavor—but time consuming. And time is money. Next time, skip the advertising. Just buy the hearts and minds of the people. It's more cost effective and you needn't sweat the voting."

A businessman, my father quickly toted how much he thought every adult vote would cost. It seemed way too expensive and he said so.

"You don't have to buy them all," his daddy explained. "You just have to buy the ones that matter most."

By the time Granddaddy had finished his master lesson, my father understood that he needed to buy only a small part of the town's voting population: the town's leaders who were for sale and its three shepherds (the reverend, priest, and pastor), whose devoted flocks tended to obey their every command.

Daddy's take on divine intervention eventually worked for him and has likewise worked for me. Of course, times change. For example, Daddy wouldn't have had much respect for a man like Squirrel. But Daddy's town didn't have Fox News, the internet, eBay, or our own weekly *Courier* newspaper. And so, in my case, I needed to keep Squirrel—deliverer of the mail and purveyor of products and opinions—close as my side pocket.

Barry Roth

I was surprised at the town's response to my interview in the *Courier*. I wasn't beaten. I wasn't cursed. I wasn't aggressively shunned. In fact, for several months I enjoyed a kind of popularity—at least with some groups of women.

A week after my *Courier* interview, I received a handwritten note in a sealed envelope that had been pushed under my front door. It was a cordial invitation to tea, signed by the wives of the town's priest, pastor, and reverend. Two days later I received a similar note, inviting me for coffee and cake, signed by the wives of the Town Council. Two days after that I received a third envelope, this time from a group called The Salon, inviting me for an evening of drinks and artsy discussion. The invitation was signed by a dozen women, each signature penned in a different colored ink and uniquely flourished.

Wondering why the envelopes had been hand delivered, I asked Allen and he said, "To avoid the notice of Squirrel and Jacqueline. In a town full of snoops, they're the worst."

"Interesting. What are they like?"

"I told you, Squirrel delivers the mail, so he's a steady guy, for all his quirks. Jacqueline is the loose cannon. Her mom ran away with some stranger in an army jacket and her father died some years ago, pickled drunk. Jacqueline never finished high school. She works in the diner and doesn't have any close friends, other than Squirrel."

"What's she like?"

"Big girl. Brunette. Stocky. Smokes too much. Wears a lot of black leather and rides a badass Harley—but I think it's all an act."

"Why?"

"I think she's lonely, scared—and angry. She acts the rowdy rebel, but I think she just wants what most women around here already have: husband, kids, home—respect."

"Have people been mean to her?"

"Maybe some of the women, when they were young ... catty girl stuff. But now I think they're just sorry for her. Maybe a little scared of her too. Alice, bless her generous heart, invited her several times to Haven House for tea—but Jacqueline never came, never even responded."

"A lost cause?"

"Alice would slap your wrist for saying such a thing. She blames herself for not reaching her."

"Hmmm. The more I learn about Alice, the more special she seems."

"And I thought you were a lost cause."

"Hey, all I did was show up unannounced."

"Unannounced? You pulled up in a red-hot Italian sports car—a convertible no less—desecrated our town's most sacred totem, then waltzed into Haven House like the la-di-da lord of the manor. And if that weren't enough, you gave an interview in which you insulted or confounded every notion cherished by the people who live here."

"I don't suppose I can get a do-over."
"What would you change?"
"I'm thinking blue sports car."
Allen shook his head.
"You're as difficult as Jacqueline."
"I don't mean to be. I'm just trying to fit in."
"Try harder."

Squirrel Evans
Jaqueline and me weren't hitched so we sometimes pulled in different directions. But we made a good team and more often than not agreed how things ought to be.

One good thing, we had the same weekday schedule. I picked her up every morning at seven. She had her own home but mostly stayed with me but didn't have a car, just an old Harley, a fat ass Electra Glide that fit her bottom just fine, so I drove us both to the Post Office, which was in City Hall, right opposite the mayor's office.

I took a lot of pride in my double duty as postmaster and mail carrier. I never missed a day and I hand-delivered everything I could easily transport. If something was too heavy or bulky, the named recipient—or an approved proxy—would pick it up at the office. Those were the rules, as stated in the Handbook and Manual given to me.

I had a special key for the large, incoming mailbox and never once did I let Jacqueline open it, though she asked numerous times, just to see what it was like. I told her she had to respect my professional boundaries. After that, she never again let me refill my own coffee cup at the diner, where she worked. She said I had to respect *her* professional boundaries, which made sense, though I knew she was just being petty.

Anyways, Jacqueline was a big help to me. Every morning, after I dumped whatever was in the incoming box onto a big, ol' wooden table, she helped me organize the great mix of envelopes and small packages into an order that matched the stops on my delivery route.

Now, nothin's for nothin' in this world, which means Jacqueline insisted on some compensation. It made no sense for me to pay her out of my own pocket, so I allowed her to keep any package marked *Current Resident,* or anything like that. Basically, this amounted to coupons and product samples, which she absolutely loved like Christmas morning. She kept the ones she wanted and sold or bartered the rest. Had herself a nice little business there.

Now, I admit I've always liked knowing what my neighbors are up to, but Jacqueline has a sickness. Because the woman is incurably nosey, helping me sort the morning mail provided her snooping eyes with yet another compensation. One time, I tested her patience by grabbing a couple picture postcards and holding them away from her prying eyes. That was a mistake. Quicker than you can flip a switch, she threw a roundhouse right that caught my shoulder and nearly busted it. After that, I just handed her all the damn postcards on a silver platter.

Eventually, people began whispering about our nosiness. That cost us some business. Now, most everyone in town hand-delivers their local postcards and invitations to keep their personal matters private.

Jacqueline
First it was the church wives, and I didn't say a word. And then it was the Town Council wives, and I shook my head.

But when I found out that a group of single ladies had invited Mr. Barry Roth to their first ever chatty Salon and didn't invite me, I blew a gasket—and I know what a fucking gasket is!

I felt invisible. Worthless. That's what I felt.

I was cursing them bitches when Squirrel said, "Honey, they don't mean nothin'. I bet they think we're married because we been together so long."

It has been a long time. Not too long, I'm not saying that. Not at all. Only, Squirrel and I have been sort of running in place, doing the same thing and not really getting anywhere. Those other women, maybe they're happy, maybe not, but I give 'em credit for one thing—they ain't running in place, I don't imagine. They're probably doing stuff they think will make them happy.

Squirrel and me? Nothing much has changed for a long time. I'm thinking we should shake things up … change as a couple. Yeah, I'm thinking marriage. That's what I'm thinking.

It's true he asked me once or twice and I turned him down, but he didn't understand my reasons. I let him think I wasn't happy about him delivering mail and going door to door selling stuff. But that wasn't it at all. I know how much money he makes. I'm always snooping over his bills and receipts and he makes more than enough for the two of us. Hell, we can raise babies on the money he makes. The problem is, he never asked me right. He was too damn casual, like he was asking me out for dinner.

Now, I know I'm not the most refined lady. I roar my Harley … fart like a truck driver … and arm-wrestle guys for free beer. Still, I'm a proud woman and insist on a proper marriage proposal. At the very least, he should take a shower, put on some clean clothes, get on one knee, and ask me nicely—with real love in his eyes. That's the way they do it in the movies.

Bottom line: I'm no women's libber. I want to be married. I want to be a wife. I love Squirrel, despite his faults and limitations, but if we're going to do this marriage thing, he has to do it right.

Come to Zee Kasbah

Alice Bouchet

    Following Lainey's lead, we ignored the signless door and uninviting street-side windows (blocked from the inside by heavy crimson curtains) and entered without hesitation.
    I didn't know what to expect, and yet, what I saw met my every fantasy. I followed Lainey through a clickety beaded curtain into a large, low-lighted room. The far-left walls were covered with dark tapestries. The far-right walls were bright murals depicting Arabian markets, minarets, muezzins calling for prayer. The large space between was divided vertically by white columns and screens of rose latticework. White sheets billowed from the ceiling. A strikingly beautiful woman in chic western garb (like a stewardess from Emirates Airline) showed us to an area in the back, sectioned off with ornate wooden panels. Inside this semi-private space was a low circular table covered with hammered tin and surrounded by a low leather bench. I panicked. I didn't think I could sit so low. If I did, I would surely need help getting up. Again, Lainey read my mind.
    "Watch your step going down. The table isn't as low as you think. It's actually quite comfortable."
    She was right and I soon settled in. Looking about, imagining myself in Istanbul or Marrakesh, I half expected harem girls to serve us, but I was not at all disappointed when a trio of dark-haired and mustachioed young men began laying silver tureens and platters on our table.
    "I arranged a tasting of a dozen different dishes," Lainey

whispered.

When the servers left, Lainey described each dish with an air of easy familiarity. She then described each condiment, pointing out which was sweet, which was spicy.

"Please," she said, indicating the exotic array of edibles. "Help yourself."

Without shame, without even self-consciousness, I devoured everything in sight: pita and hummus ... couscous ... baba ganoush ... Fattoush salad ... chicken shawarma ... Yemenite curry... jujeh kabobs ... fluke ceviche ...

When the dishes were cleared, Lainey asked if I'd like coffee, tea, or espresso. I'd never had espresso, so I asked for it, with all the insouciance of one who enjoys it daily.

Lainey Roth

We had a great afternoon, stuffing our faces and sharing stories. Alice told me more about Three Corners, her military family, Freedom Hall, and her special friends, Allen and Emily. I told her more about my Barry, my Wednesday pro bono work, and my friends at the Parkside East Synagogue. By the time I called for the check, we both felt heavy and exhausted.

We were a dozen steps from the door when I saw *him* ... dining alone ... as handsome as I daily remembered. Only, now he was real and (curse my luck) I was fat from a tencourse meal and with a friend who was even fatter and badly dressed. I hurried out the door (as if to outrun my conscience), praying he hadn't seen me.

Morris Fine

I saw her ... and the vision of her retreating figure became fixed in my mind. When I'd last seen her (how could I forget!), she'd been standing on the dark sidewalk, the light from the open door of the synagogue directly behind her, like a theater spotlight. That was nearly six months ago.

Lainey Roth

Leaving the restaurant, feeling Morris' questioning eyes on my retreating figure, it was all I could do to maintain my composure. Once outside, Alice thanked me again for the Kasbah experience but begged to postpone our shopping expedition for another day.

"I'm stuffed. No sense shopping for clothes after a meal like that. I couldn't fit into a potato sack!"

"Would you like me to walk you back?" I asked.

"No, I'm fine. I just want to stroll a bit. I'll call you tomorrow."

"Perfect," I said. And I meant it. I adored her, but I'd had enough Alice for one day. I needed to clear my head so I could focus on Morris. Had he seen me? Was he happy to see me? Why hadn't he called? Should I call him?

Morris Fine

Six months earlier, Lainey had contacted me directly (not through my publisher, publicist, or agent), reaching me on my cell while I was in New York, planning my next trip. She told me she was a big fan of my books and invited me (on behalf of her sisterhood) to speak at her synagogue about my work with marginally subsistent Jewish communities around the world.

[When I was about eight and just beginning Hebrew school, my grandfather Chaim, long deceased, told me the first of his many harrowing tales of the Russian village of his boyhood, focusing on stories of Jews who'd been dragged away for no crime—other than being a Jew—and not one Gentile raising a hand in defense or assistance.

In his stories, my grandfather was always the same age I was, forcing upon me a strong sense of identification and empathy. His stories made me very sad and very angry—surely his intent.

In large part due to my grandfather's inculcation, I grew up with a strong Jewish identity, though I am not religious. I have little interest in knowing—much less obeying—the Talmud's 613 mitzvot, or commandments. Quite frankly, even the ten basic *Thou Shall Nots* seem too restrictive to me. Throughout my sixty-two years I have abused nine of them, sometimes with great relish. But I've never killed anyone, though I'm sure I could—if necessary—to protect myself or someone I loved.

So, cutting to the chase, I grew up a secular Jew with a giant chip on my shoulder. After several professional false starts, I eventually found my calling: protecting the world's most exotic and endangered Jewish settlements—from the Brazilian rainforest to India's northeastern border states of Manipur and Mizoram.

Inasmuch as Jews are called the People of the Book, I suppose it's not surprising that I wrote about my adventures. In fact, I was quite successful. Magazines were eager to publish my articles, which—because I have a good eye with a camera—were always accompanied with arresting and provocative images. As my writing style matured and my experiences grew more varied, I began writing full-length books, which also found willing publishers and ready readers.]

"We need four to six weeks to prepare for the event," said

Lainey. "But after that, any early evening, Monday through Thursday, would do. We'd love to have you."

She sounded smart, sexy, buoyant.

"I have other commitments.... I'm busy planning my next trip.... But I'll check my schedule."

"That would be great. By the way, we pay $5000 and—following your presentation—we could set up a table for you to sell and sign your books."

My current book, *A Minyan in Madagascar,* wasn't selling as well as expected and my upcoming expedition to Tasmania promised to be expensive.

"Thank you. If my schedule allows, I'll send you some possible dates."

"Great. I'm looking forward to meeting you."

A few days later, we settled on a date for the event, six weeks out. After that we communicated sporadically by email to arrange the wording on the invitation and the design of the poster. Three days before the event, I received a second phone call from Lainey.

"Hi Morris. Everyone is looking forward to the show. Normally, a presenter arrives a half hour early to get comfortable with the microphone and lights. But since you're also using a projector, I'm thinking you should arrive at least an hour early. What do you think?"

"Will you be there?"

"Of course."

I imagined that she'd be beautiful ... and she was ... and is.

Three days later she greeted me with a warm handshake and showed me around the reception hall to review the technical particulars. After deciding on the lights and the placement of the lectern and screen, we still had forty-five minutes before the show. We spent the time as on a first date, sharing the facts of our lives, beginning with the basics and leading, incrementally, to mildly revelatory details. And then it was show time. People starting arriving—singles, couples, groups—many holding copies of my books. We pressed each other's hand and gave each other a look that implied *To be continued.*

***

My presentation went wonderfully well, audience members laughing and groaning, oohing and ahhing, exactly on cue. Following the sustained applause, I invited questions from the audience. When that spirited interaction began to wane, the temple president came on stage to thank me for an informative and moving experience. He then reminded the audience of the following week's Yizkor services, Mindy Birnbaum's upcoming bat mitzvah, and that I would be signing and selling books at a table near the coffee and cakes.

Lainey joined me there as my assistant, handing me open books to sign, her soft, naked fingers occasionally brushing mine.

In a hundred ways Lainey had facilitated the challenges of that day to make it successful. She was beautiful and wonderfully competent. And yet, something restrained me from asking, or even suggesting, that we see each other again. Yes, I was seeing someone else, but that had never stopped me before.

Lainey Roth

When the book-signing line had dwindled to the final two or three, Morris asked me in a whisper if I could retrieve his coat and wait with him outside while he called an Uber.

I thought this was devilishly calculated: the two of us alone together. By the time I brought his coat, he had signed the last of the books and was ready for parting handshakes and goodbyes.

Outside the synagogue, we stood close enough to whisper. It was chilly and I turned up my collar. Morris wore his long coat unbuttoned and it billowed in the breeze like a theatrical cape.

While he checked his phone for the status of his approaching ride, I stared at his craggy, handsome face, wondering if I should invite him somewhere. But all I managed was, "So, where do you like to eat when you're alone in New York?" At that moment, his Uber pulled up. He opened the rear passenger door as if he hadn't heard me or couldn't be bothered to answer. But as he slipped inside, he turned and smiled. "The Kasbah," he said, closing the door. The Uber drove away and I had no good reason to believe I would ever see him again.

Days later, when I realized the Kasbah was only a few blocks away from Barry's apartment, I began visiting my son more often, peeking into the Kasbah whenever time allowed, which was often. But I never once caught sight of Morris ... until the day I dined there with Alice.

Alice Bouchet

I walked home alone from the Kasbah, choosing my own route, deciding spontaneously to go left or right, plowing into shops and stores without reason. The experience was exhilarating but when its novelty wore, I felt lonely and abandoned, despite the irony of being surrounded by a million people.

Just then, feeling the need to check my phone map to establish my precise location, I realized how close I was to the East River though I had no sense of it. Imagine being so close to a large river without being able to hear it or smell it? It takes buildings like giant ramparts to block out a river, though I suppose the noisy cars and crowds also factored, and the very air itself. As to that, I'm used to the scents of pine, hyacinth, and red cedar, but that day my sensitive snooter was overloaded with the smells of gasoline, garlic, and curry. And no wonder, I was surrounded by as many restaurants as cars. Everywhere I looked—indoor, outdoor, takeout—there was a place to eat!

I continued wending the noisy streets, swiveling my head like an owl, all the while thinking: *Oh my God, look at this … look at that* and half-expecting Allen's response, which, now that I think of it, was the most natural thing in the world. I mean, I'd spent more time with Allen than with anyone else in my life and think of him as family.… Well, maybe not family, more like a best friend. But that's not right either. Truth is, I don't know what I think of Allen. I've never understood my feelings for him. But I know this: Allen is never far from my thoughts. Emily too.

Emily Schnyder

I panicked when Alice said she was going to New York. I could not imagine life without her.

"I know, that's why I'm leaving."

"But why? You haven't said why."

She paused for a moment and then asked, "Why do you build your snow globes?"

That surprised me. I'd never thought *why*.

"I'm an artist. I like to make beautiful things. Besides, we sell them at Freedom Hall."

Alice demurred. "The patriotic ones sell—the White House, Uncle Sam, the Bald Eagle, the Liberty Bell—they sell and they're wonderful. But they're not your best. The French cafés with the Eiffel tower; Moscow with its red and green minarets; the Wailing Wall in Jerusalem, the New York skyline—those are your best."

"They don't sell as well."

"No, but they're your most beautiful and creative designs and despite the fact that they don't sell, you continue to make them. Why?"

"I don't know. I suppose I'd like to visit those places someday."

Alice nodded. "I hope you do. I want you to be happy. I want you to be fully you. In part, that's why I'm going away."

"You're going away because of me?"

"No, I'm going away for me, but you figure into it. One day you will go away too."

"No!"

"Paris … Moscow … Jerusalem … New York. They're calling you."

"I can't even imagine."

"But you do. That's how you build your snow globes. You're just not ready to make the leap. Heck, it took me almost sixty years. But you're smarter than me and in your own way, you're stronger too."

"I am not! You are Alice Bouchet!"

Alice was silent awhile before she spoke again:

"Why do you think I kept your parents' house perfectly maintained all those years you lived with me?"

"I'm not sure."

"I knew you must return to your own home—your own life—as soon as you were ready. You couldn't live in Haven House forever. It's simply not for you. You need your own life. And, in time, you will leave Three Corners to discover where you really want to live the rest of your days."

"What if I don't want to leave?"

"Then you won't. But your decision should be a matter of informed choice—not a default based on fear."

"I can't imagine going away alone."

After a long pause, Alice asked, "When you imagine visiting those far-off places, are you alone?"

"No…. But I'm not with anyone in particular."

"But you're with someone. A friend? A partner?"

We'd never had this conversation before and it made me uncomfortable.

"Yes, I suppose. It always feels like someone is with me."

Alice looked at me tenderly. "I want happiness for you. I want happiness for me. Sometimes we have to look for it. Sometimes we need someone to help us find it. I waited too long to understand this. No reason you should make the same mistake."

Morris Fine

After long correspondences and much preliminary research, I had a good idea of the challenges facing Tasmanian Jews and was prepared to help any way I could. A week after my arrival, I made arrangements with two more sources on the mainland to ship kosher wine. I also arranged with a rabbi in Melbourne to travel to Hobart to perform circumcisions and bar mitzvahs.

I wanted to do much more in the way of finding suitable teachers and bakers, but with each passing day, thoughts of Lainey increasingly sidetracked my brain. Quite frankly, I couldn't get the woman out of my head. She was always there: brushing her naked fingers against mine as she handed me a book to sign ... standing on the dark sidewalk, spotlighted against the portal of light from the temple's open door ... looking at me with tragic eyes as I sat in the back of my Uber, ready to depart.... These swirling images were so distracting I was unable to give Tasmania's struggling Jewish community my best effort. I had no choice but to cut short my trip and return to New York.

***

Home two months, I still hadn't contacted her, afraid she might be angry or disappointed because I'd left so hurriedly and without explanation. But what could I have said? *I feared your irresistible charm would disrupt my important work.* Could I have said that with a straight face, even if it were true?

I spent two days drinking merlot and staring into the depths of my psyche, drifting through mists of past and present. In those harrowing divines I saw nothing I might latch onto.

Next morning, staring at my naked face in my bathroom's bulb-brightened mirror, I saw myself looking older than I remembered and realized I must act soon while I still had some vestigial good looks to trade on.

I lunched that day at the Kasbah—and Fate smiled on me.

Lainey Roth
   "Lainey, how are you?"
   "Morris is that you?" I asked, though his name had come

up in my phone contacts.

"Indeed, it is. I saw you fly out of the Kasbah the other day. You were in a rush ... and with a friend ... otherwise, I would have called out."

"What a coincidence! First time I've been there in ages!"

It was a white lie but a good one, as we both happily agreed that the Hand of Fate had brought us together.

We talked tentatively, as if we each were afraid of having our true self discovered. For my part, I was anxious to see him in person, to cut through the bullshit. But then I remembered how long he had kept me waiting and it made me angry. I mean, we'd shared some intense moments before and after his show ... and then—*poof!*—off he was with nary a fare-thee-well. Day after day I waited, but he never texted, never called, never emailed. What's up with that? He couldn't spare five minutes to say hello? Every poor Jew in the world is more important than me? Really?

Then I remembered his lecture (all the far-flung and dangerous places he visited in order to help desperate Jews cling to their lives and traditions), and I considered how remote and dangerous his recent situation might have been, and my heart swelled with respect for the brave man.

And then I thought, *Wait a second. He was due back a month ago. And if he was healthy enough to dine at the Kasbah, he sure as hell could have called me earlier.*

I went on this way until it tired and bored me. Fact is, I wanted to see him. I didn't want to stand on ceremony. I didn't want to play games. But I also didn't want to sell myself cheaply. What I wanted was to bide some time ... and that's when I thought of Alice: "She's new to town," I said to Morris, referring to my dining partner at the Kasbah. "I've promised to help her shop and settle in." Before I knew it, I was chatting her up, without exactly knowing why.

"She sounds very interesting," Morris said, sounding entirely bored with the subject of Alice and Three Corners. But that irked me and I doubled down: "Here's the kicker ..." And I told him, at length, how I met Alice through my work at the Manhattan Landlords Association and how it happened that she and my Barry had swapped homes. When even that story failed to excite his interest, I took it very personally. I mean, I'd been talking about my Barry!

For that crime, Morris sank in my estimation.... But I'm a forgiving sort. I believed he might yet clamber back into my good graces, but I needed to see his selflessness, beyond the fact of his helping needy Jews. I needed to see him sweat on my account. Alice's role in all this became suddenly clear.

"How about we double date?"

"Double date?"

"Sure," I said cheerily. "Let's get reacquainted. Only, I'm busy with Alice for the next few weeks. She doesn't know a soul here, other than me. Can you help?"

"What exactly are you asking?"

"Do you have a nice friend for her?"

He paused two scant seconds. "Off the top of my head, I can't think of anyone."

"Think harder. She's my new best friend. And she's a special lady: funny, interesting ... smart as a whip."

"What else I should know?"

"She's nearly sixty and not Jewish."

"That doesn't widen my pool of possibilities."

"C'mon, you must know a million people."

"I'm more of a loner than you think."

"You're not a loner. You have a legion of devoted readers."

"They're not all friends."

"Granted. But you're popular. C'mon, find her a nice guy."

"All right," he said with a whiff of reluctance. "I'll try. For you."

"Great! Let's go someplace fun, and a little exotic. She'll like that."

The First Day of the Rest of My Life

Emily Schnyder

At twenty-one, I left Haven House and returned to my own home. I tried working as a tailor, but without the steady work from the former Institute's cadets and officers, I did not make enough money.

I thought again about going to college. I've known all my life that I have some talent for drawing and draftsmanship, but I never wanted to leave Alice, which is another way of saying I didn't want to be alone, for while I had no close friends in Three Corners (other than Alice and Allen), making new ones, even friendly acquaintances, has never been easy for me. For example, there were three popular girls in town—Melissa, Regan, and Darla—whom I've known all my life, though I've never been close to them. I say *them* because they speak and act like a group, like a three-headed monster, which is not nice, I know, but they've never been nice to me. In fact, they have been monstrously insensitive. They did not come to my parents' funeral, even though it was held at Haven House. They never said they were sorry to hear the news. They just pretended I didn't exist. And I knew Melissa, Regan, and Darla better than I knew any of the other girls—so you see how hard it is for me to make friends.

Anyway, though I did not go to college, you'd be wrong to think I lack a higher education. During my years in Haven House, Alice was a scrupulous and exacting mentor, as all the Bouchet women had been when it came to preparing their daughters for life. But Alice wanted more for me and insisted that I learn (as she had) everything a military cadet must learn, save for the actual engagement of arms. From her own private experience, she thought I would do well to understand life in terms of battlefield strategies and so she enhanced my training with Sun Tzu's *The Art of War,* a book she had discovered in her grandfather's library. I keep an inscribed copy (a present from Alice when I turned twenty-one) on my night table, alongside whatever else I'm reading. If ever I write a book I will dedicate it to Alice, using the same words Faulkner used to dedicate *Go Down Moses* to his childhood mammy, Caroline Barr: "… who gave to my family a fidelity without stint or calculation of recompense and to my childhood an immeasurable devotion and love."

***

To say I'm undemonstrative is an understatement. Spend a day with me and you'll see that I'm withheld, interior, and secretive. I think I've always been this way, growing up in the shadows as I did. But my isolating character did not depress me or even make me sad. I like who I am. I'm different, and I like me that way. My secret hope was to meet a man who was engaged by my differences. Alice knew how I felt and said, "Vive la différence!"

Several years after returning to my own home and seeing me struggling, she offered me the opportunity to work at Freedom Hall as a docent and in the gift shop. Several years would pass before I was inspired to create my handmade snow globes.

***

Sitting at my kitchen table in my pj's and robe might have inspired another drear painting of self-examination (*Self Portrait with Still Life, #31*), but on the day that I read Barry Roth's interview in the *Courier*, I burst out laughing.

That day was the first day of the rest of my life.

The Interview

Allen Briggs

Knowing that Squirrel ended his shift at the Post Office at four o'clock (just as Jacqueline was preparing for the early dinner crowd at the diner), I greeted Squirrel at the bottom of the Courthouse steps.

"Got a minute? I'm buying."

"Works for me. I'm thirsty."

We walked side by side to the Red, White, and Brew. As usual, everything inside was dark: the walls, the floor, the windows, the air. In a town where everyone craved everyone else's secrets, this was the one public place where secrets were shared and bartered. All who entered checked their better angels and conscience at the door.

Gavin Lissome sat in the back, in the shadows of the dark, checking his receipts on his back-lighted laptop. As usual, he drank ginger beer. Some thought he might be a recovering alcoholic; others said he was wise enough to avoid his own watered-down swill.

While I ordered us a couple real beers, Squirrel chose a table against the far wall, as far from Gavin as possible. As soon as we were settled, I got down to business.

"So, what's the verdict? People willing to forgive and forget?" I was referring to Barry's interview, published a week earlier in the *Courier*.

Squirrel, who had just begun sipping his beer, wiped the foam from his mouth with the back of his hand.

"Jury's split, which surprises me. Quite frankly, Barry said nothing to excuse his behavior and what he did say was silly, vague, or insulting."

"It wasn't that bad."

"Really? How about Alice sleeping in his bed? How'd you like reading that?"

I shook my head. With each passing year, I was more resigned to taking my love secret to the grave. Still, it rankled.

"That was despicable," I said. "She's the leader of our town.... The Bouchets are our Founding Fathers." I was walking a tightrope, balancing my good-standing as a Three Corners man against my promise to Alice to watch over Barry.

"Well, I did what you asked," said Squirrel. "I gave I him an opportunity to explain himself—but he did nothing to help his case."

"So, where do we stand?"

"Jury's split: men want to hang him; women want to hug him."

I must have stared cross-eyed. "Hug him? What for?"

"You can't see?"

I searched my brain. "Because he's from out of town? Is that the attraction?"

Squirrel shook his head. "We get out-of-towners all the time. But they're mostly like us. Barry is different."

I nodded. "I get that. But I figured his differences would make him unappealing."

"I'd say our men are mostly suspicious, but our women are mostly curious."

I chewed on that. I'd lived nearly sixty years in Three Corners and no one (other than Alice or Emily) had ever asked my opinion, much less a personal question. I resented Barry's social ease.

"So, despite his unpopular opinions, he skates on his differences."

"Your friend is incredibly dodgy," said Squirrel. "His answers were as clear as a foggy mirror. Who is he? Why is he here? No one seems to really know, not even you. The men are wary, but the ladies—at least the single ones—seem to find him sexy... exotic."

"Oh for chrissake, he's from New York, not Paris!" With a pang, I recalled that Alice was in New York. "I never liked New York."

"You've never been there," said Squirrel, who was better traveled, having already visited St. Louis and Kansas City.

"Well, I don't think I'd like it. And I don't think it's exotic or sexy."

Squirrel shrugged.

"What about Jacqueline?" I asked. "She find him sexy?"

"Don't know. She doesn't read the *Courier* and he hasn't yet been to the diner. She wasn't invited to any of the soirees."

Squirrel Evans

Jacqueline is smart enough in her way, but she is very impressionable and insecure, which makes it easy for me to praise her with ironic or backhanded compliments.

One day I told her, "You're the acme of the diner's waitstaff," which she liked hearing, despite being the diner's only waitress ... other than old Melinda, who filled in whenever she was unwell, which was never ... which is still true, by the way, and which still drives me batshit crazy. I mean, Jacqueline eats like a sow, smokes like a thief, brawls like a

Mick, and she's the goddamn picture of golden health. Me? I take my vitamins, exercise like an acrobat, and always have a cough or some other achy complaint. I once pointed out to Jacqueline her exceptional wellness, saying she's as healthy as a horse … which earned me a sharp jab to my right pec, which stung for a week. I later apologized, saying all I meant was that she had a strong constitution, which I knew would confuse her further. And I was right. From that day forward, Jacqueline referred to herself as a strong patriot, inside and out, whatever that means.

For the record, I know my petty jibes say more about me than they do about Jacqueline. I'm the one who is weak and insecure. For many years I heard jokes and slights that cut her, and never once did I make the jokers pay for their cruelty. A cowardly fool, I took my pain out on her.

The Interview

Nice to meet you, Barry. Please answer the following ten questions:

What's your full name?
I go by the names Barry Roth and Baron Rothschild.

What brought you to Haven House?
The desire to excite my life; the possibility of finding love.

How long do you expect to stay?
A year, more or less; I'd like to vote in a national election.

Where is Alice Bouchet?
Let's see, midnight in New York—she's probably asleep in my bed.

What were you doing on top of the Honor Stone?
Attempting to fast-track my destiny.

What do you do for a living?
Eat, sleep, take my meds, write stories.

What church do you belong to?
All of them, except the ones with gods and snakes.

Why drive a red Fiat?
The self-driving ones are still in development; they were all out of blue.

What does the Second Amendment mean to you?
I can bear arms but not children.

Do you want to help make America great again?
I want to improve America; I want to make the world a better place.

Barry Roth

My tea with the church wives felt more inquisitorial than conversational. They were only three, but they sat upright on a Shaker sofa whose straight back and sleek wooden armrests reflected the simple and unyielding strength of their shared core beliefs. I sat on a stiff ladderback chair, facing them.

"Is it Mr. Roth or Mr. Rothschild?" asked the hostess, seated in the middle.

"Please, call me Barry."

"Thank you, Barry. And welcome to Three Corners."

"Thank, you. It's nice to be here."

"How are you finding our town?"

I smiled. "Easily enough. There's only one main street and I'm on top of the hill. Haven't got lost yet."

First pause.

"I mean, what do you think of Three Corners? I suppose most people are proud of their towns, but we have good reason to take special pride in ours."

"It's certainly unique. Alice told me the town's history, especially about the George Long Military Institute and Freedom Hall. Very interesting."

"Alice? You call her *Alice*?"

"Yes. Isn't that her name?"

"Everyone in town calls her Miss Bouchet."

"Not everyone," said the second wife.

"That's true," said the third wife. "There's Allen Briggs and that strange dark girl. But everyone else."

"She asked you to call her *Alice*?"

"I don't recall that she asked me. It just seemed natural that we would use our first names."

"Did you enjoy meeting her?"

"She's delightful. Very interesting ... and a great sense of humor. But I never actually met her. We've communicated only by phone, email, and text. But I understand she's enjoying her new life in New York."

"Isn't it dangerous?" asked the Reverend's wife.

"Aren't there addicts and prostitutes?" asked the Pastor's wife.

"Those poor souls are everywhere," I said.

"Not here!"

"Not in Three Corners!"

"God forbid!"

"Well, perhaps not here. But I'm sure Alice will be fine. It's a low-crime neighborhood."

Shocked silence.... Then, as if to lift the conversation: "What about churches?"

"What about them?"

"Are there churches in your neighborhood?"

"Hmmm. That's a good question. I suppose there must be."

"You don't know for certain?"

"I can't say that I'm a regular church-goer."

"But you do go to church?"

"I've been to many churches."

"There are three churches in Three Corners."

All three women smiled.

"Stop by on Sunday."

"Visit all three. You'll meet our husbands, Pastor Pitchford and Reverend Morgan, and Father Steele."

"In Three Corners, we have one faith but three different doors."

"Something for everyone," I said. "Thank you."

***

The Town Council's wives were more interested in my worldliness than my soul.

"Do you actually use both names, Barry Roth and Baron Rothschild?"

"I do."

"How did you come by *Baron Rothschild?*"

"It came to me, so I adopted it."

"Very interesting."

The women exchanged meaningful glances.

"According to your interview, you attempted to wrest the sword from the Honor Stone in an attempt to fast-track your destiny. How'd that go?"

"Again, I'm so sorry for that awful spectacle. It was entirely unintentional, I assure you. But, to answer your question, though I clearly failed to draw the sword, the experience reinforced my belief that I have a destiny … possibly a great one."

"Really? How so?"

"Well, in order to be great, I think one needs to overcome great challenges."

"The Honor Stone was a great challenge?"

"Not exactly. More like a preview or a metaphor of my future challenges."

"What challenges are those?"

"I don't know. I just assume I'll face some."

"You mean here? In Three Corners?"

"I suppose, here and elsewhere."

Another exchange of glances, followed by a pause and then a question that changed the mood:

"Do you usually drive foreign cars, like your red Fiat?"

I smiled, happy for the new line of questioning.

"Well, not in Manhattan, where I'm from. Parking is very difficult there."

"Aren't there parking lots and garages?"

"Yes, but not enough. It's much easier to take the train or a taxi."

Pause.

"Most people here have never taken a train or a taxi."

I thought of my father. He made a show of avoiding the

subway.

"My father always kept a brand-new Cadillac garaged about eight blocks from where we lived. Whenever he wanted to drive, he took a taxi to his car. When he returned his car to the garage, he took a taxi home."

"That's crazy!"

"Wasn't that expensive?"

"More of an annoyance. But yes."

Meaningful glances ... and then:

"So, what do you plan to do in Three Corners?"

I smiled. "You know, widen my horizons ... make new friends."

The hostess waved off my insincere vagueness:

"I meant, what kind of work do you plan to do?"

Apparently, she did not believe I told stories for a living.

"I write."

"And that pays the bills?"

"It has," I said with a smirk. "And then some."

Reverberating silence.

"Besides," I added, "I have savings ... and family money, if necessary."

The women looked at each other with wide-open eyes.

***

When I received the invitation from the ladies of The Salon, I noted it was an evening affair. That gave it a certain elan. And when I saw that each of the ladies had signed the invitation with a uniquely flourished signature, I had the feeling they were competing for my attention. That added a certain frisson. But when I learned that all the women were *single* and anxious to meet me to discuss *the man and his books,* the event projected as my kind of bacchanal: a dozen motivated women hanging on my every word.

***

For the most part, the ladies had primped to impress. For sure, some swigged beer out of cans and some from bottles … one flicked cigarette ash into a floral saucer … and many had visible tattoos … but there were three (apparently unmarked by ink) who sat closest and caught my attention with their prettiness. Left to right these were Melissa, Darla, and Regan, according to their nametags. I gathered the one in the middle was the hostess and that we were in her parents' parlor.

"So, you're an author. You write books," said Melissa, a brunette.

She must have googled me. Perhaps the invitation had been her idea. I liked her.

"Yes. I'm a novelist."

"What kind of novelist?" asked Regan, a freckled redhead with country curls.

I knew what she meant. I'd been asked that question a thousand times.

"If you don't mind, it's easier for me to say what I don't write."

"Have it your way, Mr. Roth," she said, smiling coyly. "Tell us what you don't do."

Looking past her enticing smile, I began to explain, "I don't write genre-based stories. Meaning, I don't write mysteries, fantasy, love stories—"

"What else is there?"

Everyone laughed.

I froze—an insect caught in the light.

To restore my credibility, I smiled falsely and said, "My books don't fit into neat categories. They may have elements of romance, mystery, and so on, but they're not formulaic. They're not—"

"Predictable," suggested the blonde whose nametag read *Darla*. "You write literature."

"Thank you, Darla." *Thank you. Thank you. Thank you.* "Yes, you could call it *literature*."

But the ladies had not come for *literature*. Someone called out:

"Cut to the chase: You married?"

Raw laughter! ... the nervous kind, as when the audience's collective funny bone is suddenly thwacked.

"No," I said when the laughter died. "Not married."

Questions came like a hail of arrows:

"Ever been married?"

"No."

"Engaged?"

"No."

"Children?"

"No."

"Cats?"

"No."

"Are you straight?"

Explosive laughter!

"Yes," I said, though with some embarrassment.

"So, what's your story?" asked Regan. "Haven't found the

right girl?"
 I looked her in the eye. "No, Mom, I haven't."
 Light laughter.
 Someone else asked, "Your mother wants you to marry?"
 "She thinks it will make me happy."
 "Listen to your mother!"
 More laughter.
 I added, "My mother wants grandchildren. And soon."
 "How soon?"
 "Yesterday."
 Loud laughter.
 I was feeling more secure.
 "She pressuring you?"
 "You kidding? She bribed me."
 "What did she offer?"
 "Her apartment."
 Pause.
 "You don't have your own place?"
 "I do—in fact, that's where Alice Bouchet is staying."
 Quiet. The audience seemed unsure how to respond.
 "But my mother's place is nicer."
 Another pause.
 "How much nicer?"
 "Let's see," I said, feigning mental calculations. "I rent a one-bedroom, five-story walk-up on the noisy Lower East Side. My mother owns a three-bedroom, three-bath penthouse with a wraparound terrace, right off Fifth Avenue, facing Central Park."
 "Sounds ritzy!"
 "What's it worth?"
 I shouldn't have taken the bait. But I did.

"At least six million. Maybe more."
Stunned silence.
I'd made a mistake. I knew it.
More questions:
"What are you looking for?"
"In a woman?"
"Hell yes! Why we here?"
The laughter spiked but died quickly. The audience wanted to hear what I had to say. I thought: *I want a best friend. I want a wife. I want a mother for my children.*
"I want love," I said, keeping it simple.
Ironically, I'd struck just the right note. The *ooohs* and *ahhhs* were palpable.
"Love," someone repeated.
"That's beautiful," said another.
"What does your dream girl look like?" someone asked.
"I don't have a type," I said, lying to the audience of gingers and blondes.
"What about religion?"
"Overrated." I meant that as a joke, but no one laughed.
"Any turn-offs?"
Smoking ... beer guzzling ... tattoos ... conservative attitudes ...
"Violent tempers ... vows of chastity."
No one laughed. The conversation had become serious.
"What about politics? Are you political?"
My eligibility was being seriously vetted: no more jokes ... nothing glib.
"I'm not one to march or rally, but I do enjoy a good political discussion."
A brief pause, and then:
"You said you'd like to vote in a national election. Do you

usually vote along party lines?"

At this point, I laughed uneasily. "Let's just say I'm predictably unpredictable."

Once again, no one laughed.

Two Bachelors

Alice Bouchet

I told Lainey I needed a few more days before I could go shopping.

"You okay?"

"Fine, just tired from the whirlwind."

I did not mention the five pounds I'd gained from the baba ganoush and couscous or how, saddle-bagged with the extra weight, I'd struggled to return to my apartment, crawling up the last flight of stairs on my chubby hands and knees, insensible to Sun Tzu's martial encouragement.

"Well, that's alright," said Lainey. "You just relax. It's only Tuesday. We'll go shopping early Friday and get your hair done late in the day. I'll have you all ready for Saturday."

"What's Saturday?"

"I've arranged a double date."

"A double date?"

"Exactly. My friend Morris Fine is picking me up at my place. He's bringing his friend Gerald Ellison for you."

"But I've never met him."

"Exactly. That's the way blind dates work in New York."

"But … but …"

"It's all arranged. Dinner and dance. You'll see … Morris is entertaining and Gerald will be a gentleman, I'm sure. We'll have a lovely evening."

"Oh my god, how do you know?"

"Because I've done this a thousand times. Trust me."

Lainey Roth

Taberna, ergo sum. I shop, therefore I am.

My friend Lola assigned me the motto as a joke and while I distrusted her Latin, I liked it. And why not? I know who I am. I'm a shopper.

I don't usually buy much, but I love browsing: home goods, jewelry, cosmetics, accessories, clothing. Especially clothing. I'm a sommelier of fashion. Ask my friends. They'll tell you I'm the go-to-gal for designers and brands, vintage and trendy. I know which lines run large, which run small, and which styles are best. Lucky me, I'm still a well-proportioned size six, so I can waltz into Bergdorf Goodman and know that almost anything in my size will fit like a glove. But I also knew that Alice would be a big challenge (if you know what I mean) and that shopping for her would require a special strategy. Figuring that Alice was about five seven and at least one seventy-five, I knew she'd be a 1-X in some lines but only a size sixteen or eighteen in others. Now, I have friends who would rather die than have it known they were wearing a 1-X, but I didn't now Alice well and didn't want to risk embarrassing her while we were shopping together, so I did some thinking and came up with a plan.

Morris Fine

I knew the double date was Lainey's way of getting back at me. I wasn't happy about it, but I really couldn't blame her: I'd left her hanging after the book event … avoided her for two months while I was in Tasmania … waited two more months after my return to call her … and even then, I think we both knew that without our serendipitous sighting at the Kasbah, we might still be two lonely hearts at large.

Afraid of disappointing her again, I took special care in choosing a date for her friend Alice.

Gerald Ellison

Morris and I weren't close but we shared close friends and were used to seeing each other at weddings, funerals, bar mitzvahs, and the occasional New Year's Eve party or fundraiser. I'd always thought Morris was a good guy, if a little aloof and sometimes full of himself.

We were both inveterate bachelors and while I used that fact on occasion to assume a level of connection between us, he'd always deflected my maneuver or ignored it altogether. It occurred to me that he saw himself as playing in a higher league of bachelors—a Major League to my Minor League. I respectfully (and silently) disagreed. When I privately toted up our respective selling points, I saw myself as competitive. I'm a successful architect, well-regarded for my design of small museums, galleries, and exhibition spaces. He's a travel writer with a specialty in saving the modern lost tribes of Judaism. In my mind, our bachelor quotients were basically even.

Well, perhaps he did have some slight advantages. After all, it was one thing to create a physical space for art (as I did) and quite another to create actual art—or something very much like it (which he did). And while I could pretend to have stronger artistic sympathies than I do, Morris's arty memoir-travelogues spoke for themselves, even though the marketing of Morris as a modern messiah was, I thought, an example of outrageous overreach. Having looked him in the eye on numerous occasions, I never saw a hint of holiness. I saw someone who'd hit on a good idea and run with it—all the way to the bank.

Really, I thought the biggest difference between us was our appearance. He was endowed with impressive height and a slender frame and could wear almost anything to advantage, equally impressive in jungle khakis as he was in jacket and jeans. Me? I had the squat thickness of a butcher. T-shirts were impossible. Any tuxedo made me look like a penguin.

Okay, I was jealous. Morris was a dashing man of the world. Me? I was a designer of empty spaces. Ironically, as an exhibition designer, I was praised as a master of negative space—the planned nothingness surrounding an artistic shape thought by some to have its own artistic merit. I was happy for the praise, but being a master of negative space is an invisible and fleeting achievement. If I wanted to crow, what could I do but point to an empty space and say "That's mine!"

Shopping Spree

Alice Bouchet

New York was enlightening and enticing, but also sinuous and intimidating. A wrong turn could easily lead me to a dark alley and death.

There were times I sought strength in remembering the accomplishments of my great-great grandma Bouchet. If she could cross an ocean and half a continent to live on top of a hill in the middle of nowhere, I could take a subway by myself to Thirty-fourth Street and Herald Square.

"No way! Are you crazy?" said Lainey.

She's a lovably pushy sort, but still.

"Why ever not?"

I'd been looking forward to taking the subway by myself. I saw it as a challenge; a visitor's rite of passage. And I wasn't used to being told *No*.

Lainey noted my querulous tone. "I mean, just not today. Not your first time," she said. "The subway is complicated. You have to buy a MetroCard … and if there isn't a teller, you have to use a machine … and the machines are confusing … and not all of them work …"

By the time she finished explaining about uptown and downtown, local and express, cross-town and shuttles, I was way past my peeve and deeply grateful for her help.

"I'll meet you outside your building in exactly one hour," she said. "I'll help you set up a Metro account on your phone. After today, you can travel about as you please."

***

An hour later, walking down the subway stairwell on the corner of Delancey and Essex, Lainey took my arm as though she thought I might fall or run away. I knew she saw me as an adorable country bumpkin—and her personal charge—but I don't think she really understood what it meant to be a Bouchet—or how much I'd learned from Sun Tzu. That would come later.

Anyway, New York's subterranean world was as dank and dirty and fascinating as I expected: I saw an old Asian man reading a foreign newspaper with red print ... a black boy wearing loosely tied gold sneakers ... a young woman with shaggy purple hair and a black nose ring.... Even the most quotidian things seemed otherworldly: an overflowing receptacle ... encaged sooty lightbulbs ... wads of gum stuck everywhere like blackened barnacles.

Lainey led me carefully to the edge of the platform.

"Avoid that," she said, pointing to a black third rail that ran beside a pair of comparatively shiny tracks. "That's the one that carries the juice. That one will fry you."

I assumed she was funning me, but I went along. "Anything else I should know?"

"Yes. If you find yourself down there, don't feed the alligators. It's against the law. Big fine if you're caught."

***

The train seemed to move quite fast, but with sudden jolts and loud clacking. After fifteen minutes, it slowed to our destination and I was able to read the various signs: *34 Street ... Broadway ... Herald Square ... Penn Station ... Madison Square Garden.* Every one of those renowned places had been described in my guide books, but when I looked about, no one else seemed excited. I held my tongue, but I was bursting!

When the train stopped and the doors opened, an equal crush of people exited and entered at the same time. Though relatively slight, Lainey ploughed ahead, an impressive blocker, giving as good as she got with hip checks and elbows. I followed her lead all the way down the platform and up two stairwells, until we reached daylight and street-level Manhattan.

"Where are we?" I said, gasping the gasoline-fumed air.

Lainey sprightly pointed to a pair of right-angled street signs, then broke into a twangy burlesque: "Give my regards to Broadway, remember me to Herald Square."

Oh my God, she was right! I was standing on the crossroads of holy ground, immortalized by the great George M. Cohan. I looked all about. Every sightline was amazing.

"This is amazing. Thank you! What do we do first?"

Lainey smiled. "As Caesar said to his legions when they were about to cross the Rubicon, "*Let's go shopping!*" With that, she pointed across the street and upwards. There, on top of the widest building I'd ever seen—an entire New York city block—I saw a giant red sign, itself the size of a big building: WORLD'S LARGEST STORE.

I was stunned. The Colossus of Rhodes could not have inspired greater wonder.

"Thar she blows!" called Captain Lainey, pointing to our destination: "Macy's! Eleven stories high … a million square feet of *shopping*. Hold on tight, my dear, we are getting you a new wardrobe!"

I didn't know what to say. Lainey was as much a whirlwind as New York itself.

Lainey Roth

I led her through labyrinths of glitzy perfumeries ... carousels of lingerie ... dress displays like tropical flora. Of course, there were shoes and tops and so much else, but there's no need for a lengthy accounting. Just know that Alice was happy.

Alice Bouchet

I'd never been so happy. I'd never felt so womanly before. Comparatively speaking, life in Three Corners had been as exciting as a horse blanket, and Haven House hadn't always lived up to its name: its Bouchet men only slightly more enlightened than the college's officers in the way they regarded women.

It was sad for us all when Mother died, but especially for me, I think. I was only twelve and had no sisters. My father and brothers were soldiers or training to join their ranks. The cadets ignored me. I really didn't have any close friends. My closest friend was Allen Briggs, a classmate, and like most boys, he was intimidated by the men of my family.

I remember Christmas being particularly sad the year my mother died. As the only female, I thought the holiday would make me feel special—in a loved and rewarded way—but I was only ever encouraged to be Mother's replacement as cook and housekeeper, and the only presents I received were holiday boxes of candy or practical gifts, like a prettily embroidered apron. Nothing personal, certainly nothing feminine. To be fair, on some rare occasions my father and brothers did gift me some wonderful books, though it never occurred to them (I don't think) to give me a copy of *Anna Karenina* or *Madame Bovary* or *Moll Flanders* or any other book with a strong womanly protagonist. It certainly never occurred to them to give me books by women about women. I don't think they knew any.

Allen was a nice boy and a good friend. He made me daisy chains. Sometimes we bumped into each other and I always hoped it was intentional on his part and that he would do it again. But all he ever did was apologize. We sometimes met in the school library or by the river that formed the western boundary of the college's campus. Allen invited me to his home only once. His father made a poor living as a carpenter and his mother was a terrible homemaker—the place was unkempt and dirty, and his father's grimy tools lay about as if the entire house were his toolshed. When I visited, I may have grimaced and Allen may have seen it and been embarrassed. I wasn't invited back for many years.

After his mother and father passed, Allen cleaned up the home mightily—made a lovely and tidy place for himself—removed all his father's tools to a revamped toolshed and set up a small office inside, where he conducted his modest business. I visited his home on several occasions, always casually, when I happened to be nearby, and was always asked to sit awhile on the porch or come inside for a lemonade or tea.

While my family lived, Allen did not visit me often, but when he did, we usually stayed on the porch or the back veranda. When it was cold or rainy, we'd go into the parlor or the kitchen. Once or twice, I showed him the library. But he was never invited to climb the stairs to the second floor. Even when I came into sole possession of Haven House, I never invited him upstairs. And so, he never entered my room. By the time we were middle-aged, I think we'd both grown afraid of the idea.

    My shopping spree with Lainey was life-changing. Other than my mother's remarks regarding my expected inheritance of her trousseau, no female had ever expressed any interest in my womanliness ... until the day I stood before a public mirror in Macy's fourth-floor Designer Collection, holding designer panties against my body. Unthinkable! Even more unthinkable, I had a date the very next day—with a strange man!

Sounds of Brazil

Lainey Roth

"Wear the black dress tonight," I'd told Alice that morning.

"Do we know where we're going for dinner?"

"We do. We're going to Picholine."

"Sounds French."

"Indeed it is. French-Mediterranean—and very elegant."

"Oooh. Sounds lovely."

"Afterwards," I'd added in a sultry undertone, "we're going downtown to Sounds of Brazil."

"Sounds wonderful…. What is it?"

"Girl, we're talking dance music—live and *hot*."

"Oh my!"

"We're talking the *Afro-Latino Diaspora*."

"Lord! … What's that?"

"Music from South Africa … Brazil … the Caribbean—the hot of the hot!"

"Oh my!"

"We're talking the home of Latin legends like Tito Puente and Celia Cruz."

"I think I know them! Will they be there?"

"Well, they're dead. But Little Pablo and Haitian Hottie will get us movin'."

"You mean dancing?"

"Of course! Isn't that exciting?"

Alice Bouchet

My dress for that evening was very daring—for me. It had

a reasonably modest front but a somewhat sunken back that left my shoulder blades bare.

"I don't think I can do it."

"Do what?"

I wasn't sure what to say. My mind was a jumble of things I didn't think I could do.

"Dance" slipped from my mouth.

"Dance? Why not?"

"I don't know. I suppose I'm out of practice."

I hadn't danced since the night of my prom ... when Allen laid his tentative fingertips on my taffeta-covered shoulders.

"Relax," said Lainey. "It's like riding a bike."

Another thing I'd never learned to do. Too afraid of losing control and crashing.

"I bet Gerald is a good dancer," she said.

That brought me back. "I've never even met him!"

"Don't worry so much. He's just another man. Just another date."

Oh Lainey!

Gerald Ellison

Morris told me we'd be meeting the ladies at Lainey's apartment for a casual pre-dinner cocktail. I thought it was a great idea. I'd get to see the top-floor apartment of one of New York's classiest pre-war buildings, with all the architectural and design embellishments I admire. I was also curious to see how Lainey furnished and decorated. Morris said she was smart and funny and passionate, and I wondered how all that might translate into her design taste.

***

The building (which had been impeccably maintained) was

everything I expected and more, but Lainey's apartment disappointed. I saw nothing bold or daring, certainly nothing whimsical. Every detail: the lampshades ... the paintings ... the perfectly faded Persian carpets ... all bespoke a quiet and self-assured elegance ... and while everything fit perfectly by color and design, the overall effect was underwhelmingly dowdy. I thought she might have saved her boldest ideas for her bedroom, but, sad to say, that room was not part of her tour.

***

I haven't yet mentioned Alice Bouchet. Nervous about meeting her, I'd all but blocked her from my mind until she came toward me, her right hand extended like an eager politician's.

"It's a pleasure to meet you, Mr. Ellison."

She was a little older than I expected (nearer my age than Lainey's), but she seemed perfectly comfortable in her silvered maturity. Her hair was shiny like freshly cut lead and hiply styled (sharply cleaved and hove to the right), and while she was a tad thickish in her black dress and pumps, she looked confident and strong and altogether appealing.

"Why, thank you. And please call me Gerald—or Gerry, if you prefer."

"I think I prefer *Gerald*. It's a lovely name. My few friends call me *Alice*. I hope you will too."

"I'm sure you have more than a few friends, Alice."

"Actually, Gerald, before coming to New York, I counted only two friends—and they both call me Alice. Everyone else I know—mostly from my town—calls me Miss Bouchet."

Then and there I wanted to hear her story, but our side conversation was interrupted with a call for drinks. Wanting to make a good impression, I sidled up to Lainey and asked if she needed help.

"Thank you, Gerry, but I'm fine. Why don't you get back to chatting up Alice." And then, "Morris, can you give me a hand?"

I was glad to get back to Alice.

"By the way, that's a lovely dress you're wearing."

She twirled once like a happy prom girl. "I'm glad you like it. Fresh off Macy's rack!"

How beautifully natural, I thought. *Like a young girl.*

"And you look quite dashing," she added.

"Me? Why thank you!"

I suddenly felt taller, and more confident.

But then there was an uncomfortable pause.

"Lainey's home is lovely," Alice said, looking about. "Isn't it?"

Her words struck me as more questioning than complimentary, and thus a tad insincere.

"Very tasteful," I said.

"I think so too."

I sensed there was something more that she wanted to share.

"What's your home like?" I ventured.

"My home?"

"Yes. Does it fit your personality?"

She paused. I thought I might have overstepped.

"What an interesting question. Let me think…."

Thoughtful, she looked even more lovely.

"I would say my home suits me perfectly because it does *not* reflect my tastes."

I was stunned. "I've asked that question before, but I've never heard a response like yours."

"I'll take that as a compliment."

"It most certainly was. Sorry, I should have made that clearer."

"That's okay. I'm just funning you. But to answer your very interesting question ..."

For a full minute she described Haven House: a home originally outfitted for an English military commander and his Francophile wife—and essentially unchanged in one hundred fifty years.

"Fascinating. Thank you," I said when she had finished. "Only, you said your home suits you perfectly because it does *not* reflect your tastes. I still don't quite understand."

Alice smiled. "The military maleness of my home camouflages my personal feelings. I like that."

"You like to surprise your enemies?"

"Being covert is almost always a potential advantage."

"Where does this thinking come from? What inspired it, if you don't mind me asking?"

With a wave of her hand, she indicated that we should both sit on the nearby couch. I happily obliged and we settled in quickly. She locked onto my eyes while she spoke.

"My home includes a large library, mostly military history. One work in particular, *The Art of War* by Sun Tzu, was required reading by all the males in my family. I read it when I was young and admired it immensely. Over the years I've applied its teachings to my own life as a discredited and underappreciated female, which is how I romantically regard my personal drama."

"Romantically regard?"

"My life isn't as bad as I'm suggesting. Besides, I'm growing muchly in recent days—taking more control, becoming more naturally me."

"I see. Just, if you don't mind, tell me a bit more about Sun Tzu. I've never read him."

"Sun Tzu wrote that all warfare is based on deception. He said, 'I make the enemy see my strengths as weaknesses and my weaknesses as strengths.'"

"And so, your military-styled home doesn't reflect who you are. It doesn't betray your weaknesses or reveal your strengths."

"More specifically, it doesn't reflect my womanliness."

"Hmmm. I'm still not sure I understand. In the context of Sun Tzu, are you saying something about love and war?"

She shook her head. "I haven't enough experience to comment. I know a little about war, having lived among soldiers all my life, but—practically speaking—I know nothing of love."

Morris Fine

It was hard to tell if Lainey enjoyed the restaurant. She seemed distracted, more interested in Gerry and his date than in on our own conversation. But something changed when we went dancing. Then she seemed devotedly mine, as if her body and hair were a whirling serenade.

After what I thought was the last dance, she boldly approached Little Pablo and asked if he would please play the Lambada—the forbidden dance. The band leader winkingly complied and the seductive music piqued an already excited crowd. I'll never forget Lainey snaking and swirling like Salome herself.

Later, after we'd settled the tab, got our coats, and reached the sidewalk, she asked me to call her a cab. When it arrived and I'd opened the door for her, she looked at me and said, "I'm sorry if I seemed occasionally distant. I was concerned about Alice. She's new here. Ask me out again, just the two of us, and we'll get to know each other better."

Gerald Ellison

Alice's eyes went wide when the food was brought to our table, every dish presented with decoration and finesse.

"Lord, this is lovely," she said. "I'm proud of my French cookery, but compared to all this, I've just been slinging burgers and wings."

Her appetite was not as voracious as her wide eyes suggested. Perhaps she was mindful of her fulsome figure. Perhaps she did not want to seem wolfish on our first date. Whatever, she took only small tasting portions of everything that was served, savoring each bite as if it were a most rare and delectable gift.

We sat alone together for the first few dances, watching Morris and Lainey cavort on the dancefloor. Morris had insisted on Sounds of Brazil, citing Lainey's claim that Alice had her heart set on it. Overcoming my personal concern (I can barely sway to a beat), I'd agreed to go for Alice's sake. When the music finally slowed, I turned to Alice. "Would you like to dance?"

Alice Bouchet

"Would you like to dance at the end of a rope?" is how I processed Gerald's words.

Of course, he didn't mean it that way. He'd been an absolute dear. But after two hours of French feasting and then two more waves of appetizers and drinks, I felt unrestrainedly fat. Loosed on the dancefloor, I feared my flabby body would flap like unbattened tarps in a storm.

But Gerald was gentlemanly and intuitively sympathetic. He asked me to dance only during slow numbers and always led me to a shadowy far corner of the dancefloor, beyond the reach of the brightest lights. He never asked more of my dancing than a simple sway. Without pretense or permission, he cradled me in his strong arms and we swayed together.

I might have rocked that way until the end of time—had our slow dance not suddenly shifted into an up-tempo mambo, trapping us on the dance floor. But I did not panic. Instead (summoning my inner Sun Tzu), my smiling eyes accepted the challenge.

Gerald's right hand moved off the side of my covered left shoulder and slid across my sweaty naked back, the better to lead me. What with all the blare and shifting lights, he had no idea how I'd gasped at his touch.

Ten-Cent Tour

Allen Briggs

I still hadn't given Barry the ten-cent tour of Three Corners. What with the *Courier* interview, his meetings with all the women's groups, and my extra shifts at the museum, we never seemed to find the time. Still, Alice had asked me to do it and I wanted to do it—for her. I'd always enjoyed doing things for Alice. In my mind, it brought us closer together.

Two years earlier, she'd showed up at my door with a serious look on her face.

"Allen, I could really use your special skill sets."

"I don't think I have any."

"Well, you do. You have business experience. You work as a general contractor."

"That's a stretch."

"Well, you're a great carpenter and you know enough about electricity and plumbing."

"Okay."

"Further, you were born and raised in this town, and even though you didn't attend the college as a cadet, you've read every military book I ever shared with you. You know as much as I do about the George Long Military Institute and Three Corners."

"Another stretch, but very kind of you to say."

"I'm not being kind at all, just truthful. And, quite frankly, a little selfish."

That gave me pause.

"Never. You're the least selfish person I know."

"Well, that's about to change. I want to ask you a favor. And it's a not a small one. It's more like a life-changing favor."

I panicked. I knew what she was going to say. She was going to ask me what I had never dared to ask her.

"I'll do anything you want, Alice. Just ask."

"I want you to be my right-hand man."

I was bustin' with love—ready to take her in my arms!

"Allen, I need you. I can't go it alone. I must have your help…."

Yes, I thought. *Anything at all. Just say the word.*

"Freedom Hall can save our town, but I can't do it without you. Whatever needs doing—the upkeep, the tours, the marketing—we can figure it out together. I can't pay a great deal, but I'll pay you all I can."

For several seconds my life had been a beautiful spinning orb—and then it toppled and lay inert.

[I know now that my joy had been unsustainable because it was undeserved. If I wanted to marry Alice, I'd have to man up and speak the words of love. But I wasn't ready at the time—even after so many years.]

But when I realized what Alice was asking, my heart soared. Freedom Hall was the next best thing that could have happened to me. To work with Alice every day … to have a steady paycheck … to be respected around town as a person of special importance …

"Alice, I'm your man."

"I think we'll be great partners," she said.

After that, I started thinking seriously about Alice and me as a couple. I'd still been thinking about it when she moved to New York.

Barry Roth

Allen made good on his promise to give me the ten-cent tour. He led me up and down Jefferson and then up and down Adams, whispering the low-down on every shop and family we passed. He saved Main Street for last. This was the town's first street, the early shops built to serve the George Long Military Institute. At the convergence of the three streets was a large, grassy common; in its center, the Courthouse, a tiny Parthenon that housed every administrative office necessary to govern Three Corners.

"So, this is where Squirrel and Jacqueline work, in the Post Office?"

"Like I said, Jacqueline doesn't actually work here. She just helps Squirrel sort the morning mail."

I nodded.

"She interests me. I like that she's a rough-riding, rebel type."

"Really?" he said. "Didn't peg you for that sort of gal."

"No no … not like that."

"She doesn't interest you?"

"She does … but as a writer."

"What's that mean? You'd like to explore her *character*?"

I didn't like his tone. "Let's change the subject."

It wasn't the first time I'd felt Allen's animosity. But I was starting to understand that it had less to do with the Honor Stone and more with me taking Alice's place, especially in her bedroom, a place he'd never been.

"Have you been to the diner yet?" he asked, moving the conversation along.

"No. Not yet."

"Well, you'll find Jacqueline there 'bout every day. You

should go and introduce yourself."

"Thanks. I think I'll do that."

"Only—"

"Only?"

"Be careful."

"Why? She'll knock me out if I get fresh?"

"She might. Or she might tell Squirrel."

"And—"

"And he has a squirrel gun."

"Squirrel has a squirrel gun?"

"Exactly."

"And … what does he do with a squirrel gun?"

"What do you think?"

I should have let it go. But I was tired of playing the stupid city slicker. Besides, the writer in me wanted details—and character motivation.

"I reckon he shoots squirrels and other varmints," I said. "Is he a good shot?"

"Deadly. His gun is fitted with a Bushnell Rimfire Riflescope."

"That's my favorite scope."

"Don't be snarky. He can take out either one of your eyes at a hundred yards. One shot. *Splat.*"

***

We'd been walking north on Main and had stopped outside Haven House. We both glanced at the Honor Stone. It was impossible not to.

"Funny thing, there's only one person who found what

you did here amusing."

"Why's that funny?" I asked.

"Because she's a friend of mine and Alice's and we're going to visit her now."

"I thought our next stop was a tour of Freedom Hall."

"It is. But I never said I'd be your guide."

Emily Schnyder

I saw him approaching from my window seat behind the display case of snow globes. It had to be him. He was walking with Allen and I knew everyone else in town.

I'd thought a lot about Barry after the *Courier* had printed his interview. He sounded daring and exotic and I wanted to know more about him, so I logged on to Facebook, because that's what I'd been told people do when they want to snoop.

I had no Facebook friends. Literally, none. I didn't even have a page of my own. A couple years before, Alice had asked me to use my computer and graphic skills to build a Freedom Hall website and link it with a fan page on Facebook. A couple years later, Barry arrived and suddenly I'm snooping him like a bloodhound … and that's when I learned that Melissa and Darla and Regan each had the hots for him—damn them to hell.

Barry Roth

Our initial meeting was perfunctory. I entered Freedom Hall in Allen's company; Emily sitting placidly behind a glass display case of souvenirs. I sensed we were alone.

"Barry Roth, Emily Schnyder. Emily, Barry."

There must have been nods and how-do-you dos, but all I recall was a pall of unease, which Allen deepened in his ham-handed way:

"Ticket sales and souvenirs are our main sources of revenue. In fact, take a gander at those snow globes, all made by our own artist in residence, Miss Emily."

Emily remained quiet, smiling vacantly. I was embarrassed for us both.

I moved closer to the display case of snow globes. On the left were Liberty Bells, White Houses, Capitol Buildings, etc. On the right, Eiffel Towers, Big Bens, and other totems of famous foreign places, each perfectly rendered.

"They're all very beautiful," I said, my words clearly meant for Emily's ears. "But I'm especially taken with the foreign ones."

"Me too," she whispered.

"How much are they?"

"Eight dollars," said Allen. "Priced to sell!"

I looked to Emily but she was blank. I turned toward the globes on the right. One in particular drew my attention: Jerusalem's Wailing Wall bathed in a wan sunlight.

"Lovely," I said. "Looks like real stones with ivy poking through."

"Thorny caper."

"What's that?"

"The plant. It's native to Jerusalem and famous for its endurance."

"Really?"

"Cut down to its roots, it still survives."

What a strange fact. What a strange woman.

"Beautiful," I said, thinking what it would be like to visit the Wailing Wall with someone like Emily.

"I'll take that one."

"Thank you," she said softly, rising to her feet.

Using a key that had been dangling from her elastic wristband, she opened the back of the case and retrieved the globe. While she put together a gift box, I noted that she was thin, a little shorter than average, and quietly pretty: no jewelry, no makeup, no visible tattoos. She had fine features and pale, blue-veined skin, which contrasted boldly with her dark eyebrows and short black hair. She wore a pair of skinny black jeans and a black t-shirt: the lithographed face of Cat Stevens on the front; the lyric *Peace Train take this country* printed on the back in luminous pink.

When she finished placing the snow globe in the gift box, I opened my wallet and laid a twenty-dollar bill on the glass counter.

"Thank you," she said again. "Twelve dollars change."

"Please, keep the change."

"But it's only eight dollars."

"You're an artist. You should be paid for your work."

Emily didn't know what to do. Her eyes sought Allen's.

"Keep the change," he said. "An American can spend his money however he pleases."

***

Emily came out from behind the display case and Allen took her place.

"Give him the deluxe tour."

I felt her cringe.

I followed her silently across the lobby … through an archway of crossed swords … to a handsome staircase whose marble steps and ancient handrail were well worn.

"We'll start on the top floor and work our way down," she said.

"How many floors are there?"

"Two. Three if you count the basement."

Right then, I decided to test the waters.

"Is that where you keep the dead soldiers?"

A short pause, then she replied:

"The dead ones are stuffed and on display. The live ones are kept out back in cages. I feed them twice a day."

"Nice," I said, admiring her quickness. "What do they eat?"

"Mostly fried bullet shells on a crispy crepe of tarpaulin, accented with black gunpowder."

I was impressed. "Tasty. What do they drink?"

"Blood."

I hadn't expected that.

"Plain blood?"

"Depends," she said with a shrug. "Most take it straight. Tough guys add Worcestershire sauce and black pepper. Some prefer horseradish. City slickers like celery, fresh dill, and lemon garnishes."

Wow. She'd drawn, shot, and holstered before my fingers had even twitched.

I felt the strong need for a restart. "I love your snow globes."

Silence. We continued walking to the first exhibit.

"Do you do other kinds of artwork?"

"I draw and paint," she said without breaking stride.

"Nice. Do you do figurative art?"

"Is that what you like?"

"Yes, I suppose."

"No. I avoid it like the plague."
We continued walking.
"Why—if you don't mind me asking."
"Why what?"
"Why do you avoid figurative art—if you don't mind."
"Not at all, it's your tour."
"Are we on the clock?"
"Tours last forty-five minutes."
"But I was promised the deluxe tour."
"Fair point."
"And I left a big tip and paid you a compliment."
"Two more points."
"So, what do I get?"
She turned to face me. "A one-hour tour."
"Excellent! How is my tour special?"
"It won't be—you've already used up the first fifteen minutes."
I smiled. She'd outdrew me again.
"Damn," I said. "You are one tough negotiator."
"Take it with up with management."
With that, she handed me her card:

FREEDOM HALL
The Story of the American Soldier
Emily Schnyder, Tour Guide and Artist
E.Schnyder@FreedomHallMuseum.com

Emily Schnyder

I hated single-person tours when the tourist (always a man) asked personal questions and stood too close. But Barry was different. He maintained a respectful distance, asked only relevant questions that sounded sincere, and seemed genuinely absorbed with all the exhibits. In one hall, he stared closely at the portrait of every Bouchet commander. Later, he seemed particularly taken with the exhibit of Haven House, which included photographs of every room—save the private quarters of the Commander's wife, which, until recently, had been Alice's bedroom and was now his.

As he looked seriously handsome in his button-down shirt and neat slacks and had been so polite and interested, I shared with him a few unsolicited details about my own life as they related to Freedom Hall. He did not pry or press for more.

I then asked what brought him to Three Corners. Without hesitation he told me about his life in New York: about his domineering father, now dead, and his meddlesome but well-meaning mother—and how she had brokered the deal that had brought Alice to New York and him to Three Corners.

"How well do you know Alice?" I asked. He said he'd never actually met her but that she and his mother were becoming fast friends.

I'd heard that he was a writer and asked him about his work and he told me about his short-lived fame and subsequent flameout. He confided that *Barry Roth* and *Baron Rothschild* were two faces of the same mask but didn't elaborate. I asked some vague questions about his social life. He replied (making it sound like a confession) that he used to date a lot and that his mother worried he'd never fall in love, marry, and give her a grandchild.

He spoke so honestly and shamelessly, I began to share glimpses into my own dark past. By the time we reached the basement exhibits, I was speaking freely of my parents' strange, outsider ways ... their inexplicable sudden deaths ... my life with Alice in Haven House ... my aversion to the town's three churches ... and my lifelong hatred of Melissa, Regan, and Darla.

Barry Roth
While returning with Emily to the front of the museum, I considered the irony that Freedom Hall's gatekeeper was a peace-loving, whip-smart, artistic goth.

"I really enjoyed our tour—even if I was shortchanged," I said.

"Regrettable, but unavoidable."

"You know what I'm referring to?"

"Of course," she said without breaking stride. "You're referring to the fact that you didn't get to see either of the splashy videos that are the hallmark of the Freedom Hall experience."

I didn't argue or deny. You can't lie to a seer. "Okay, but can you at least explain?"

"Of course. It's very simple. We spent a lot of time in personal conversation, which I'm sure neither of us regrets. But that time cut significantly into the time of the tour. If we'd been alone, I would have happily led you to the videos."

"We were alone."

"Not really. Allen was waiting for us in the lobby. He knew to the minute when we should return."

"And you weren't going to give him anything to wonder about."

"You've already created a stir. You don't need any more bad press—and neither do I."

"I thought he likes you. He told me you're friends."

"We are, in a sense. My closest friend is Alice and his closest friend is Alice. That and Three Corners is what we have in common. It's not much—but for us, it's a lot."

I nodded, taking it all in. "Okay, but I still didn't get the whole tour."

She laughed. "Guilty as charged. I'll make it up to you. I promise."

Three Unholy Bitches

Emily Schnyder

Another Monday, another edition of the *Courier,* hand-delivered by Squirrel. This time, rather than remain behind my kitchen curtain, I waited for him on the high ground of my raised porch.

"Good morning," I said, avoiding his name.

The bastard would not even say *Good morning*. Instead, "How did your friend enjoy his tour?"

I didn't wonder how he knew. After all, this was Three Corners. "Why don't you ask Mr. Roth?"

The bastard smiled. "Actually, the Baron's my last stop. I'll speak to him soon."

"You're referring to Barry?"

"Is that what you call him?"

I took the *Courier* from his hand and turned towards my front door. As I walked away, I heard:

"Did you know he's having lunch this week with Melissa, Darla, and Regan?"

That was cruel.... I shouldn't have exposed my back.

Barry Roth

I'd been invited to lunch by Melissa, Darla, and Regan via a private note skipped under my front door. Once again, the note was calligraphically penned, each of the three women flourishing her name in a different colored ink: violet, peach, and scarlet.

As there was no return address, email, or phone number, I hadn't a clue how to respond. I finally decided to show up at the diner the next day at noon, as invited, and let nature take its course.

In a way, I felt like I was doing my sworn duty, fulfilling a pact made with Lainey, who'd sent me on this mission to find committed love. In that spirit, I thought it best to leave no eligible woman unturned, though I assumed Emily would not approve.

Jacqueline

Well, la di dah, them three unholy bitches—Melissa, Darla, and Regan—came waltzin' in like it was an everyday thing—and trust me, it wasn't. Our regulars were men who mostly wore fishin' or huntin' caps and who ordered the same eggs or pie every day.

"Table for three?"

I didn't smile. I wouldn't give them the satisfaction. And why should I? Not a one of them ever said my name or greeted me in a kind or normal way. And they all knew me. Bet your sweet ass they did. We'd all gone to the same schools. I just I hadn't run in their circle. Big deal. I hadn't run in anybody's circle. I had no circle.

"Actually," said Darla, the peachy blonde, "we're expecting a fourth."

Damn if they didn't giggle like schoolgirls.

"This way," I directed, like some prissy English maid.

While they settled, I left to get four menus, four waters, and four place settings. While my back was turned, I heard the door's tinkle-bell and looked over my shoulder to see who'd come in—and damn if I didn't get a little jolt, like seeing a famous person.

I recognized him right away because Squirrel had described him exactly so, right down to his button shirt and pressed trousers. But he was better than advertised: he looked extra smart, the way some people do who wear glasses. And he looked like he might be a big tipper. I was about to go over and give him a big greeting when I heard, "Mr. Roth! Over here!"

Barry Roth

As the three ladies had squeezed together on the far side of the booth, I positioned myself in the middle of the bench facing them to balance the conversation. Unfortunately, the three women talked over each other, vying for my attention. Swiveling my head left and right, trying to look three ways at once, I confused which facts belonged to which woman. After twenty minutes I'd gleaned only this: one had sowed enough oats to seed a hundred acres ... one believed she had enough relational experience to write a bestseller ... one relished sex in complete darkness, to the sound of running water. I believe one or all were engaged or had been, and one (Regan, the redhead with the country curls) had a daughter or someone's niece living with her.

When I didn't respond to their seductive-sounding advances, they took a very different tack, explaining how each of them belonged to a different one of the town's three churches.

"Now that you're settled in, you must come to church on Sunday," one of them said.

"Visit all three!"

"Choose the one that speaks to you."

"But you absolutely must go."

"See you Sunday!"

"Rise and shine!"

"Come as you are!"

"Wear your Sunday best!"

"Mass begins at eight and ends with Holy Communion."

"Our Lutheran service starts a half hour later and ends with a singing of psalms."

"First Baptist begins around nine and ends with a wonderful sermon."

"In nice weather, each church has a luncheon."

"You don't have to bring anything because you're new around here."

"Besides, you're a man. No one expects you to cook."

"So, see you Sunday!"

"By the way, are you actually a Rothschild or just related to one?"

Love Is a Hoped-for Thing

Allen Briggs

Every week I received a shiny, colorful postcard from Alice. She never mentioned the famous place pictured on the front, but on the back, in the tiny space reserved for messages, she always shared trivial greetings in a handwriting I barely recognized, the words larger and scratchier than I remembered—as if written in haste.

She signed each postcard, *Yours, Alice* ... but I wondered at that. Truth is, I'd never felt less certain of that hope.

Alice Bouchet

For two days my nape and shoulders glowed hotly from the heat of Gerald's touch. I was thrilled and wanted Gerald to know what he'd done to me.... I was ashamed and hoped he would never know.... I was a confused schoolgirl whose father was, and was not, the town's Commander, depending.

Gerald Ellison

For many years, I had the sad feeling that Manhattan women liked me but always thought they could do better. That really hurt. Following that script, I knew I'd never find love. So, I decided to change the script. And that's why I agreed to the blind date.

Alice was the best first date I ever had. She listened to me like I was the only man in Manhattan. When we danced close, she looked happy.

Morris Fine

I didn't realize I'd been living a lie until I saw Lainey's apartment. Everything she owned—every painting, every chair, every bowl, every tchotchke—marked her home as unmistakably hers.

In comparison, my apartment was a fraud: a hodgepodge of nondescript furniture, surrounded by souvenirs and totems of existentially challenged Jews from around the world, along with self-serving ephemera (mostly posters and photos) memorializing my career. I suppose it patched together pretty well—I have a solid sense of design—but I knew it didn't reflect my emotional self.

I felt Lainey's presence in her apartment, and it drew me the way an oasis beckons the starved and thirsty. I sensed I could be happy there, with Lainey.

Lainey Roth

Despite his public press, I did not see Morris as a heroic adventurer and saver of souls. I saw his professional life as more of a calculated career choice than a passionate calling. And I was well aware of his track record with women. No, I didn't snoop or stalk. I didn't have to. You see, despite its reputation as a center of world finance and culture, Manhattan is a relatively small island of neighborhoods and cliques. Residents active in similar social and cultural circles are bound to meet or, at the very least, know some of the same people. Because Morris and I are close in age ... and both Jewish ... and both relatively well-to-do ... we had dated people who knew each other—and Jewish women love to talk.

My first romantic impression of Morris—before I'd met him—was that he was a player; meaning, he liked to date women ... love women ... and leave them when it suited him. But none of that bothered me. Quite frankly, I wasn't so different, except that I liked men. Thing is, I knew I had a good and loving heart and sensed the same about Morris. I assumed he hadn't yet settled down because he hadn't yet found the right woman. I sensed I might be the one. I had a tingling feeling that I could save this handsome Jew who was famous for saving other Jews.

Personal Accounts

Barry Roth

Emily and I exchanged cell numbers and emails.

"Don't you have a personal email account?" I asked.

"What do you mean?"

"Your email address is your Freedom Hall account."

"That's the only email I have."

"What if I wanted to send you something personal?"

"Like what?"

"Like … I don't know … but I'm reluctant to send personal email to a business server."

"I never considered that. I guess I've never received a personal email."

I let that go, for the time being.

"I'll tell you what," I said. "You show me the two films I missed at Freedom Hall, and I'll help you set up a Gmail account."

"Gmail is Google, right?"

"That's right."

"Is the account free?"

"It is."

"Well, I bet Google archives personal emails."

Emily was like an onion. The more I peeled back, the more intense she seemed.

I said, "Google has several billion user accounts, so they won't take much notice of you and me. How many accounts does Freedom Hall have?"

"Counting everyone who has ever worked there?"

"Yes, everyone."

She grew quiet, as if toting up a large number.

"Three."

"Three? In total?"

"Wait," she said. "Let me recheck my math." This time she used her fingers. "Yup. Just as I thought—three."

"Let me guess," I said. "You, Allen, and Alice."

"Bingo!"

Emily Schnyder

I made good on my promise.

"I owe you for the two films you missed during your tour."

"You're a woman of your word."

"Meet me Sunday morning at ten. At the backdoor of the museum."

"The backdoor?"

"I don't want to take any chances."

"With what?"

"With people seeing you marching about while they're at church service."

"If they're at church, they won't see me marching about."

"Of course, they will. They have a sick sense."

"A *sick* sense?"

"Yes. It's intuitive and it's sick."

He let that go, for the moment.

"They won't mind that you're not there?" he asked.

"I attend lots of church-sponsored events, but I never go to services."

"Why not?"

"I'm not sure. My parents never went."

"Did they ever talk about it?"

"Not that I remember. But I sensed it wasn't for them."

"Did it bother you that they didn't go to church?"

"Not exactly ... but kids would tease me terribly and say awful things about my godless parents. One teacher—in front of the whole class—said my parents worshipped the devil."

"Oh my god. What did you do?"

"Nothing. I just sat there and let them burn me at the stake."

Barry was silent for several seconds ... and then: "Did you hate your parents for making you an outsider?"

"No. Never. In fact, that's the central irony of my life, I think."

"What do you mean?"

"I mean, I didn't want to be despised.... I wanted friends.... But at the same time, I relished my outsider status. It made me feel unique."

"Is that why you avoided going to church?"

"Again, it's complicated. I wanted to be accepted by all the kids who did go ... but I had no desire to go myself. I seem to have inherited my parents' reservations—without understanding their reasons."

"Did it ever get better?"

"Ironically, it got a little better after my parents died."

"Yikes. How'd that make anything better?"

"When my parents died, I went to live with Alice. Her mother had died earlier and she was also hurting."

"What was it like living with her?"

"Living in Haven House gave me a weird status. It protected me from the taunts of the other kids, but it effectively increased my isolation."

"I can see that. I'm so sorry."

"Don't be. And don't get me wrong. Alice saved my life. I don't know what would have happened if she hadn't taken me in."

"Did you like living with her?"

"She was wonderful, like a wise older sister or a loving aunt. But—"

"But?"

"Her father and brothers were always busy at the college or away on duty, so it was really just the two of us. And that could be trying."

"She had no close friends, other than Allen?"

"None. After a while, I realized she was almost as lonely and isolated as I was—the curse of the women of Haven House. She needed me as much as I needed her."

"Tell me more. Give me an example."

"Okay…. When I was old enough to consider college—which would have meant leaving Three Corners to go to State University—Alice shared her opinions and then let me decide for myself."

"That's a good thing, right?"

"Not in this case. She always framed the conversation in a way that forced me to see the inevitable reasonableness of what she thought best—but never actually said."

"Which was for you to remain in Three Corners."

"Exactly."

"Was that fair to you?"

"Hard to say."

"Please try. I'm very interested."

I believed him. I sensed Barry had his own otherness, which helped him understand mine.

"Okay," I said, gathering my thoughts. "To my knowledge, my parents hadn't any close friends or relatives, and so, young as they were—not yet forty—they'd named Alice executor of their will, which established her as my ward and legal guardian until I reached the age of twenty-one."

"But the question of college came up when you were around seventeen."

"Exactly. On the one hand, Alice worried she'd violate her responsibility as ward if she allowed me to go away to college."

"On the other hand—"

"She had personal reasons for keeping me close."

"Which were?"

"Look, Alice is an extraordinary person. Generous, brilliant, and self-reliant. But for all her independence, even she needs someone to talk to."

"She had Allen and her brothers."

"Allen is sweet, in his way, but he never stepped up. And her brothers were older and never that interested in her."

"No one else—in all of Three Corners?"

"No."

"What about the priest, the reverend, the pastor?"

"Oy! Don't get me started."

"Did you just say *Oy*?"

"Did I? I sometimes do. Alice has pointed it out. Weird, right?"

Barry let that go.

"So," he said, getting back to our conversation, "Alice felt an ethical compulsion to keep you at home *and* a strong personal need for your companionship."

"Yes, that sounds about right."

"Well, you're clearly educated. What did you decide about college?"

"Alice applied to State University for permission to mentor me in a distance-learning curriculum."

"Is that like home schooling?"

"Yes, but now they say *online learning* because it's mostly done with computers and supported by a live mentor. But it wasn't uncommon around here, even then, to be home schooled through college. Lots of people with special needs or special situations went that route."

"I assume Alice's application on your behalf was accepted."

"Never any doubt. Having taught various courses at Long Institute, she was well-credentialed to be my mentor. She also had incredible connections—right up to and including the governor himself."

"So, her application was accepted and you continued to live with her."

"Exactly. All told, I lived with Alice nearly ten years."

"Who took care of your parents' home while you lived in Haven House?"

"As per the will, Alice maintained my parents' house, drawing on their modest savings."

"Did you go there often?"

"I had a key and could go whenever I liked—but I never went inside alone."

"Too depressing?"

"Too traumatizing. I was afraid I'd relive my parents' horrible deaths."

"God, I'm so sorry."

"Thank you. Anyway, when I turned twenty-one, I assumed full responsibility for owning and maintaining my own home."

"You were psychologically and emotionally able to go back there?"

"By that time, yes. Over the years Alice had prepared me—with some help from Sun Tzu."

"The military writer?"

"Yes. Good for you!"

"How'd that work?"

"Alice knew I sensed my parents' angry spirits in the house and never argued with me … never made me feel like I was crazy. When she sensed I was ready, she helped me chase their spirits away."

"And Sun Tzu?"

"He provided the strategies—and helped steel my nerves."

"Can you share specifics? This is a key part of your life. I'd like to understand."

My heart smiled. Only Alice ever asked me probing personal questions. It felt wonderful.

"Well, as to strategies, we'd spy on the house during the day and make reconnaissance runs at night. We'd also secure the perimeter—checking the fencing, the garage, and the toolshed."

"You ever go inside?"

"Of course. We were thorough. And get this: Alice had used her connections to get a copy of the original blueprints, which we used to check every room, every closet, every crawl space—basement to attic."

"What exactly was your goal?"

"To make sure no one was there and no one could get in."

"Did you ever go in by yourself?"

"Yes, but only after many years of training. Eventually, Alice ordered me to enter alone while she waited outside."

"Were you scared?"

"Are you kidding? I was petrified. As soon as I got close to my door, I froze. All my training vanished in a flash."

"But you did it. What got you through?"

"I chanted some Sun Tzu mantras…. But mostly it was knowing that Alice had my six."

"You appear to have conquered your demons. Was there a specific turning point?"

"There was. One day, right before my twenty-first birthday, Alice said I was ready to spend a whole night in my old room—alone."

"Wow. How did you react?"

"I panicked. Which is crazy, 'cause I knew we'd been building up to that point."

"What did you do?"

"I shook my head and stamped my feet like a little kid: "No. No. No!"

"What did Alice do?"

"She went all Patton on me. She grabbed me by the shoulders and shook me like a rag doll. 'Stop it! Just stop it! You're a grown woman with a college degree—and you've been trained for this mission!'"

"What a character! What happened?"

"I had no choice. I did what I had to do. I walked up my front steps … crossed my porch … unlocked my door … kicked it open … ran upstairs to my old room—and locked the door behind me."

"Geez Louise. What next?"

I took several seconds to remember.

"It was night. And very dark. I sat cross-legged on my bed and pulled the covers over my head. I thought that would protect me ... but I still heard their horrible sounds."

"Whose sounds?"

"My dead parents. I heard their moans and howls ... their retching."

"What did you do?"

"Nothing. I just sat there.... Once again, I did nothing to help them.... Eventually, I fell asleep...."

"Did you dream?"

"I don't think so. I don't remember.... But when I woke at sunrise, the house was peacefully quiet, and I remember thinking: *My parents are dead and gone—but I'm alive and well.*"

The tears came in a rush and Barry let me cry it out. At some point, I felt his hand on my back, rubbing soothing circles.

"And then?" he asked.

I knew what he meant.

"And then I was free."

"And now?"

I dried my eyes with the heels of my hands.

"And now I love my home."

"What changed?"

I took a deep breath. "I cleansed it from the inside out. I began with the front room, which used to be the dim storefront of my parents' tailor shop. When I was little, I'd sit on the floor, in the shadows, playing with buttons and scraps of fabric. My first memory of Alice is looking up from the floor and seeing her, so tall and regal looking.... Anywho, now it's a sunny parlor. I can see out and people can see in—although, to be honest, not many people walk by and I get very few visitors. Still, I love the room. This is where I sip mint tea, read, and sketch."

"What about your old room, you change that too?"

"It's still my bedroom, but I painted it daisy yellow and replaced the old heavy curtains with white lacy ones. When I open the windows, even a little, the curtains billow in and I pretend to have visitors."

Barry looked uncomfortably skeptical. "What kind of visitors?"

"The usual suspects: My parents ... God ... Prince Charming."

He changed the subject: "You change anything else?"

"The bathrooms, for sure. I had the toilets ripped out and replaced ... the floor tiles scoured ... the walls repapered."

"What about your parents' room?"

"I tossed everything. Then I stripped and revarnished the floors ... whitewashed the walls ... had a skylight built into the ceiling. Now it's my art studio ... my haven of ordered chaos."

"You spend a lot of time there?"

"Of course. It's where I work, when I'm not at the museum. It's where I keep my easels ... my paints ... my canvasses."

"Do you display your art?"

"On almost every wall of my home, even the hallways."

"I'd love to see your work."

"You will."

He paused several seconds and then said, "I suppose your paintings are very different from your snow globes."

I gave that idea a cold shrug. "Snow globes are a different kind of art—more of a craft, really.... Anyway, that brings us full circle. You still want to meet Sunday at ten to see the films?"

"Beats going to church."

"Were you planning to go?"

"No. Though I was invited."

"I know."

"You know what?"

"I know that the wives of our three church leaders invited you … and that Melissa, Darla, and Regan also invited you."

He didn't ask how I knew. He was catching on.

"Yes. They were all kind enough to invite me."

"Well, you're free to go—or not—as you please. But if you're going to meet me on Sunday morning at the museum, I suggest you do so discreetly."

"I'll see you Sunday," he said firmly. "At ten—at the museum's backdoor."

I smiled.

"I'll be inside, waiting."

Sunday Matinee

Emily Schnyder

I wasn't sure how to dress. At last, I decided to primp a bit, as I always did for special events, just to please Alice and Allen. Of course, I wasn't expecting them. I knew Allen would be at First Baptist, sitting behind the empty Bouchet pew, and God only knew where Alice was. All her life she'd attended Sunday service with her family, but now—her family gone—she was somewhere in New York, doing God knows what. I tried to picture what she might be doing but hadn't a clue and soon gave up. If she thought of me that Sunday morning, she'd likely have imagined me in my front parlor, sketching and listening to music on my headphones. I wondered what she might say if she knew I was about to sit in the dark theater of Freedom Hall, alone with Barry Roth, the only man in Three Corner history to mount our cherished Honor Stone and ride it like his own bucking bronco.

Barry Roth

I easily could have walked to the museum but didn't want to appear like some heathen idler, shambling about while everyone else was in church, praying … so I drove my little Fiat the equivalent of several blocks and parked in the museum's rear lot, in the shadow of its back entrance.

Stepping out of the car (which still glowed spitfire red from the dealer's excellent waxing), I stood for a moment, looking about. Straight ahead (facing north) and to my left were a dozen lovely homes, mostly former lecture halls and barracks of the defunct military institute, many with their original ivied bricks and mullioned windows. Off to my right was white-steepled First Baptist and from its open windows the thundering voice of Reverend Somethingorother reached my heathen ears in thin drifts.

Though freshly shaved and cologned, I hadn't taken any special pains to dress sharp. I didn't want to make too much of the occasion.

Emily Schnyder
I watched Barry arrive in his shiny red Fiat—like a little boy sneaking into a room with clanging cymbals. Clearly, he didn't get Three Corners. He didn't fit in and never would. Just like me.

My palms were sweating but don't think I was anxious to show him the films. I didn't give a shit about the films. I just wanted him … on that Sunday morning … when the museum was closed … when everyone was in church … to be with me … in the dark.

Barry Roth
Walking toward the museum's rear door, I was reminded of the countless times I'd walked into a Manhattan apartment building to pick up a date. I recalled Lainey saying to me:

"How can they all be wrong? You must have liked one of them."

"I like them all," I'd said with a straight face. "I have a hundred girlfriends. What are you so worried about?"

She hated when I was flippant.

"A hundred is not as good as one."

"Actually, it's a hundred times better."

"Oh yeah? Name one girlfriend. Name one woman you care about."

I paused, spluttered—and then gave up....

Having lived awhile in Three Corners, I saw the advantage of being a big fish in a small pond. For one thing, all the female fish took notice of me so I didn't have to spend a lot of time baiting and casting. Still, the pond was not exactly well stocked: after factoring in marital status, age, and attraction level, I saw only four possibilities: Melissa, Regan, Darla ... and, of course, Emily Schnyder.

Emily Schnyder

I watched nervously as he opened the museum's rear door.

"Good morning."

He sounded chirpy but looked nice in his buttoned shirt and clean slacks, his hair combed. I wore black jeans and my old AC/DC t-shirt with its hell-fire lettering and power-bolt. I'd washed my hair but left it unbrushed so it would look spiky wild.

I made sure we didn't kiss or shake hands in view of the glass window.

"Thank you for being prompt," I said.

"Thank you for the special viewing."

I led him to an area on the first floor we hadn't entered on his first visit. We walked in darkness. Normally, all the lights would have been on.

"Where would you like to sit?" I said, entering the small theater.

"Normally, last row—far corner."

I winced. It was not the time for wisecracks.

***

We couldn't take our eyes off the screen (or didn't want to) for with our eyes on the screen we both could pretend to be captivated by the martial music and scenes of patriotic bluster and soldierly sacrifice—and ignore the fact that we were sitting so close our arms and hips caressed, and our breath commingled.

Allen Briggs

At the back of the church, behind the altar, are two bathrooms, *Men* and *Women*. From the opened window in the men's room, I saw Barry's red Fiat, parked in the museum's rear parking lot, close to the door. I watched until I saw Barry and Emily emerge from the museum … not exactly holding hands (that I could see), but walking close, like they had some history.

I wanted desperately to discuss the matter with Alice. I'd been trying not to think of her, but the sight of Barry and Emily together, looking so much like a couple, made my heart long for what it didn't have.

Leaky Secrets

Jacqueline

Beasley Wilson owned the diner and was my best friend, besides Squirrel. When I was little, he used to drink and fish with my Pop on Sundays. After Pop died (I was fourteen; Mom was long gone, as in vamoosed), he used to come by the house at the end of a long work day, bearing leftover wedges of fruit pies, the dregs of a huge pot of goulash, or some dented tin cans. Sure, they were things he could no longer sell—perishables past their prime—but they kept me fat and saved me a lot of money.

Knowing I'd taken over Pop's plumbing business—and that it wasn't much of a business—Beasley said I could waitress at the diner whenever I liked, so I did.

I liked Beasley and his wife Mavis a lot. They never had kids and Mavis treated me sweet. She gave me beautiful presents on my birthday and Christmas, girly things like only a mother would know to give, and when I'd hug her to say thanks, she'd always turn her head, her eyes filled with tears.

I knew Mavis kept the books and was damn good at it, accounting for every penny, making sure the diner always turned a profit. After Mavis died suddenly (having eaten something foul), Beasley asked if I could help with the bookkeeping. I didn't hesitate one second, as I'd loved Mavis and Beasley both.

As to the bookkeeping, Beasley kept it simple: every dollar earned had to be accounted for and the balance had to square at the end of the day.

Without Mavis to share his personal errands, Beasley was often away from the diner for an hour or more, leaving me alone with the customers and the cash register. I never dishonored his trust. One evening at home, telling Squirrel how my honesty made me feel better about myself, he ruined my mood by calling me *scrupulous*. I was just about to bust his mouth when he explained how it was a compliment.

Squirrel usually had my best interests at heart and over time I learned to be more patient and less sensitive. Beasley and Squirrel were all I had before I became chummy with Brenda.

Brenda Lissome

Like most girls who stayed local after high school, my romantic options were pretty much limited to Marion and Three Corners—which is to say, they were slim pickings.

Given that I could never have loved a priest, pastor, or reverend—and would have rather died drunk and alone than marry a bloody butcher or a greasy mechanic—I figured I'd scored the pick of the mangy litter when Gavin popped the question after a romantic getaway in Jefferson City when I was twenty-two.

It was like one of the those love stories you see in the movies. Gavin gave me flowers and took me to a French-like restaurant with tall, lighted candles and bubbly champagne in real glasses with long stems. That same night we went to a show—a play with real live actors—and they all came out at the end, bowing and sweeping their arms, and I jumped up, along with everybody else, and clapped like crazy, even though I hadn't caught every word and had a dozen questions about what the hell I'd just seen. That was the night Gavin proposed. We'd only been going out a month or so, but we'd seen each other plenty times around town and I liked him well enough and figured I wasn't likely to get a better offer. Yeah, he was already a little paunchy and bald, but he was bright enough to have had a rich daddy who'd left him the second largest house in Three Corners, along with a general store and two gas stations. By the time I got to be friends with Jacqueline, Gavin already had some other businesses, including the Red, White, and Brew and an egg farm in Marion.

Jacqueline used to ask me how it felt to be so rich. I told her it was boring, that there's only so many times a week I can get my hair or nails done. She asked me lots more questions. She was very curious about my life. I told her that Gavin didn't like me to work, so I had lots of time to kill before I had to feed him each night. I told her that with so many choices and so much time, it was hard to know what to do each day. She asked me if I belonged to the ladies' book club, but I told her the truth: that reading hurt my eyes and gave me a headache. She asked me if I went to church on Sundays, and I told her I did one better: I wrote a big check to all three churches every Christmas.

I'd got to know Jacqueline pretty well. I never liked her in high school because her father was a drunken plumber and her mother had run off and none of the other girls liked her neither. But I liked her more and more when we were older and I'd got used to sitting in the diner most afternoons, sipping coffee and eating pie, chatting with her about this and that. It beat watching TV alone at home. Gavin and me had no kids.

All in all, I suppose life was generally tolerable with Gavin, though I didn't trust him as far as I could throw him, and I couldn't have lifted the fat bastard if my life depended on it.

Gavin Lissome

I think most people live with at least one dark secret they hope to take to the grave. I have several but one in particular that still gives me the heebie-jeebies.

***

The light but steady traffic on Marion Pike was enough to support two gas stations, one in Marion and one in Three Corners, both of which I'd inherited from my daddy. The one in Marion benefitted from its location right off the Interstate; the one in Three Corners from its proximity to the Long Institute and later, to Freedom Hall. Both had mini-marts that sold more chips, jerky, soda, beer, and cigarettes than the gas stations sold gas.

As I'd learned from my daddy, I checked my business inventories the first and fifteenth of each month, always beginning with the level of my gas tanks. One day, mid-month, I noted that my 10,000-gallon tank in Three Corners was more than half full, but my 12,000-gallon tank in Marion was down 80%, having lost more than 9,000 gallons in the past two weeks.

I suspected the worst. Both tanks were old and had just passed their thirty-year warranty. Because each tank would have cost at least thirty thousand dollars to replace (and I was then low on cash and collateral), I'd rolled the dice, hoping to squeeze a few more years of service from each.

I stepped slowly and nervously all about the Marion station but found no evidence of a gasoline leak. That worried me more than stepping my new shoes into an oozing black puddle. The gasoline had to go somewhere. Like water, I figured it had flowed downward. Unfortunately, the downward slope from my property led to a small poultry farm, where Gil Nethers sold fresh eggs at a well-known, roadside egg stand.

I had an old friend named Bucky Moorland who owed me a big favor for having once helped him out of a singularly ugly mess. I'd rather not relate the sordid details; let's just say it involved Bucky, a bloody hooker, and his unsuspecting wife of twelve years. Now, I knew Bucky's brother was a project manager for a waste-spill, clean-up site outside Jeff Station, a town about forty miles south of Marion. I called Bucky and discreetly explained the situation. Bucky called his younger brother Danny, who called me to say that he and a friend would see me the following day. Seeking to avoid even the hint of anything amiss, I told Danny to pull into the Marion gas station like he was just another customer looking to top off his tank. He said no; it made no sense to waste time. He said he was almost certain what the problem was and would arrive with an excavation machine and a truck to pull up the tank. At that point I was shittin' bricks. I didn't need the whole damn world to know I had a leaky tank, which was what Danny suspected. Danny said he would arrive at dawn and likely be gone by breakfast, and that was the best he could do. Long story short: when Danny and his friend pulled up the tank, they found a nickel-sized hole on the bottom.

As a waste-site, cleanup manger, Danny was something

of an expert on the subjects of clean-up costs, insurance payments, state regulators, possible fines, and potential criminal liabilities.

I said to him, "Dannyboy, theoretically speaking, if you were in my place, how would you make this sticky situation go away?"

Squirrel Evans

Though Gavin Lissome and me played baseball together as kids, we did not run in the same circles, despite our monthly meetings at the Red, White, and Brew.

Gavin had initiated these meetings some years before when his daddy Clyde was still breathing. I'd then been the newly appointed postmaster, though I hadn't yet branched out with my boutique sales business or yet launched my career as publisher of the *Three Corners Courier*. Still, as postmaster, I had the unique opportunity of meetin' and greetin' every adult resident in town, including its powerbrokers—Commander Bouchet, the mayor, clergy, and council members. I knew that's why Gavin had sought me out. In fact, after several meetings of easy chatting over burgers and beers, he mentioned—in the most casual way—that he'd love to know whatever inside dope came my way concerning our town's leading lights. When I asked, naively, how this might benefit him, he boldly confided that he was following his daddy's theory of social politics: it was easier to influence a few agents of authority than gladden the hand (or turn the heart) of a thousand voters.

As Gavin was the only person of importance ever to take a strong professional interest in my doings, I gladly did what he asked, sharing with him whatever gossip and news I'd picked up on my daily rounds.

Gavin valued my input, slipping me cash incentives twice a year, on Christmas and my birthday. A few years later, when I told him my idea to buy cheap products from eBay China (to be repackaged and resold as part of my daily mail route), he offered to loan me two thousand dollars to fund my dream.

We had ourselves a nice, friendly, wink-wink arrangement.

Jacqueline

Squirrel knew Beasley was teaching me some electronic, spreadsheet bookkeeping but had no idea he was also teaching me how to use the computer in his tiny office at the back of the diner. That's how I came to be so good with search engines—which I liked to call snoop engines. Damn, the stuff that's out there!

Hudson Yards

Morris Fine

I was touched when Lainey had said to me: "I'm sorry if I seemed occasionally distant. I was concerned about Alice ... she's new here. Ask me out again, just the two of us, and we'll get to know each other better."

I'm not sure which impressed me more: Lainey's concern for Alice, her beautifully personalized apartment, her seductive dancing, or the simple directness with which she expressed her wishes. And then I realized: *I don't have to choose. I can adore them all. They're all perfectly Lainey.*

It then occurred to me that Lainey was altogether a better person than I was, and I began to worry that her honesty and altruism might prove incompatible with my shady egoism. I wondered: *Could I improve? Could I become more deserving of her?* I didn't think so. But I knew I had to try. I'd seen the old man in the mirror.

Lainey Roth

Bert never wasted any time explaining himself. "Do as I do!" was about the only advice he ever gave to any of his associates. That it served him so well is testament to his inflated balls and egoistic drive to lead by example.

Aside from Barry and my co-op, Bert's leadership style is the only part of his legacy I claimed proudly. Like Bert, I wielded power easily and shamelessly. For example, as president of my temple's Sisterhood, if I wanted something done,

I just went ahead and did it. Sure, there were occasional dust-ups and petty arguments, but my many successes (profitable gala events, newsworthy charitable funds, a high-profile author series) convinced most members that their active involvement was appreciated but unnecessary.

I managed my relationship with Morris with similar efficiency. Knowing he was a life-long bachelor and professional solo act who'd struggle with compromise, I worked hard to discover the razor's edge in our deepening relationship that would leave me committed, even compromised—but still effectively in charge.

Gerald Ellison

After my date with Alice, two ineluctable facts danced in my brain: *she let me hold her* and *she looked happy*.... I thought: *To hell with past is prologue. This is a new dawn. I'm not going to wallow in doubt and piss away another opportunity.*

I began planning a second date—just the two of us. After much internal debate, I chose an itinerary that would bask me in a series of favorable lights.

To begin, I planned that we'd meet at Hudson Yards, Manhattan's newest neighborhood, which I'd helped shape as part of a committee of landscape architects and space designers. Next, I planned a stroll south on the High Line, the westside's park in the sky, a botanical boulevard built on a two-mile stretch of disused elevated train track, which I'd helped conceive as one of the original Friends of the High Line. After exiting the High Line at Gansevoort Street, I planned to show Alice the soaring lobby of the new Whitney Museum, whose vaunted design included several of my suggestions, having been invited by architect Renzo Piano's assistant to share my thoughts.... Finally, the date's *pièce de resistance:* an early dinner at nearby RH Rooftop Restaurant, managed by my friend Phillipe Landau, who'd promised to personally greet us and (later) have his sommelier present a silver bucket of iced champagne.

Alice Bouchet
Oh ... my ... God. Never did I imagine such a day. I mean, living in Manhattan was amazing, but keeping company with such an intelligent and attentive gentleman—who had personally done so much to shape New York's cultural landscape—well, let's just say this old gal from Three Corners, USA, was living the dream.

Gerald Ellison
Everything went wonderfully well, from Hudson Yards to the Whitney Museum. Every time I explained a point of interest, Alice weighed in with astute observations and fearless assessments. Dinner at RH Rooftop was a nearly perfect experience. For someone who had never known fine dining, Alice exhibited extraordinary natural graces. When the French sommelier presented a champagne from the town of Epernay, fifteen miles south of Reims, her eyes welled with tears. I found her mysteriously fascinating.

Two hours later, when exiting the restaurant, she looked into my eyes. "Glorious," she said, stretching the word into three languid syllables. "But I think the bubbly went to my head."

Outside, in the cool early evening, I placed a steadying hand on the small of her back. Minutes later we approached a wide cobblestone street. Despite noting her sensible flats,

I suggested the footing might be dangerous and took her hand, which she withdrew in a flash. I thought all was lost—but her hand returned quickly, as if changing its mind.

We were laughing our tipsy heads off when we came to a three-story public school. The windows on the first two floors were covered with an iron mesh that mostly obscured the display of students' drawings and posters. On the sidewalk, to the right of a pair of red-painted metal doors, was a large sign that read *Voter Registration* in English and Spanish. To me it seemed a heaven-sent prompt, almost too good to be true. You see, our dinner conversation, while entertaining and free-ranging, had skirted the topics of ex-lovers and politics—despite my best efforts to drive our talk in those directions. I did not want to seem pushy or prurient; still, having already dined twice with Alice without having learned anything really personal, I did not think (given my age) that I could afford to spend too much more time with her if I thought she would prove sexually or politically incompatible.

Like many Americans at that time, I was preoccupied with politics. With the orange dunderhead in office and the nation reeling from a viral pandemic, I regarded the upcoming presidential election, still months away, as an existential crisis: as if a large asteroid was on course to obliterate Earth and only America's most intelligent, coordinated response could save humanity from destruction. And so, all in all, standing beside the voter registration sign, I thought my direct question to Alice was reasonably tempered: "So, what do you think of the upcoming election?"

Alice Bouchet

Of course, I steered our conversation away from my

romantic history and politics. Hell's bells, what could I have said? That I was a virgin? That I'd been kissed only once—and not since my prom? That my family was largely responsible for creating the most conservative town in modern America? That in large part I'd left Three Corners so I would not have to vote FOR the vilest presidential candidate in American history or AGAINST the perfect uniformity of political opinion that was the hallmark of my town and its economic *raison d'être*?

I'd been looking at the voter registration sign when Gerald fired his broadside, "So, what do you think of the upcoming election?"

"Such an important question," I said. "So much to say. But right now, it's too much for my tipsy head. Another time, shall we?"

I gave him my hand and he took it.

I felt like I'd dodged a bullet.

Farm Fresh Eggs

Barry Roth

We'd left the museum together but in silence.

"So?" said Emily, locking herself into the passenger seat of my spiffy red Fiat. "What are you thinking?"

I didn't know where to begin, so I said, "Where to begin?" hoping to buy some time. She didn't respond.

"Do you want my opinion of the films?" I asked.

"I don't give a shit about the films."

I drew a deep breath. "Okay.... Is there someplace you'd like to go?"

"Anywhere. Just go."

I drove down Washington Street, which I'd begun to refer to as Main, as the locals did. "Which way?" I asked when we'd reached the turnpike.

"Make a right."

The road was familiar. It was the road I'd traveled the day I first arrived. That day had been all about City Mouse and Country Mouse.

We drove with the top down, passing through dappled tunnels of overhanging branches. I didn't think she had a destination in mind, but when we saw a hand-painted sign for *Fresh Farm Eggs* she said, "Pull over there."

I parked and followed her out of the car, towards a wide, planked table, behind which stood an old country couple: overalls, gingham frock, straw sunhats—the whole bit. On the left side of the table were handmade wicker baskets, horseshoe trivets, and potholders embroidered with homilies like *Have a Blessed Day*. On the right side were several egg cartons open for inspection. Hanging from the lip of the table was another sign: *Farm Fresh Eggs, $4/doz*.

Emily made a show of examining the wicker baskets and trivets while stealing hard glances at the old couple and the eggs. Though this went on for a weirdly long time, I knew, instinctually, not to comment. Eventually, she quickly grabbed one of the cartons and paid with four single dollars. The old man closed the carton, slipped it into a paper bag, and presented it to her carefully.

"Where you from, dear?" the old woman asked.

"Far away…. New York."

"Well, you come a long way for fresh eggs. I hope they're worth the trouble."

We walked back to the car without speaking. When I started the car, Emily said, "Turn around. I want to go back."

I made a U-turn and headed back.

She was silent for a full minute, and then, "They're not the same."

I didn't understand. "What do you mean?"

"The people aren't the same. The eggs aren't the same. Everything is different."

I let it go, figuring we'd get to it later.

A couple miles on we passed the famous billboard: *Three Corners / America's Most Conservative Town*. A hundred yards further, I turned left on Main Street.

I didn't have to wait long for my next instruction. I assumed it would be my place or hers.

"My place" was all she said.

Emily Schnyder

I'd entered the theater like tinder in a lightning storm. You want explanations? Look at my childhood.

Look at me sitting in the shadows between two looming parents, both tailors, hunched over their monotonous labor, tossing me their discards: broken buttons; blemished stripes; damaged braids and chevrons ...

My parent's dross was my treasure. From their discards I shaped clothes and accessories for my dolls and imaginary friends.

But those years in the shadows distorted my reality, stunted my social skills. I was the odd-ball kid (of odd-ball parents) who never went to church, never decorated a Christmas tree, never painted an Easter egg. I taught myself to dance—but never danced with a boy. In ninth grade funny Eric tried to kiss me. I thought it would be nice but he tried to swallow my tongue, so I stomped his foot and ran.

There I was, in the museum theater on a Sunday morning, alone with Barry Roth. I wasn't exactly sure why he'd come to Three Corners or what the hell I was doing with him, but there we were, our eyes fixed on the screen (soldiers saluting, salvos exploding) and he was so close and looked so adorable, I jumped his bones. I think that's the expression.

I truly thought he'd like it, but he slipped my every move like an oiled wrestler. Frustrated and embarrassed, I looked him in the eye and whispered, "What's wrong?" And he said, also in a whisper, "We just met. Let's talk."

Barry Roth

Don't get me wrong, I was flattered and excited—but also scared shitless. Since my travesty on the Honor Stone (and the ensuing interview that had only made it worse), I felt the town's evil eye wherever I went. I had no refuge. Not even

Haven House, which drew everyone's eye.

Also, I had no close friends. Allen could be helpful, but we weren't close. And while some of the women looked at me as at some shiny new thing, I knew they didn't trust me.

But I saw warm possibilities in Emily. I liked her goth look and gender-defiant hair. I also liked her vulnerable slenderness and the fact that she was an artist—and an outlier. And so, when she jumped my bones, I demurred, not out of any scruple (other than my fear of being discovered and publicly shamed), but out of a sense that she was special and needed to be handled with care.

Emily Schnyder

I'd thought it would be a beautiful day but my spurned advances and unsettling experience at the egg stand conspired like a gathering of dark mists. By the time we arrived home, I was in no mood for deep conversation. I just wanted simple.

"You want coffee?" I asked.

"Sure. Thank you."

Just then, I decided to make the eggs. I hadn't eaten eggs in many years and had never made them myself.

I recalled my mother's porcelain mixing bowl, a wedding gift from her mother that she'd promised to give to me when I was grown up. I hadn't seen it in years. I was thrilled to find it in a box in the back of the pantry closet.

I put up a pot of fresh coffee and placed four slices of bread in the toaster. I readied a frying pan with a thick pat of butter.

I placed a paper towel beside the bowl, cracked four eggs, and poured the icky yolks into the bowl, the towel catching the drippings.

I recalled that my mother added salt and a little milk. There was something else, but I couldn't remember.

I looked about for my mother's egg beater. I recalled it was a hand one—not electric—a whisk, that's what she called it. I checked all the familiar drawers and shelves but couldn't find it. I could have used a fork, but I wanted that beater.

Meanwhile, the coffee was boiling, the toast browning, the butter melting—and still I hadn't found the beater. And then I remembered—bacon! That's what was missing! I'd never bought bacon in my life, yet I opened the refrigerator and searched behind every carton, inside every container, growing increasingly frustrated ... until I recalled a little-used drawer above the pots, and there I found the beater, along with a can opener, two extension cords, and a couple fuses.

By then the toast was burning—the butter, bubbling black. Furious, I grabbed the damn beater and whisked those eggs so savagely, the yolk spun round the bowl like a golden blur—and the bowl flung from my hands.

I stared in seething astonishment as the bowl sailed across the room, struck a cabinet and exploded....

Shards and bits of my mother's heirloom lay everywhere; a vomit-like ooze, dripped down the sides of the cabinets, mottling the floor.

My gorge rising, my stomach heaving, I lurched into the nearby bathroom—where my mother had died.

Barry Roth

I heard retching so agonized, wails so plaintive, I feared for her life.

"You okay?" I said through the closed bathroom door.

There was no response, except for the reassuring sounds

of splashing sink water.

Minutes passed. I checked my phone for messages.

"Can I do anything?" I asked for the third time.

Still, no response.

I figured she was embarrassed or had fallen asleep. Perhaps she was still on the floor, still clutching the toilet bowl. I left quietly.

Worlds Colliding

Lainey Roth
I missed dancing with my big Bert. Despite being tall and bearish, he'd always presented an accommodating dance frame and led with care and confidence. When it came to this one tiny sector of our relationship, Bert had been considerate.

After a suitable period of mourning, I returned to the dance floor. Many of the men (mostly divorced or widowed) moved well enough but were not good leaders, which meant they were not good dance partners.

Morris was an exception. He led decisively, perhaps a tad too insistently. Because I liked him—because I thought he might be a keeper—I decided to set him straight. At the very least, I would insist on a compromise. The second time went to Sounds of Brazil, I said to him as we took the dance floor, "My turn to lead, big boy. Try to keep up."

Morris Fine
Lainey seemed surprised that I acquiesced so easily, but she didn't know how my career of saving far-flung Jews had worn me to a nub. She didn't understand that at sixty, my mind was jaded, my strength and nerves diminished. I wanted her to know that I was done living out of suitcases and backpacks, that I was ready for the comforts of a beautiful home … and if those comforts included the company of a beautiful woman like her, I was more than ready to follow her lead—in life, as in dance.

Alice Bouchet

I didn't know what to do. I liked Gerald in so many ways and I admired his progressive politics—but they also frightened the bejesus out of me. I mean, he told me he cried during the entire televised funeral for Civil Rights leader Elijah Cummings and how a *60 Minutes* segment on the caged children at the Mexican border had sent him into a week-long depression. Lord! How could I tell him that every voting adult in Three Corners had voted for the President in 2016, except a very few who had cast blank ballots, including me? Would he see my lack of opposition as cowardly? As passive complicity? How could I tell him that I was liberal pacifist who opposed most military traditions but would never, ever, publicly disavow my family's legacy? Would he understand that? Could a man who celebrated the power of empty art space understand the hard edges of my conservative world?

I thought I should tell him the simple truth: that coming to New York had been (in large part) my passive-aggressive solution for wanting to avoid another presidential campaign and election back home; that by voting Democrat in a Blue state, I would avoid betraying my conscience, my town, and my family.

Bottom line: I'd rather die a thousand deaths than betray my Bouchet heritage. Family is family! … But then I thought: My family will die with me. I'm the end of the line. There is no collateral issue. When I die, my family falls like the House of Usher—no bang, just a whimper, and maybe not even that … unless Allen is there to mourn me.

Allen Briggs

Alice never sent me an actual letter—or even an email—

just those touristy postcards that said *Thinking of you! Thanks for holding down the fort!* ... or something along those lines. I figured she was enjoying herself and had no time for me.

Mostly, I took the high road: Good for her! I thought. She deserves great happiness. No one deserves it more. Just look where she came from. I mean, Haven House was no haven. I'd seen first-hand what it had been like to live there. Plenty times I played in Alice's backyard or (when I was older) kept her company on her front porch, and sometimes—when I least expected it—one of her parents or brothers would invite me inside for lemonade or iced tea.

You might think I felt rewarded by their hospitality but I never did. Inside, I always felt her family's close scrutiny, like I'd stepped into a confessional, like they were reading my mind and I could read theirs: *Don't think for a second that we can't see your dirty little thoughts.* Now, no one ever said anything like that to me. I'm just saying that whenever I had even the tiniest bit of interaction with Alice's father—the Commander—or one of her officer brothers, or even her mother—the Commander's Wife—I felt like they were grilling me with personal, probing questions.

I can only imagine what living in Haven House must have been like for Alice. I mean, it was a top-down, regimented organization with a hundred rules on how life should be lived. I know it wasn't easy for Alice, though I think the effect on her was a mixed bag: emboldening her in some ways, hobbling her in others.

But what was my excuse? I was raised in a normal house with a normal family. Why was I emotionally crippled? Why did I struggle to tell Alice how I felt about her?

I think her family made it damn hard on us both. But

that's weak, I know. And it doesn't explain the fact that years after Alice's father and brothers had died (her mother having passed some years before), I still hadn't declared my love. And then Alice was gone. Just like that. Of course, her choice to go was a lifetime in the making and decided only after she had saved the future of Three Corners by closing the college, selling off its buildings, and creating Freedom Hall.

Everything Alice did to save our town was amazingly impressive, but I was even more amazed by her decision to go to New York. Of all places, New York! I'd never heard her say a word about it. Not even a passing comment. Nothing. And then she was gone.

I could understand why she might not want to write and receive long letters, but I couldn't figure why she sent me such brief, impersonal postcards. Didn't I mean more to her than that? And then it occurred to me: perhaps she's not happy in New York. Maybe she's lonely. Maybe she's homesick. Maybe she needs a little reminder of home to help her appreciate where she is and what she left behind. I thought: Be the damndest thing for us both if I paid her a visit.

Gerald Ellison

Alice nearly jumped out of her skin when I'd asked about her personal history. Apparently, my questions cut close to the bone. Still, it made no sense for me to pressure her for more fulsome responses. We all have scars and skeletons. And it wasn't like she'd been completely reticent. She'd told me plenty about why she'd come to New York. What she didn't mention is what she'd left behind. But what could I do? I couldn't twist her arm. I couldn't sneak into her closet to see what secrets she kept in the dark. Besides, what I did know about her was wonderful. And that's no small thing. And so, since I wasn't dating anyone else, I decided not to rock the boat, to let the relationship unfold slowly, in its own time.

Still, I felt the occasional need to be provocative. When these feelings hit, I led her to the city's edgier entertainments, where emotionally promiscuous minds could toe-step into the Dark. Over the course of one month, I took her to Dream House, Surreal Elevator, Boroughs of the Dead—thinking the mind-blowing experiences they advertised would be my best chance of getting Alice to dish on her tightly guarded past. As it happened, we always enjoyed ourselves, but the experiences never resulted in any revelatory disclosures, as I had hoped.

During this period, it occurred to me that New York must seem a very strange place to Alice. How long had she been here? A few months? That's a cup of coffee after a lifetime on Main Street.

I imagined walking in her shoes. Would I find New York copasetic? Was it too loud and busy? Was there too much sensory overload? Would I want to live here if I were her?

And then, to switch the roleplay, I imagined walking about her hometown in my own shoes. I liked the idea. I liked the thought that I might learn about her formative influences—especially as they related to her ideas on love and politics.

I think we can learn a lot from a change in perspective. That's the centerpiece of my design philosophy. I've always preached it. I thought it might be a good time to apply it to my personal life.

Quid Pro Quo

Barry Roth

Several weeks after meeting the three salon ladies at the diner, I received an invitation to meet them there again. As a postscript (but without the *P.S.*), one of them wrote in a flamboyant cursive, "We need another meeting to decide which of us you should date first."

Though tempted, I hadn't yet contacted any of the ladies, avoiding, for the time being, the possibility of further complications.

I'd also been tempted to contact Emily. I hadn't heard from her since her meltdown. I really wanted to speak with her, but I didn't have her phone number. Her only email address was the museum server, but I didn't want to write anything that Allen might read. I considered writing a letter, but I knew Squirrel and Jacqueline would see it at the Post Office. I could not walk to her house—or drive there in my red Fiat—without alerting the town's early warning system. I'd been thinking about Emily when the second invitation from the salon ladies arrived. A few days later I went to the diner to meet them again for lunch.

Jacqueline

As soon as that scrumptious new fella walked in and took a booth seat, I brought him a fresh cup a joe.

"Here you go, sweetie—milk, two sugars."

"You remembered," he said, sharing his adorable smile.

"I take pride in my work," I said.

He was about to respond but I cut him off: "I have good news and bad news."

"Oh?" he said, lookin' like a sad little puppy. "What's the bad news?"

"Your three lady friends just called and left a message. They can't come today. They said they'd reschedule."

"Oh, okay. And the good news?"

"One second, honey."

I walked behind the counter, grabbed the plate I'd quickly prepared, and returned.

"The good news," I said, laying down half an apple pie and two forks, "is that I have some free time."

"Well, thank you, Jacqueline," he said while I settled into the seat opposite his. "I'm Barry Roth."

"I know who you are," I said, straightening my blouse and hair, "but how'd you know my name?"

"I take pride in my work."

I looked at him suspiciously.

"Which is what, exactly?"

"I write novels."

"And you know my name because—"

"Because I ask lots of questions about what's what and who's who. That's how I get ideas."

"You writing about me?"

"It's possible. I'm still getting to know the town and some of the people who live here."

"Yeah, well, what do you think you know about me?"

"I know you ride a Harley and don't take crap from anyone. I'm always interested in meeting unique people."

"So," I said, dipping a shoulder and batting an eye. "You want to get to know me?"

He laughed nervously.

"Sure," he said. "That would be nice."

Squirrel Evans

It's not so much that we hear things in this town, it's that we hear *everything*, sooner or later. In Three Corners, a secret is just a private truth not yet publicly revealed. So, when I heard something about an egg stand and Emily Schnyder getting sick, I mentioned it, off-the-cuff like, to Gavin Lissome. I'd long suspected his involvement in those half-dozen cases of local folk who'd died after eating eggs from an old chicken farm just below his Marion gas station. Anyway, I wanted to see how he'd react. Thing is, Gavin had something on everyone—including me and Jacqueline—and I figured it would only help my bargaining position if I held at least one card he couldn't read. Besides, I owed him the info. We had ourselves a nice, profitable quid pro quo, by which I'd agreed to share hearsay picked up on my delivery rounds, especially as it related to our town's powerbrokers. Now, Mr. Barry Roth and Miss Emily Schnyder weren't exactly powerbrokers, but they both had significant connections to Alice Bouchet—which made them persons of interest to Gavin.

On a separate score, Barry Roth was on my own personal radar, having heard from Jacqueline (and others) what a swell time she'd had with him in the diner, chattin' up a storm. I mostly trusted Jacqueline, but I knew she'd use any means at hand to goad me into marrying her. Quite frankly, I'd intended to do just that when the time was right, but I didn't like to be pushed. Meantime, I was thinking that Barry and me might have ourselves a conversation to set matters straight.

Gavin Lissome

My daddy Clyde was still alive when old Esther Higgins died at her breakfast table in Marion, her three-egg omelet only partially consumed, according to Sheriff Herb Stanchion and the coroner, Box Bailey. Herb and Box were old hunting buddies of daddy's and always treated to cigarettes and beef jerky when they filled up at the station. Their conspired Coroner's Report cited *old age* and unspecified *pre-existing conditions* as the reasons for Esther's sudden demise. Over the next couple years there were several similar deaths, likewise ascribed to *pre-existing conditions*. In one case *heart attack* was cited because the deceased was known to have a weak ticker and no one had insisted on an autopsy.

Now, let me be perfectly clear: there was never a jot of forensic proof to tie any death in Marion to the consumption of local tainted eggs. Still, when Jack and Carol Schnyder of Three Corners died suddenly and there was some whispered suspicion of tainted eggs, I felt a black threat bearing down on me. As if fulfilling my own sense of impending doom, I was soon approached by Sheriff Herb Stanchion, coroner Box Bailey, Three Corners' mayor Peyton Carson, and Colonel Karl Bouchet, who insisted I do everything I could to forestall any future allegations or criminal suits that might hurt the reputation of either town.

The way I saw it, I'd already taken my civic duty seriously—and it had cost me plenty: more than a hundred grand, which I'd been able to borrow (with the help of the Town Council) at very favorable terms. But don't think I profited from this fiasco. I'd used every penny to excavate and remove my old empty gasoline tanks, buy a pair of spanking new tanks, fill in the cavity with fresh soil, hook up the new tanks to the existing pumps, and then hope to God that whatever had already leaked into the soil would dilute or evaporate or seep into the watershed and be washed away.

When Squirrel mentioned what happened to Emily Schnyder, I sensed he was trying to poke the bear. I wouldn't have admitted it, but I was a little unnerved.

Brenda Lissome

Gavin and me had an arrangement that worked for us both. So long as I kept the house dustless and cooked him a decent supper six days a week, he generally left me alone.

His laissez faire extended to the bedroom and that was fine with me ... although, as you might expect, certain yearnings of mine tended to build up over time. Eventually, these yearnings became predictable enough to be scheduled: enter Billy Acers. Or, I should say, enter Brenda Lissome, since I was the one who entered the Red, White, and Brew, having learned from Jacqueline that its new bartender was a smoldering hunk, who did not smoke and who always wore a clean white shirt and black pants, like a professional uniform. I liked that. That kind of positive self-awareness projected well, I thought. Anyway, one day, when yearning and curiosity had got the better of me, I sauntered into the Red White and Brew real casual-like, looking about like I was expecting to see someone, and when I saw no one, I sauntered up to the bar, real ladylike, and asked:

"I'm looking for Gavin Lissome. He told me he'd be here."

"Well, he's a lucky man to have such a pretty lady asking for him. And what might your name be?"

"It might be Marilyn Monroe ... and it might be Brenda

Lissome."

"Brenda Lissome. I'm thinking kid sister."

"Think again."

"Wife?"

"I suppose. That's what the license says."

Billy Acers smiled; his teeth even whiter than his clean shirt.

"What are you drinking? The first three are on the house."

***

Billy was a good talker and smart too. Before I knew him five minutes, I used *laissez faire* twice to show I was his intellectual equal.

Billy took note of my high standards and raised me one: Squatting low behind the bar so I could no longer see him, he rooted about until he came up smiling like a deep-sea diver holding high some prized discovery.

"I've never showed this to anyone else," he said, drawing a thick spiral notebook from a crinkled paper bag. "It's my greatest work. My masterpiece."

***

Billy was a poet—and a great one! He lived modestly in a tiny house in a tiny town (even by Three Corners standards) and that suited him just fine because great poets are visionaries—they can see past the trappings that define boring, middle-class life. Billy saw higher things. Some even higher than the sky, which he called the *empyrean*.

Billy had decided to write a coming-of-age novel because he'd learned that all writers start that way. He made his narrative a quest story because he knew it would be a commercial success and make a good movie. He made the lead character a young woman because he'd read somewhere that women buy and read most of the books and he thought feminism was a hot issue he could hang his hat on. He wrote the novel as an epic poem because he really was a poet, first and foremost, and knew he needed a hook to capture the world's attention. In addition to being crazy good at rhyming, Billy understood market trends.

***

Billy liked bartending at the Red, White, and Brew because it gave him plenty time to write. He was also able to bring home some food, which saved a lot of money—not that he needed much help with that. His family owned and operated Golden Orchard and he received a stipend, whether he worked or not.

Billy described the orchard work as seasonal, which made me think there was a lot of slow time when his family didn't need his help. But I would learn that Spring (strawberries), Summer (blueberries, peaches), and Fall (apples) were the busy selling seasons … and that Winter was intense with inspecting, trimming, pruning, repairing, planting…. When I mentioned that running an orchard seemed a daily, year-round challenge, Billy added that it was also wonderfully satisfying … and then helped me see the sacrifice he'd made by giving up farm work to focus on his writing career.

***

That first day, we knew we shouldn't get too crazy, though that didn't stop Billy from carrying me into the supply room and taking down my pants and sitting my bare ass on a low stack of liquor boxes.... It was wild and I didn't regret it, but I knew it was dangerous and somewhat beneath us and told him so. That's when he told me about the orchards: hundreds of acres of trees and bushes, along with scattered out-buildings—rarely visited in their off seasons.

***

I was seduced as much by Mother Nature as I was by Billy. I mean, you ever visit an orchard on a bright sunny day? The sights of blueberry blues, peachy yellows, and strawberry reds are stupendous; the scents of a million budding fruits are overwhelming. Adding the musk of an excited man, a toolshed that reeks of iron-girded baskets, and the tang of steel tools is just overkill. I know. I just swooned!

***

Billy taught me a lot, if you know what I mean. "We're so lucky," he said one day when we were sweaty and catching our breath. "What's that, baby?" I asked, my flushed face resting on his rising and falling pec. He said, "These orchards are like our private woods, and each shed is another pied-à-terre." I thought *how lovely*—though, to be honest, I didn't understand *pied*-à-*terre* and was picking splinters out of my ass.

For all that, Billy was the complete package: talented, beautiful, sensitive—and passionate. We had a good thing even if we had no idea where it was going. I knew it was important to keep our relationship a strict secret, so I made sure I didn't tell a soul—except Jacqueline, my new best friend.

Jacqueline

That Squirrel thought he could keep his arrangement with Gavin a secret from me was just the cutest thing. I mean, *really?* I read the man's face like a newspaper. I read his mind like I was his therapist. But most efficiently, I read his mail, checked his phone, and studied his daily business ledger—where he entered sidenotes more suitable for a private journal or a Dear Diary. How did I discover all his keys and passwords? What can I say? I'm a born snoop and had perfected my gift through years of dedicated practice.

But don't think bad of me. Quite frankly, Squirrel had only himself to blame. Knowing me as he did, he should have taken better precautions against my snooping. That he didn't was another sign of disrespect. Men should take their women more seriously.

And this brings me to Brenda. I knew she wasn't happy with Gavin, so I threw her Billy Acers like a tasty bone. I liked Brenda. She was my new friend. But I just hated that she was rich and married and I wasn't. That shit just isn't fair.

***

Mr. Barry Roth was in my head like one of those damn song worms. Now, I had no serious designs on that pretty boy and didn't think anything would ever happen between us, but I liked holding tight to the possibility that fancy dreams could come true.

Still, it made me feel guilty. Like maybe Squirrel would read my mind (the way I read his) and get so mad he'd leave me. That thought was terrible. So terrible, I had to act real quick to stop Squirrel from reading my mind. So one day, as if out of the clear blue, I accused him of having sexy feelings for Brenda.

Squirrel Evans

My first reaction: Jacqueline was getting back at me 'cause I'd accused her of getting all chatty-like with Barry at the diner. But my very next thought was: *How the hell did she know?* I mean, Brenda came into my head often enough, but I almost always made an effort to chase her away on account of me and Gavin being business partners. So how did Jacqueline know? Perhaps I'd smiled a little too hard at Brenda once or twice, or maybe I pressed her hand a little too warmly on occasion. I know I stared at her twitching ass whenever I could.... If Brenda sensed something sly and told Gavin, that would not be good for me. Gavin was not the man to cross.

But I was just as afraid of Jacqueline. To get the idea of me and Brenda out of her head, I had to set her bloodhound nose in some other direction. So, I gave her some real juicy gossip to distract her: I told her my suspicions about Gavin's involvement in all the egg deaths. I gave her a few particulars, just enough to put her on the scent.

Angel of Death

Emily Schnyder
I was at a crossroads and didn't know what to do. I didn't know left from right. The only thing I knew, and it was an intuitive thing, was that I had to start moving away from my past and towards my future, whatever it was. I suppose I thought—or hoped—that Barry would remain in my life. At the very least, I thought he might help me see what my next steps should be. So I called him, not on his cell (I didn't have his number) but at Haven House—and not on the kitchen phone but on Alice's private pink phone, right beside her bed, where I'd sat a thousand times, crying my heart out.

Barry Roth
I was reading in bed when the phone rang. I knew it was my mother. She had used that number when first speaking with Alice (before she came to New York) and often used it to call me in the evening.
"Hi, Lainey. How's life in the Big Apple?"
She didn't answer. I thought it might be a wrong number.
"Who's Lainey?"
Pause. "Who's this?" I asked.
"I asked first."
"Emily?"
"Depends. Who's Lainey?"
"My mother."
"You call your mother Lainey?"
"That's her name. What did you call your mother?"

Silence…. I bit my tongue.

"Sorry, bad question," I said.

"No, it's an okay question. I just don't remember. I think I called her mommy."

Emily Schnyder

It was a good conversation. Barry asked how I was but did not refer to our last meeting.

"I owe you a meal," was the highlight of my scant remarks.

"I'll tell you what," he said, sounding happy enough to move forward. "There's something I want to do—need to do—and I'd like to share it with you. It involves a meal, of sorts. But it might be easier if we did it here."

"No dice. Whatever it is, let's do it together at my place. I owe you."

"Fair enough. We have about two weeks—plenty time for us to prepare."

"For what?"

"The Angel of Death. We'll need to sacrifice a lamb and smear your door with its blood."

"Really?"

"No. Of course not. But we have a ritual feast to prepare, and I have to rehearse the story that goes with it."

"I have no idea what you're talking about—but count me in."

Feng Shui

Lainey Roth

Morris and I both liked dancing, theater, and foreign films. But mostly he liked to stay home, which meant my place. Without invitation—or even discussion—he stayed for days at a time. In fact, he'd essentially moved in, returning to his own apartment only to dust, water his plants, and retrieve his mail. Having spent decades helping far-flung Jews establish *halachic* lives, he'd become quite the homebody.

Mostly, I loved his company. Mo was a wonderful conversationalist, freely sharing his strong opinions on just about everything, including his adventurous past. On several occasions I tested him, just to see how far I could go (how many women have you slept with? were you ever attracted to another man? have you fathered any children? do you believe in a Jewish God?). He answered all my probing questions fully and frankly. Thing is, I had to ask. He never revealed the personal stuff casually.

In turn, Morris asked many questions about my life but very few about my son, Barry, and even fewer about my ex, Bert. He was, however, very curious about my finances, often inveigling information at opportune moments. For example, I might say, "Isn't that a lovely building?"

"Co-op or rental?" he might ask.

"Definitely co-op."

"Pricey?"

"Must be."

"What do you think a three-bedroom goes for?"

"Depends on the floor," I might say. "With a great view—at least three million."

"Really? What's yours worth?"

***

One day he asked for his own set of keys. I was stunned (though I shouldn't have been) and said yes. I spoke too quickly. I should have waited. Had I waited, even a little bit, he might have felt a little less empowered. As it was, a week later I experienced my first pang of regret. We were both in my living room. I was reading; he was pacing about, as if surveying the room's dimensions. Suddenly, as if directed by an epiphany, he turned the tall, triangular planter in the far corner ever so slightly.

"Something wrong?" I asked.

"I just fixed an affront to the room's feng shui."

I was astounded. Not because he was wrong (he wasn't), but because the change was so small—barely perceptible—and he'd made such a big deal of it. Why?

***

Had I addressed the situation calmly (or ignored it altogether), it might have passed as a misunderstanding—a minor first offence. But no, not me. I let it fester until I felt violated and victimized. Looking back, this was not surprising. After all, I was Lainey Roth, autocratic President of the Park East Sisterhood, whose fellow sisters admired my successes but did not admire me—or even like me. I punished Morris with three days of tense aloofness.

***

During those three days I thought more about Barry than I had in several months. I really wanted him to be happy. It occurred to me that my plan to help him find happiness had resulted in him living in Three Corners ... Alice living in his apartment ... and Morris living with me. I called him and we had a good conversation.

"How's my favorite, left-leaning son making out in America's heartland?"

He laughed.

"Well, considering my rocky start: pulling on that stupid sword ... riding around in a hot red convertible ... sleeping late on Sundays and skipping church—"

"You fit right in?"

We both laughed.

"Actually," he said, "now that we're well into the election year, things are starting to heat up here. It's a long way to November, but folks are already pounding the drums."

"Why so early?"

"Remember, this town is uniquely conservative: one hundred percent, dead-red Republican—and they work hard to keep it that way."

"There must be other small towns where everyone votes the same way."

"I think every town has its outliers and naysayers—except Three Corners. Here, everyone who votes, votes the party line."

"Why's that?"

"Everyone here votes their pocketbook: money talks, conscience walks."

"That's just a slogan. And people everywhere vote their pocketbook."

"Fair enough. But the people here are economically incentivized to vote Republican."

"How so?"

"Simple: the town's survival is entirely dependent on the success of its military museum, Freedom Hall. Without the museum, the town is not self-sustaining. And there aren't many other business opportunities nearby. Without Freedom Hall, most people in Three Corners would be forced to move."

"But why do they need to be one hundred percent conservative?"

"Simple: the town's advertised motto, *Most Conservative Town in America!* is what attracts the tourists, who spend their money at Freedom Hall—and at the diner, the grocery, the gas station—which basically keeps the town alive."

"Okay, I get it. But what if another town became one hundred percent Republican? Surely, that's possible."

"At this point, the best another town could do is a statistical tie, which would be meaningless. Three Corners was the first to claim itself as America's most conservative town, so it's their motto—their brand—and they'll do anything to maintain it."

"Okay, I get that too. But now I have to ask: what are *you* going to do on Election Day? Won't you be a marked man?"

"Let's not go there—just yet."

As he said nothing more, I tacked with the question nearest my heart: "Okay, what about the social scene? Have you

met anyone special?"
"I expected him to be flippant or coy.
"Actually, I have."
"*What?*" My heart leaped with joyful possibilities.
"Easy, Lainey. Don't get your hopes up. It's way too early. Besides, she has issues."
"Don't we all," I said, supporting the case for my future daughter-in-law.

As soon as the call ended, I began fantasizing about the wedding—and the bride's ensuing pregnancy. I remembered my promise to gift Barry my apartment as soon as he made me a grandma.... Then I thought: Why wait? Why not offer him the apartment as a wedding gift? ... And then: Why not as an engagement gift? What an idea! ... Let's see how Morris likes that. Feng shui my ass!

Morris Fine

I should have known better. For all Lainey's intelligence and showy power, her main source of pride (other than her son) had been her perfectly appointed home.

So why had I challenged her decorating aesthetic? Because, wanting desperately to live with her, I thought it would help my case if she saw me as an equal partner, someone who might freely offer a strong opinion about all aspects of our shared life. But I'd acted prematurely (as evidenced by her cold silence) and understood clearly that with a single pointed finger I could be shown the door.

Intuiting that a simple apology would not suffice, I vowed (to myself) to make it up to her in a more meaningful way. But what to do?

For months she'd been asking me to accompany her to

one of her synagogue's cultural events but I hadn't wanted to go, feeling done with the Jewish thing and wanting to move on. On the fourth day following our tiff, she brought it up again—this time gift-wrapping her request.

"You must think the synagogue's events are worthwhile, you lectured there almost exactly a year ago. That's how we met, remember?"

I don't recall exactly what I said. Something like: *After the lecture, I remember looking up at your beautiful face when I entered the cab.... I carried that image all the way to Tasmania and never let it go.... I hoped we'd meet again, but my work was consuming. When I returned, I was burnt out. That's why I didn't contact you. I didn't think I was ready. But Fate thought otherwise, and brought us together at the Kasbah. Now, I'm ready to return—with you—to your synagogue.*

Switching Places

Alice Bouchet

I'd learned much during my time in New York, but nothing so profound as the certainty that I would find love there. I could sense it getting closer, the way I could sense the increasing nearness of a flowing river.

With my sixtieth birthday fast approaching, I thought I should hurry Fate along. Sun Tzu says that opportunities multiply as they are seized, so I decided to encourage the two men in my life to discover what they needed to know about me—and hoped they'd act on it soon.

***

Gerald and I were enjoying the fusion fare of a Cuban-Chinese restaurant in Lower Midtown. The thought of culinary atoms exploding in my mouth made me feel sexy. Then again, I knew nothing of real sex. Having waited nearly sixty years, I figured I could hold out a while longer.

While enjoying dessert, I set part one of my plan in action:

"Gerald, I've told you about Freedom Hall, our military museum in Three Corners."

"You have indeed. And I've seen the website. It looks wonderful. Congratulations."

"Thank you. It's been a big success, and lately more popular than ever."

"Because of our crazy national politics?"

For the moment, I wanted to avoid any further questioning of my personal politics. "I'm sure that's it. But I'm concerned about the museum. Its success is my responsibility. I expect business to be great until the election—but after that I fear it will drop off dramatically."

"I'm guessing you have a plan."

"Not quite. But I have an idea for a plan."

"Okay, I'll bite. What's your idea?"

I put down my dessert spoon and wiped my mouth with a fresh napkin.

"As I said, I expect a downturn in business after the election—especially if the Democrats win. But the town can't afford a prolonged downturn. We need a steady a business from the museum to survive."

"Okay. What's your idea for a plan?"

"We need many more new customers and a compelling reason for previous customers to return—again and again. I hadn't really considered that when the museum was originally designed."

"Makes sense. Do you have some specific ideas or directions?"

"Not really. But I'm thinking big. Not just tweaks and updates—but expansion. Maybe a new wing."

"You have the budget?"

"I might. If our current business holds from now until the election, we'll have record profits, and I'm willing to reinvest most of it back into the museum."

"And you have that authority?"

"Yes, I am sole owner and director. But I need your help."

Gerald Ellison

She said I was perfect for the job.

She said, "You work with galleries and museums. You're an expert on design space. Also, your politics are … oppositional. I think that's a big plus."

"Interesting" was all I said.

She said, "If you could suggest new ideas to expand our exhibits beyond the strictly conservative … I think that would be great."

I held my tongue.

She said, "And think big—at least to start—we can always scale back. But our enhanced museum must remain essentially conservative—we can't risk losing our base. Still, I'd like our new look to appeal to a broader range of Americans. I think that's key."

I kept silent, gathering my thoughts.

She said, "So, that's my idea. It's vague, I know, but there's one thing I know for sure. If you take on this project, you must go to Three Corners. You need to meet the people who live there and the tourists who visit. You'll also need to see the current exhibits up close and consider the possibilities for expansion. Just so you know, I own adjacent land parcels, north and east. I can send you the surveyor's report."

Still, I stayed silent.

She said, "I can arrange for a place for you to stay—no charge. And you won't need a car—everything is within walking distance…. I will pay you a very fair consulting fee."

Still silent, still processing.

She said, "Here's my final two cents—and then I'll shut up: I read somewhere that successful businesses serve current demands while hoping to discover future trends. I'm not sure what that means for us specifically, but I'll leave that up to you. So, what do you think?"

I'd never seen her so animated. So sexy.

"I see this as a win-win for us both," she said, preempting my response. "I'll learn more about you and you'll learn a lot more about me. I think you'll need about two weeks in Three Corners."

I smiled.

"I'm in," I said, thumping the table. "I have some time free time coming up, so I can plan to leave soon. But I have one condition."

She gave me a nervous look. "What's that?"

"I'm waiving my consulting fee."

Her face relaxed into a widening smile.

"In that case," she said, "this meal is my treat. And that's nonnegotiable."

Allen Briggs

The Lord moves in mysterious ways. Alice called me last night—on my home phone—right after I'd convinced myself to go to New York. Sounds crazy, but I recognized her ring, even though she was calling from a different world.

"Hi, Allen. It's Alice!"

Thank God she sounded happy. I'd prepared myself for the worst.

"Alice, how are you?"

I didn't care if my voice quivered. Save for those stupid postcards, I hadn't heard from her in the longest time—and had begun to fear terrible things.

"I'm fine," she said. "Really, all is good."

We exchanged more pleasantries and assurances … and then, out of nowhere, she said, "Allen, I want you to come to New York. Soon! I miss you. I want to show you the city."

I was stunned.

"Me? New York?"

"Yes, you! Happy sixtieth! I know it was last week, but I wanted to wait and surprise you."

"Thank you, Alice! But what about the museum? We're so busy. I can't leave now."

"That's part of my surprise. I spoke to Emily and she agreed to work extra hours ... and she spoke with Barry, who said he'd help too."

"What about all the things I clean and fix—there's always stuff to do."

"I know that. That's why I spoke with Jacqueline. She said she'd visit the museum before and after her diner shifts to do whatever's needed."

Alice never ceased to amaze me. "You're about the only person in town she might have obliged."

"She has a good heart. I've always known that…. So, we agreed? You coming to the Big Apple?"

Pause. "Have I ever let you down?" My words ended in a quiver of emotion.

"No, Allen. You never have. You've always done all I've asked."

She paused. I think her voice had a quiver too. But she soon got back to business.

"I've arranged a flight for you on the 14th out of St. Louis, returning two weeks later, on the 27th."

"No one plans like you do, Alice. I just don't know what to do first."

"You don't worry about a thing. I'll send you an email that explains everything. I'll make it real easy. All you have to do is drive to the St. Louis airport and pick up the ticket waiting for you. Bring your ID."

"How will I know where to find you in New York?"

"Silly boy, when you get to LaGuardia Airport, you just give a cab driver my address. He'll drive you to Manhattan, straight to my door. I've already found you a nice little hotel—right near my place in the Lower East Side."

I had a catch in my throat and couldn't say another word. Alice must have known that too.

"I have to run now, dear," she said. "You just pack sensibly. You won't need any suit, but bring a sport jacket and some of your nicer shirts and pants."

"What about my hunting cap and fishing tackle?"

She laughed. "You leave those home, dear."

Holiday Eggs

Emily Schnyder
 I never liked Easter. My parents discouraged it and I knew not to argue. Except one year, the school was having a contest to see who could paint the most beautiful Easter egg. I asked my mother if we could do it together but she said no, she was too busy. She said this while watching television, so I knew she wasn't busy. But I also knew I shouldn't ask again if I knew what was good for me.
 I already knew I would not be dressing up on Easter Sunday and parading up and down Main Street like all the other girls. But I didn't want to give up on the Easter egg contest. It was my chance to feel normal, like I belonged.
 The contest was on a Thursday. There was no school the next day because that was the day Christ was crucified—though I was fuzzy on the details and felt I shouldn't ask. Anyway, the important thing was that everyone was going to bring in their special, painted egg. I knew I'd feel terrible if I was the only kid too poor or too stupid not to participate. Besides, I knew I could win. I was the best artist in the whole damn school and winning would make me special.
 The night before the contest I practiced my design on a piece of a paper. I didn't include anything about Jesus or the Cross but I painted a beautiful hill with a golden sunrise behind it and some daisies and bunnies at the bottom. I practiced it several times, using only a few watercolors because watercolors are pretty and quick to dry. When my design looked perfect, I rolled a piece of paper into a cone so

I could practice painting on a curve. When I perfected that technique, I knew I could paint an egg.

Next morning, before I left for school, I took an egg from the carton in our refrigerator and placed it carefully in a small cardboard box that I'd lined with cotton. There were five eggs left and I didn't think my parents would miss one.

I left for school about ten minutes earlier than usual and when I got there I didn't wait in the playground for the bell, as I usually did, but went inside to the bathroom, which was unusual, but not weird enough for anyone to notice. I chose the far stall, pulled down my pants and underwear (so no one would think I was doing anything but my business), and quickly painted my Easter egg. When I was done, I blew on it like I was whispering and then laid it carefully in the box. It was dry and perfect, and I knew I would win.

Barry Roth

I'm not religious. I went to Hebrew school like most of my friends but rarely returned for prayer services after my bar mitzvah. Bert didn't give a damn and Lainey was busy with her teas and galleries. She hadn't yet joined the Park East Synagogue—that came later, after Bert died, when she discovered she had more time and money on her hands than she knew what to do with.

At first, I made fun of Lainey's synagogue work because she took it so seriously and we both knew God had nothing to do with it. I think she enjoyed expressing her authority and leadership, impossible in her marriage to Bert.

Like Lainey, I loved being Jewish—even without God. I especially loved those holiday feasts that required no accounting of my moral register or ethical record. For me, being Jewish was social, cultural, historical. Admittedly, I've had many Jewish moments that felt divinely profound—as if I'd experienced something pure and greater than myself—but I've always been loath to acknowledge God.

***

My favorite holidays were Purim and Passover because they involved a good story and lots of food. I especially loved Passover, because of its many rituals and songs. When I left New York for Three Corners I'd packed two Haggadahs (Passover handbooks), just in case I met someone to invite to my personal seder feast, which, according to that year's calendar, would occur during Easter week.

Emily Schnyder

After agreeing to meet Barry for some kind of ritual feast, I saw him every day for two weeks. Sometimes he came to my home, sometimes I went to Haven House. I was comfortable (or uncomfortable) in either place, depending on my mood and other factors I little understood. Suffice to say, my behavior was unpredictable, which was hard on us both.

We were in the kitchen of Haven House. I had mostly good memories of the place. Barry had made a fresh pot of coffee and had arranged a half-dozen cinnamon sticks in a glass creamer like a stack of bivouac rifles.

"Tell me more about Passover," I said. "Why so much preparation?"

"Passover is my favorite holiday," he said, smiling. "Even better than Thanksgiving—and I love Thanksgiving."

"Hard to beat stuffed turkey and all the fixin's."

"Agreed. But you can enjoy turkey and fixin's all year. Passover's ritual fare is unique. Besides, there are prayers and songs. You'll see—just two more days."

"Does Passover always occur during Easter?"

"It's always this general time of year, but the date varies."

"So, is Passover like a Jewish Easter, the way Hannukah is like a Jewish Christmas?"

"Whoa, hold it right there. Hannukah has nothing to do with Christmas—except the shared time of year. Passover and Easter, however, do share some biblical history."

"Okay. I have a lot to learn. But let me ask you this: Why don't Jewish holidays occur at the same time every year?"

"Because of the Jewish calendar."

"There's a Jewish calendar?"

"Yup."

"Jewish people have their own calendar?"

"Yup."

"Do Jewish people believe in months and days of the week?"

"Of course. They just have different names."

"Hmmm. Is there a Jewish New Year's Day?"

"In the fall."

"The fall. Why the fall?"

"Something to do with the harvest."

"Makes sense. What date is the Jewish new year?"

"It varies."

"Well, how do Jews plan for it?"

"They check their Jewish calendar. Actually, most American calendars list the major Jewish holidays."

"But ... I still don't understand ... why are the calendars not the same?"

"The common calendar—the one we both use—is a solar calendar. The Hebrew calendar is a lunisolar calendar. The months are based on lunar months, but years are based on solar years."

"Does the Jewish calendar have a leap year?"

"Yes, but it's like every two to three years … and it's a leap *month*."

"A whole month! A thirteenth month?"

"Yup. So, if I'm ever late, I can say I was on Jewish time."

"Funny.… Do you follow the Jewish calendar?"

"No. I don't even know the months of the year. Only religious Jews who speak Hebrew use the Hebrew calendar."

"Fascinating. You are quite exotic."

"By Three Corners' standards. There are a million Jews where I come from."

"Are they all as smart and adorable as you?"

"Depends who you ask. According to Lainey, I'm number one."

"Well, you're number one with me."

That's when we kissed for the first time.

Barry Roth

Through Amazon I'd acquired a new Seder plate; a brass menorah; three small silver wine glasses; and a large bottle of Manischewitz Concord Grape wine. I'd had Lainey send me a box of matzahs, my bar mitzvah yarmulka, and the afikomen cover I'd embroidered in Hebrew school when I was eight or nine. To avoid her third degree, I told her I'd be observing Passover alone—a lone bastion of Yiddishkeit in a goyishe world. Because of the extensive preparations, I'd convinced Emily to come to my place.

***

Because it was Easter Sunday and most of the town would be walking back and forth between their homes and First Baptist Church, passing Haven House along the way, I'd opened the windows but drawn the blinds for a balance of fresh air and privacy.

I expected Emily at High Noon. I gave no thought to what she might be thinking as she walked to Haven House on that Easter Sunday, nodding hello to all her passing neighbors.

She arrived wearing a white, long-sleeved blouse and a blue skirt: no makeup, no jewelry; her short hair neatly brushed. She looked pious ... and incredibly sexy.

The dining room table was set; everything ritualized according to ancient customs. Emily's eyes were drawn first to the lighted candles of the seven-branched menorah and then to the three silver wine cups.

"You expecting company?"

I laughed. "A symbolic invitation to the prophet Elijah. Every year we hope he returns with news of the coming messiah and with answers to all our unresolved questions."

"You're gonna need a bigger wineglass."

I laughed again. She reminded me of me. But she was quicker, sharper—and more damaged.

I invited her to sit and thanked her for coming.

"This was my home for many years," she said, staring in wonderment at the exotic presentation.

I wasn't exactly sure what she meant.

"Well, I'm happy you're here," I said. "I've never missed

a seder."

With that, we got down to business. I gave her one of the two Haggadahs.

"Passover celebrates the traditional story of Moses leading the captive Israelites out of Egypt. This book, called a *Haggadah,* tells the story and includes lots of information about how and why the holiday should be celebrated."

"It's a pretty big book."

I laughed. "Don't worry, we're not going to read the whole thing. Trust me."

"Whatever you say, Mr. Seder Chairperson."

"Besides, we usually do this in the evening, when everyone's tired."

With that, I began the seder service with the recitation of the Kiddush, proclaiming the holiness of the holiday over a cup of wine....

Through the many blessings and ritual enactments, Emily grew increasingly attentive and serious. She looked like she had something to say but held her tongue.

Emily Schnyder

I felt a sense of increasing dread, made worse because it felt dimly explicable. Dim seemed key.... Barry had drawn the blinds against the outside world.

"Let's get down to business," he said. "The Haggadah instructs us to ask four questions. The provided answers tell the story of Passover."

"I ask the questions?"

"Yes. How did you know?"

"I'm the youngest?"

"Yes, and apparently the brightest."

Barry paused to look at his notes. "Here," he said, handing me a single sheet of paper. "These are the four questions, printed in phonetic Hebrew and in English."

I read the first one, slowly:

"Ma nishtanah ha-lailah hazeh mikol ha-leilot?"

"Beautiful," said Barry.

And then I read: "Why is this night different from all other nights?"

***

I read the rest of the questions, each one drawing me deeper and deeper towards some forgotten time….

There were more blessings, more washings, more wine. More stories of wise rabbis, angels of death, unleavened bread, and manna from heaven.

We ate a bitter herb and then a paste of minced apples, wine, and cinnamon in a tiny matzo sandwich. At long last, Barry said we were ready for the actual seder meal, which begins with dipping an egg into salt water.

Barry Roth

I turned the large, round seder plate like it was a Lazy Susan so Emily would have the honor of picking up the egg and dipping it. But rather than pick up the egg, she stared at it for quite a while without moving. When she finally reached for it, her hand was trembling. I might have acted at that moment but didn't. Instead, I watched her lift the egg nervously… bobble its unexpected slipperiness … and scream as it slipped from her fingers.

Emily Schnyder

In that moment (expecting the falling Passover egg to shatter), I experienced a swirl of disturbing images: Sunday omelets in a dim, curtained kitchen ... my parents' bathroom groans and retchings ... sitting on my night-bed; immobilized, terrified ... whisked eggs flying across my kitchen, splattering ... my mother's smeared porcelain bowl, smashed to pieces ... my painted Easter egg crushed in my teacher's hands, its slimy ooze dripping through her shocked fingers—all the students laughing at me.

Having slipped off my chair and fallen onto the floor, I heard Barry's entreating voice—and sensed his hands reaching towards me.

Seniors in Love

Lainey Roth

Morris was so conciliatory, I figured he'd suffered enough penance. Besides, I was anxious to show him off to my sisters at the Park East Synagogue. I had only to choose an event from these remaining lectures on our schedule:
"Does Reconstructionism Go Too Far?"
"Can Women Be Great Rabbis?"
"Are Jews White?"
"What Was David's Secret Chord?"
I assumed each lecture would be informative and entertaining, but as the last lecturer was the only female, I thought Morris would appreciate the lower-level threat. Besides, the last lecturer said she'd be discussing romantic relationships and I thought our pot could do with a little more stirring.

Morris Fine

I used to love appearing before large groups of women who'd read my latest book or knew of my heroic exploits. For such events I'd prepare like a diva but dress with casual dash.

Suggestion had been the secret ingredient behind my successful presenting. The more I'd downplayed the dangers of my work (the more I'd diminished my supporting role in my stories of struggling, far-flung Jews), the more I was admired as a selfless angel. On a slow night, a half-dozen women would slip me a phone number, a business card, or even a hotel key.... But I'd had my fill. Over the years such experiences had glommed into a pall of sad sameness. I'd grown jaded, tired, old.

My last trip—all the way to Tasmania—forever drained my desire to play a Yiddishe Indiana Jones. And even though Hobart was not the Brazilian Amazon, or even suburban India, it was enough to tax my sixty-year-old body. On arriving home, I saw in the mirror of my medicine cabinet the reflection of the aging man I'd long feared seeing: vestigially good looking, haggardly handsome … but cheeks and neck-flesh incipiently creased and droopy.

Returning to an audience-packed synagogue no longer excited me. I was proud to be remembered as the author who had lectured there more than a year before, and even more proud—and grateful—to be introduced by Lainey as her *special friend*. It was more than I expected and—I dare say—more than I deserved.

Gerald Ellison

In addition to finding me a Three Corners' home for a two-week stay, Alice provided me with a solid cover story: *Chicago architect recovering from a bout of pleurisy, requires two weeks of country fresh air for complete recuperation.*

I was meant to be transient and invisible. With the presidential election only four months away and political tempers running feverishly high, I was free to make repeated visits to the museum and to talk to townsfolk and tourists as much as I pleased.

I asked hundreds of people what they liked best about the museum and what they thought might be expanded or added. Many conservative males wanted to see exhibits of next-gen super weapons: electromagnetic rail guns; satellite-guided lasers; and high-speed, AI-enabled drones. The few liberals I met suggested exhibits featuring diversity and inclusiveness, females in the military, and advances in veteran's health care for wounds of the mind and body.

All in all, gathering information for a report on how Freedom Hall might be expanded was easier than I had thought. But I wasn't nearly done. Learning about Alice's personal past proved infinitely more difficult.

Most Three Corners citizens regarded the Bouchet family in much the same way as American patriots regard our nation's Founding Fathers, which is to say, whatever their remembered flaws, in death they are beyond reproach. Further complicating my research, all the Bouchets (excepting Alice) were interred in an elaborate, gated cemetery, suggesting (to me) that the family legacy was sealed at an inviolable remove. There would be no easy wresting of personal insights from these silent sources.

Lacking familial testimony, I turned my attention to Allen Briggs (widely acknowledged as Alice's oldest childhood friend), only to discover that he had recently left for a trip to New York. That stopped me in my tracks. Still, though it was impossible not to see Alice's hand in this, I decided to table all conjecture until I had more information.

With a little more sleuthing I learned of Alice's special relationship with Emily Schnyder and her peculiar fondness for a waitress named Jacqueline. Those sources would prove invaluable, as would Haven House, Alice's historic, childhood home.

***

"Which way to Haven House?" I asked a passerby.

"Top of the street. On the right. You'll see the sword in the Honor Stone."

I'd already walked past the house several times but had never noticed an Honor Stone, much less one with an implanted sword. This time I stopped and looked about, and there, jungled behind some overgrown hydrangeas, I saw an inscribed boulder and its protruding sword, much as I'd imagined it. I was toying with the boyish idea to give the sword a tug when I heard a voice through an open window.

"Forget it. I tried—and still haven't lived it down. Come on in."

Barry Roth

Gerald had called me earlier that day and our first conversation had been a doozy. I'd learned that his name was Ellison (not *Emerson*), that he was from New York (not Chicago), and that he knew Lainey and was "well-acquainted" with Alice Bouchet. That's a fine how do you do!

"Lainey send you here to check on me?"

"Actually," he said, ignoring my sarcasm, "Alice sent me. I'm an interior space designer. I do a lot of work with galleries and museums. Alice has some ideas for enhancing Freedom Hall and hired me to assess the possibilities. By the way, if you don't mind, please don't tell anyone of my personal association with her."

"I'll take it to the grave. But why the cloak and dagger?"

"We both feel I'll gain more reliable input if our association remains private."

"It's a deal. My lips are sealed."

"Thank you."

"Of course."

We were now seated at the kitchen table, both of us nursing a cup of tea. "So, Gerry, you said earlier that you'd also like to explore Haven House. Is that still on your agenda?"

"Gerald, please ... and yes, I'm interested in information that might relate to the George Long Military Institute—and thus to Freedom Hall. I'd love a tour of the house; after which, I'd like your permission to spend time alone in the library. Alice said I'd find materials there that are not referenced in the museum. She said my perusal might take at least a week."

"Happy to oblige."

"Thank you. And, just so you know, I plan to speak with an Emily Schnyder, who works at the museum."

"I know her. We work together. What are you interested in learning?"

"Anything she can tell me about the museum and Alice would be worthwhile."

"Understood. What else can I do for you?"

"What can you tell me about Allen Briggs? I understand he's been part of the museum staff since the very beginning."

Barry Roth

Over the next ten days I saw a lot of Gerald. I liked the guy, though I sensed he was holding something back, which I guessed had to do with Alice and Allen. I tried to imagine the relations of these three senior citizens but their gray and demure ways unplugged my curiosity. Besides, I didn't have a horse in the race. I wasn't rooting for one romantic pair over another. It was all I could do to figure out what made me happy. I mean, I had a strong sense that Emily might be right for me, but I knew she had some serious shit to work out. Then again, I strongly sensed I might be part of the help she needed.

One thing I knew for sure: whatever troubled Emily was wrapped in her parents' shadowy peculiarities and in her disturbed associations with eggs. I encouraged her to talk more about her past. I even suggested we go away for a few weeks for some new perspective—maybe New York. But with Alice and Allen gone, the museum's success—and the town's fate—was in our hands, and Emily would do nothing that might harm the town that meant so much to Alice.

Field Research

Alice Bouchet
I may have been terribly naïve when I first arrived, but I wasn't half the greenhorn Allen was. I loved the man, but he could be a sore embarrassment. It wasn't just the things he said, it was how he said them. During our first walk around the Lower East Side, he kept yelling out "Oh, for the love of God!" and "Dontcha like that!" Worse, he kept pointing at things, which drew everyone's attention, which embarrassed me terribly.

Allen was my closest friend—sweet and innocent—and still I'd been tempted to throw him under a smoke-belching bus as it roared by.

Allen Briggs
Alice always looked out for me. She asked me to the prom when I lacked the courage to ask her … and when I was barely getting by as a carpenter, she asked me to help her run Freedom Hall … and when I turned sixty, she put me on a jet and flew me to New York. After our initial walkabout, she said to me, "Allen, it's so nice to have you here."

I was happy to be there … happy to see her … but my head was spinning from everything new.

"What would you like to do while you're here?" she asked. "The possibilities are endless."

I know she didn't mean it, but it was a hurtful question. How should I know what to do? I'd never been to New York.

Then I realized: I should have done some planning ... taken some initiative ... not relied entirely on her, as I'd always done. But Alice—ever thoughtful and prepared—was ready to save me from myself, yet again.

Alice Bouchet

I said to Allen, "How about I make some suggestions and you tell me what appeals to you?" Knowing he'd agree, I drew a folded sheet of paper from my purse and confidently read aloud my ideas, one by one. I knew he'd like them. In many ways, I knew Allen better than he knew himself.

Over the next twelve days we visited the dinosaurs at the Museum of Natural History ... Central Park ... Yankee Stadium in the Bronx ... the Cloisters in Upper Manhattan. We experienced the World Trade Center footprints, the subways and ferries. We lunched at Fraunces Tavern, where Washington bid farewell to his officers at the end of the War. We strolled Times Square ... the Theater District ... Hudson Yards ... Lincoln Center. We ate glazed duck in Chinatown and sipped cappuccino in Little Italy. We sat in the United Nations' General Assembly, listening to an African leader speak of drought and genocide. Near the end of his visit, after having toured the Intrepid Museum (an aircraft carrier docked on the West Side) and hiked the Brooklyn Bridge, I was exhausted and nearly depleted of hope: for not once during our twelve days had Allen taken my arm or held my hand, much less kissed me—not once, despite dozens of intimate opportunities.

I gave him one last chance. I'd saved our most romantic setting for our last evening. I was thinking: *I'll bring him to water. I'll hand him the damn ladle. If he's thirsty, he'll drink.*

Emily Schnyder

Given the circumstances—me on the floor, having succumbed to some sudden and mysterious vertigo—Barry remained impressively calm. When I was ready, he helped me to my feet.

"Would you like to freshen up? The bathroom is to the left and down the hall."

"I know where it is. I lived here ten years."

When I returned, he asked again if I were okay.

"I'm fine," I said with ridiculous nonchalance. "Are we done with the prayers and reading?"

"We are. You were great. We can eat now—if you're up to it."

***

Monday morning, we were back to work at the museum, as if nothing unusual had happened between us. During the previous weeks, having accompanied me on a dozen different kinds of tours, Barry had made himself into a very good docent. Not only could he recall everything I'd said as a tour leader, he was friendly, funny, and could improvise. If he didn't know an answer, he'd go off script and come up with *something* that would satisfy. Everyone seemed to like him.

I wasn't jealous at all. I didn't have Barry's social skills and didn't envy them—except, perhaps, his salesmanship. Whenever he joined me in the lobby, standing with me behind the glass display of my snow globes, he'd sell them like hot cakes at a county fair. "Step right up and see the miniaturized wonders of the world!" he'd shout like a carnival barker—and then introduce me as the *artiste*, as if I just happened to be there on that very day to answer questions about my inspiration and technique. Barry was outrageously engaging. He made me feel very special.

"You know," he said one late afternoon when we were alone and looking at the globes, "the real McCoys are even more amazing. We could see them together. We could start small, like a visit to New York."

I didn't encourage him, nor did I shut him down. "Hold that thought" was as much commitment as I could muster.

Gerald Ellison

Emily Schnyder agreed to meet me at her home on a Sunday morning when the museum was closed. Per our phone conversation, she expected questions about the museum, but I'd also prepared her for some questions about Alice Bouchet, who had hired me and who would be judging the merits of my proposal. "The better I understand her," I'd said to Emily, "the better my chances of delivering what she wants."

I didn't have to knock. The door opened inward as soon as I'd crossed her porch.

"Good morning," she said. "Let's talk in the kitchen."

I followed her through a sunroom and then a living room, before arriving at the kitchen, which seemed oddly muted, the blinds drawn against a sun that was still rising and not yet particularly warm.

Emily began talking as soon we were comfortably seated with our coffees. She needed no prompts, not even simple questions. She just talked … and talked.

"My parents died when I was twelve and left me this house. They'd also left a will naming Alice Bouchet my guardian until I turned twenty-one. For nearly ten years—the decade of my teens—Haven House was my home and the Bouchets were my family. They were nice, in their distant way. Anyway, Alice maintained this house—subsidizing a stipend provided by my parents—until I was ready to return."

I nodded, hanging on her every word.

"I redid this house to make it mine and to help me forget some of my darker memories. The changes helped in some ways, but they also created new contrasts that helped preserve my worst memories.

"The room you first entered—the sunroom—was my first big change. The living room used to extend to the front door and served my parents as both foyer, where they greeted customers, and work area, where they bent over their ceaseless tailoring.

"Most of the work they did was delivered by Alice, who oversaw the manufacture and maintenance of all the Institute's uniforms. I was usually on the floor when she arrived, sitting in the shadowy space between my parents' work stations, playing with the scraps and flawed insignia that fell to me.

"I recall Alice as tall, regal, and backlighted against the bright front windows. She always said hello to me, speaking my name. One day, she sidled past my parents and knelt to speak with me. My parents were shocked. But on another day, not long after, she actually sat on the floor beside me and we played together. After that, she visited often and we became friends, despite the obvious age difference.

"My parents died on a Sunday morning, apparently from something they ate. It's never been made clear. But clearly, I was orphaned. No family or friends called to claim me or even to extend sympathy.

"There was no church funeral service. Instead, the service was held in Alice's backyard. Only the Bouchets were there. Maybe a couple other people. Maybe I'm projecting or misremembering. But I remember two things distinctly: I remember Alice telling me that my parents were going to be buried back East. From the way she said *back East* I understood that it was far away and I wouldn't be able to visit them until I was much older. She also made it clear that I would live with her in Haven House. She said we would always be friends and she would do all she could to make me safe and happy."

Emily pushed back her chair, stood, then refilled my coffee cup—hers remained untouched. She then sat again and continued her story, as if there had been no interruption.

"I have mostly good memories of Haven House. Besides me, Alice was the only female, but I can hardly say she ruled the roost because no Bouchet woman ever did—not in that macho military family. But it was even harder for Alice because she wasn't a wife or mother, just a daughter to the colonel and a kid sister to her brothers. Still, I know she always pushed herself when she was young. Her parents saw how naturally smart she was and allowed her to learn everything in the cadet's curriculum, except for their actual military training. Even then, having discovered her grandfather's copy of Sun Tzu's *Art of War* in the family library, she taught herself a great deal about the martial mindset and war strategy."

"Did she go away to college?"

"No. She was home schooled. In fact, she did so well, she eventually taught some courses to the younger cadets."

"What about you? Did you go away to college? Did you

leave Alice and Three Corners?"

"We discussed it. I think Alice encouraged it, and then maybe she didn't. I felt like the choice was mine, and then maybe it wasn't. Bottom line—I stayed here with Alice."

"Was that fun? What was it like?"

"I wouldn't call it fun. It was just our lives."

"Not an easy time?"

"No, not easy. Alice was my only friend and she wasn't very popular either."

"Why's that?"

"She's a Bouchet. Her father was the Commander. She lived in grand ol' Haven House, at the top of the hill. People saw her as entitled, and they resented her.... Despite her smarts and good heart, Alice didn't get the respect she deserved for a long time."

"What changed?"

Emily looked down and shook her head. "In a single tragic year, her father and both brothers died suddenly."

"Oh my god. I didn't know that. Was she terribly bereft—or worse?"

"What's worse than bereft?"

"Broken—at least for a time."

"Not her. Not Alice Bouchet."

"Still, she must have grieved terribly."

"I'm sure she did, but in her way. No one saw it, including me, so I couldn't say for sure. But I know she wasn't bereft. And she sure as hell wasn't broken."

"How do you know?"

"She took over Haven House. She took her father's place on the Town Council. She used the situation to grow into her full self. And then she rose to the occasion."

"What occasion?"

"A few years after the death of her family, after she'd had time to study the Institute's finances and tax records, she determined that the college was failing—going under financially. She tried to save it—but it was too late. When she told the Council, they nearly panicked, and likely would have, had anyone but Alice been in charge. She told them, "Don't worry. Give me some time. I have some ideas." A few months later she'd figured out how to save the college—by reinventing it."

"The birth of Freedom Hall."

"Well, its conception…. In any case, by resurrecting the spirit of the dying college, Alice saved Three Corners."

"Which had been dependent on the college and is now dependent on Freedom Hall."

"Which is why she wants to do all she can to perpetuate its success."

"Which is why she invited me here."

"Presumably."

"Presumably?"

"I don't know all her reasons for inviting you here. I don't really know you. Alice hasn't talked to me about you. In fact, I've heard very little from her since she went to New York."

"Do you feel slighted?"

"I did, early on. But I generally trust my instincts where Alice is concerned. If she wanted a break from Three Corners and me, she undoubtedly thought it would be best—for us all."

Jacqueline

Gerald didn't know my phone number or anyone who did

and so had no way of contacting me other than coming into the diner for a cup of coffee and slipping me a note. I sort of recognized him 'cause he'd been hanging around the museum, asking folks what they thought about it. Everyone in town had took notice and been wondering what the hell he was up to. We always took notice of strangers, but what with all the crazy politics and so much at stake for our town, we were all on a kind of high alert.

"What can I get you?" was all I said when he walked in and sat down at a booth.

I brought him coffee and neither one of us said another word. When he was finished, he came to the register and gave me a five-dollar bill folded over a small piece of paper, which I assumed was a note. I shoved the note into my apron pocket and didn't read it until I was closing up and all alone. The note was neatly written and said: *My name is Gerald Ellison. I'd like to speak with you privately about Alice Bouchet. This is my cell number.*

As soon as I got home, I went to my bedroom and closed the blinds. You can't never be too careful. Then I dialed the number and nearly jumped through the roof when I heard his voice after just one ring. Who answers after one ring? He must of been waiting for me.

I was prepared not to reveal anything too personal. I know how these people operate. But he cut right to the point, saying who he was and how he knew Alice and what she'd asked him to do for her about the museum. I asked him a couple clever questions about how Alice looked, just to make sure he really knew her—and it seemed he did. All in all, he sounded just the right amount friendly and professional, so yeah, I mostly trusted him.

He said he was headed back to New York in a few days and wanted to meet me as soon as possible. That gave me the creeps. But then he asked me to pick a time and place to meet and that helped lower my nerves.

But I couldn't decide where to meet him. The diner? My place? The Red, White, and Brew? I even considered Marion, but even there I thought someone might see me and the news get back to Squirrel. News about me was always getting back to Squirrel and he always had some damn advice or criticism for me. I was tired of it. And we weren't even married!

I took out my frustration on Mr. Ellison. "I don't know you. I don't trust you. What do you want from me?" And he said, "I'm so sorry. I didn't mean for you to feel anxious. I met Alice in New York a few months ago and we've become close friends. She's thinking of ways to improve the museum and wants my help—I do a lot of work with museums and art galleries. But if you are uncomfortable about meeting, I suppose we can talk on the phone, as we're doing right now. I have some questions about the museum and about Alice herself." "Why are you asking me about Alice if you already know her so well?" "That's an excellent question," he said, which made me feel real good, because I don't get all that many compliments about my intelligence. "Because the better I understand Alice," he said, "the better I can help improve the museum and help Three Corners."

He seemed so smart and polite I decided to meet him. Still, I felt like I needed some insurance and came up with a plan. For Squirrel's last birthday I bought him a brand-new squirrel gun, as he's had his old one since he was a boy. He loved the gift so much he just about cried. He took his brand-new zoom off his old gun and fixed it on the new one. I asked if

I could have his old squirrel gun. "What do you want it for?" "For my protection," I said. "I might need it sometime if you're not around." My answer was pure bullshit, but I guess he liked it 'cause he gave me the old gun, saying, "You need to be careful. You can kill someone with this." And I said, "I'm counting on it. No one will mess with me if I'm locked and loaded." And so I told Mr. Gerald Ellison, "Meet me by the river, just west of town. Walk north about two miles. I'll be the big girl with the Cardinal's cap and loaded rifle."

Gerald Ellison

How does one dress for the woods? I had no hat—certainly no hunting cap or baseball cap. I had a sport jacket and a sleeveless cotton shirt, which looked nice and casual—but for the woods? And what about my feet? Good thing I'd packed my moccasin-style loafers; they would have to do. I just hoped I wouldn't have to run downhill or hop mossy stones across the river.

***

The hike had been arduous but she'd been easy to spot: standing soldierly before a pink flowering dogwood … red baseball cap … a rifle cradled militia-like across her ample chest.

"Nice to meet you," I said, gasping.

"You okay?"

I was bent forward, breathing heavily, my hands cupped on my damp knees where they'd contacted a sudden slope of slippery riverbank.

"Just fine," I said. "Beautiful country."

Jacqueline

He looked harmless, nothing like that rabid dog that'd parked itself outside my house one day, the one Squirrel called "a clear and present danger" and shot between the eyes. Nothing like that—more like a banker that'd got himself lost in the woods looking for a golf ball. But I'll grant this: he looked smart and I could see him being friends with Alice.

"So, what do you want to know?"

He looked all about. "Is there a place we could sit? A dry place?"

I led him to a big flat rock, smooth as a tabletop. We both sat down but he looked miserable. I think he had a bony butt, but I let it go, thinkin' it evened the sides.

"Is there something specific you want to know?" I asked again. "I don't know where to start."

Before he spoke, he shifted side-to-side and when that didn't work, he took off his jacket and made himself a comfy cushion. That seemed to do the trick.

"Okay," he said, turning his attention to me, now all polite and professional. "If you please, tell me about Alice and what is was like growing up in Three Corners."

Maybe it was the sunshine pouring through the dogwoods … or the background rush of the river … or that no other man had ever let me spill my guts without interruption or correction—whatever, it worked, and I rambled on and on.

Gerald Ellison

She told me about her mother who'd liked listening to the radio and reading movie magazines but had little interest in housework and even less in her husband and daughter. I gathered it hadn't taken much for a woman like that to latch onto something new and run with it—which is exactly what had happened. Her mother met a handsome stranger in an Army jacket and left with nary a goodbye ... never to return, never to be missed, according to Jacqueline. I knew there must be much more, but I let it go.

"Tell me about your father."

She said she'd loved her daddy something special. He'd been kind and they'd been buddies. When he'd worked as a plumber, she'd often been by his side, watching and learning. Same for his tinkering with old and broken motorcycles. By the time she was twelve, she could rebuild a carburetor, rewire an ignition coil, install new brakes—disk or drum.... Sometimes they went fishing, sometimes hunting. She was (she said smiling) a deadeye shot and had bagged her share of snipe, woodcock, geese, deer—and plenty squirrel.... She said she'd loved her daddy, even if the rest of the town decried his drunkenness and the dirty motorcycle parts that littered their yard.

"Tell me about you and Alice."

From the way she drew a deep breath and then stretched the muscles in her neck, I gathered it was an emotionally complex story and that its telling would be strenuous.

She began at the point when she was young and motherless: Alice invited her to Haven House for comfort and improvement but she'd felt sadly singled out—the truant who must pass the gauntlet of student scrutiny en route to the principal's office—and rarely replied to Alice's invitations.

Later, after losing her father and dropping out of high school, she was even more uncomfortably aware of Alice's largesse, even though the latter's outreach had become more subtle: finding odd jobs for her at Haven House or at the college to make sure Jacqueline was kept warm and well fed.

Though sometimes tempted to bite the feeding hand, Jacqueline came to appreciate Alice's many acts of kindness and generosity, which prepared her for the next and perhaps most important maternal relationship of her life. Enter Mavis Wilson, who, along with her husband Beasley, owned the town's diner and been her father's best friends. Husband and wife, who were childless, took Jacqueline under their wings, hiring her as a waitress and teaching her life lessons, professional habits, and bookkeeping. And while both were caring and influential, it was Mavis who taught Jacqueline the soulful lessons of holiday gifting and other secrets of the feminine heart. Mavis would likely have become the nurturing mother-figure Jacqueline craved more than she knew … had she not suddenly died of food poisoning.

Jacqueline talked through her tears.

"The coroner's report said *old age* and *pre-existing conditions* but Beasley didn't buy it. It reminded him too much of what'd killed Emily's parents. But what could he do? No one made any waves. Not the sheriff, not the mayor—not even Alice."

I handed her a tissue but she just rolled it into a ball and locked it in her fist.

Gavin Lissome
Thrilled by the idea of the museum's expansion (which promised to raise the sales and profitability of his several local businesses without costing him a dime), Gavin privately vowed to do all he could to make sure the expansion went through, and though he was generally confident, several de-

tails concerned him.

For one thing, there were two new people in town: an older gent, who spent a lot of time at Freedom Hall and Haven House, and the latter's current occupant, Barry Roth. (Or was it Rothschild? He'd never got that straight). In any case, it did not escape his attention that both men were connected to Alice Bouchet, who herself was noticeably absent, having suddenly left town months before without saying goodbye to him or to anyone else on the Council.

Though he hadn't been singled out, Gavin saw the situation as a personal slight—and a potential problem. Ever since the mysterious sudden deaths of a half-dozen persons in Marion and Three Corners—followed by his hurried appeal to the Council to approve his request for a large bank loan for "business upgrades"—he'd sensed a vague antipathy from council-member Alice, who'd proposed a formal inquest into the deaths before the bank loan could be discussed—and been voted down. They'd never had words, but Gavin believed Alice suspected him of foul play.

So, here it was: now only three months before the presidential election and there were two persons in town whose votes Gavin did not control and could not account for. Word was the older gent would be leaving soon. But that still left Barry Roth.

Having spoken to the mayor ... and the sheriff ... and the reverend, pastor, priest ... and to Squirrel (whose job it was to report all relevant scuttlebutt), Gavin was certain Barry would vote Democrat, which would ruin Three Corners' perfect voting record and tarnish its brand as America's most perfectly conservative town. That was something he could not afford to let happen.

Gerald Ellison

Having completed my research, I prepared for my return to New York. I thought the work had gone well. I'd collected and prioritized all the serious comments for new exhibits (both traditionally conservative and cutting-edge progressive) and included content, design, and space recommendations—including preliminary specs and plans. My report would note that the museum could easily be extended on its north side, appropriating much of the current parking lot; the remaining parking lot could be extended even further north—and expanded—if necessary. Requisite land was available and affordable.

I wrote a personal note to append to the eventual report:

I congratulate you on the success of the current museum. It is very well designed—which is not to say it couldn't be expanded and improved. But as with most important decisions, success may be dependent on timing. And these are tumultuous times. While your state is likely to vote Republican, there are strong polling indicators to suggest that Democrats will win the presidency. Also, as you likely know, it appears that at least one person currently residing in Three Corners will vote Democrat, which could impact the museum's marketability, which might adversely affect your town's economy. Whatever you decide, it was a pleasure and privilege learning about your museum, your town, and you.

A Good Wingman Is Hard to Find

Alice Bouchet

Put up or shut up sounds crass, but I suppose I had in mind some sort of showdown with Allen. I certainly dressed the part: a sexy black thing with a low neckline—hardly plunging, but scooped enough to reveal two inches of my high, ample bosom. On Lainey's advice I'd bought a pair of two-inch heels, eschewing my sensible flats, which would have been all wrong for the deluxe dinner cruise I'd splurged on: an all-glass boat with 180-degree sightseeing views of New York City. And that wasn't the half of it. We had ourselves a private table and French sparkling wine in long-stemmed flutes while a black pianist played Harlem jazz and the lighted Statue of Liberty faded in our wake. After dinner, we strolled the shadowy deck, with plenty opportunity for hand-holding and sweet-talking....

My poor, dear Allen. I think he really did want to seize the day. But that elegant cruise had boxed him tighter than the OK Corral.

Allen Briggs

Why would she ask the waiter a question in French? And what the hell was so funny that they both laughed ... and me sitting there like a dumb yokel.

The whole night had been like that. I felt ridiculous. I wanted to go home... Three Corners had everything I needed—when Alice was there.

Lainey Roth

Of course, everyone at the synagogue had adored Morris. He was incredibly social and presentable. But not so much when we were alone. Then he could be aloof … self-sufficient … self-satisfied. He didn't make me feel like I was the rarest flower in the world. I didn't get that from Morris—or not nearly enough. Bert had adored me, but he'd been a boorish putz and none too exciting. Bert and Morris were sort of opposites. Could Morris be my romantic wingman 'til death do us part? I needed to know. I needed some way to test his devotion.

Meanwhile, I missed my Barry. I wanted to see him, if only for a visit. I thought he might return for Election Day. That would be lovely. Even better if he stayed for Thanksgiving: I imagined him walking through the door with a pretty young woman, anxious to meet me.

Gerald Ellison

Gathering information for the report had been the easy part because it had been practical and straightforward. Acquiring insights into Alice's personal life proved way more complicated—and troubling. She must have known I would speak with Emily and Jacqueline. Each loved Alice in her way—and each suspected her of withholding some vital information. Why would Alice set me on that trail? And while we're at it, why did she have Allen visit her in New York while I was visiting her hometown? What game was she playing?

Shady Conniving

Billy Acers

I loved working at the Red, White, and Brew, what with its slow business that gave me time to write and its odd acoustics that allowed me to eavesdrop on whispered conversations ... so long as folk didn't huddle in the far corner beyond earshot, which they rarely did, knowing how it would suggest shady conniving.

On the day in question, Squirrel Evans and Gavin Lissome took a table in the middle of the room, against the far wall, thinking their privacy reasonably assured. No one else was present, except me. After bringing their beers and a fresh bowl of peanuts, I retreated to my station behind the bar, where I made a show of writing intently in a new spiral notebook, hoping the pose would encourage them to be careless with their whispering. Very slyly, I lowered the main fan and the house music by imperceptible degrees.

I didn't hear every word, but I gathered that with the election only weeks away, it was time to save Three Corners from unwanted interlopers:

"Barry and Jacqueline ... drinking coffee ... laughing."

"She serves everyone coffee."

"Everyone don't make her laugh."

"Someone saw Brenda ... and a guy ... at Golden Orchard ..."

"Who?"

"Some guy … coming out a toolshed."
"… that Barry fellow?"
"Could be."

"… overheard some questionable shit … museum tour."
"What he'd say?"
"… unpatriotic shit."
"We can't be havin' that shit. Not now."

"It don't seem right … the two of them … Haven House."
"Two commies … plotting."
"… Alice knows?"
"You shitting me?"
"… it's her town too."
"You seen her around?"

"Second Amendment, baby!"
"… protect our own …"
"… can't take what's ours."
"Here's to our President!"
"To Freedom Hall!"
"To Three Corners!"

Brenda Lissome

Jacqueline liked coming over for lunch 'cause our house was pretty and Gavin let me buy all sorts of sweet things which I set out after we'd had our sandwiches and coffee. This time we had a special lot to discuss because Billy had told me what he'd overheard our men say to each other.

"Gavin told Squirrel you're spending a lot of time with Barry in the diner, laughin' and jokin'."

"That's nothin'. What else?"

"Squirrel told Gavin someone saw me at the Orchard with a man—coming out of a toolshed. I just said, 'Don't be stupid. I was just buying flower seeds for the garden.'"

I was glad no one suspected Billy, but I knew we'd have to find a new place to meet, which wouldn't be easy. Meanwhile, Jacqueline took it like she was flattered to be seen laughin' with someone so smart and good-lookin' as Barry ... but after a bit she looked worried 'cause she knew Squirrel could get himself crazy jealous and she worried what he might do.

"Billy says they also talked some politics. Says Gavin called Barry and his older friend a couple o' commies who needed to be taught a lesson."

Jacqueline

I love Squirrel and would never do nothin' to hurt him but I do believe he is capable of some pigheaded thinking, especially when a mean bastard like Gavin has his ear. Also, that Barry Roth fellow has been nothin' but nice to me—always talks straight, never gets fresh, always is interested in what I have to say—a damn good tipper too! I'd never let him get hurt, if I could help it. Besides, I sort of like Emily Schnyder and I can see they like each other. I like when two strange ducks fall in love. She was always one of the strange girls in town—like me, but quiet and smart.... I remember when her parents died. Not long after, my mother left ... not long after that, Mavis left too. I feel a sisterly connection with Emily—though I'd never let on.

Electoral Integrity

Barry Roth

For months, while my relationship with Emily had been so consuming, the three salon ladies had been mostly out of sight, out of mind—hence my surprise when they asked to meet me again, though this invitation sounded more sedately purposeful.

Once again, I was asked to Melissa's home and led to the room where we'd had our literary salon. I don't think the women were aware how judgmental they now appeared, the three of them sitting together on the sofa while I sat alone on a stiff-backed chair, facing them.

"Looks like we're swingers now," Megan began.

One blushed. One giggled. One coughed into her hand.

"Swingers?"

"Our state has been red for many years," said Regan.

"Red?" I asked.

"Reliably Republican."

"Yes, of course," I said, nodding agreeably, but without any idea where the conversation was going and why I'd been invited.

"We have more big farms now, but fewer farmers," said Darla. "Many families have moved from rural areas to the cities."

"Lots of young people have moved too," added Regan.

"The cities tend to vote Democrat. That means blue, as I'm sure you know," said Melissa.

"So the press says we're purple now. We're a swing state," said Regan.

"We're swingers!"

"Oh," I said. "That's what you meant."

"What did you think we meant?" asked Darla the shaggy blond.

A chorus of giggling.

"Ladies, he may not be the gentleman we supposed."

The three of them laughed.

"All kidding aside," said Darla. "It's very important that we vote solidly red—up and down the ticket."

"Especially up," said Regan. We must keep the White House."

"We lose the White House, we lose the soul of our nation."

"The Dems are a slippery slope to socialism."

"We can't lose the White House."

"It all starts here."

"We have to do our part."

"It's do or die."

"We can't afford to slip—not even by a single vote."

"We can't have our perfect record blemished."

"It's our business model—our life blood."

"The secret sauce of Freedom Hall."

"One hundred percent *Made in America!*"

"So, can we count on you?"

Emily Schnyder

For as long as I can remember, Squirrel had delivered mail-in ballots to every voting-age resident of Three Corners. The inside joke was that no one in our town had ever returned the ballot by mail. Instead, come Election Day, nearly all eligible voters walked proudly to Courier Day (the town's primary and middle school), where the Town Council and volunteers sat at a long table near the back of the lobby, collecting the ballots. Because the ballot was a trifold to be inserted into the narrow mouth of a locked steel box, the vote was anonymous. This was important to my parents. I recall their solemnity upon receiving their ballots in the mail: how they carefully removed each from its envelope, slowly read its contents, and then carefully refolded it, licking the gluey part to seal its privacy. On Election Day (but never on Easter, or any other holiday), I'd accompany my parents on a very public march from our home to the school, where I'd proudly watch while they consecrated their ballots to the inviolable strongbox. Years later (after I'd been allowed to leave Haven House and return to my own home) I realized my parents had always submitted a pair of blank ballots. To this day, I don't fully understand their reasons, but I like to think they always voted their conscience.

Barry Roth

Before leaving Manhattan, I'd already investigated the process for obtaining a provisional ID that would allow me to vote in Three Corners, though I left wide open the idea that I might still return to New York to vote on Election Day, as I always had, since turning eighteen.

Voting in New York meant continuing with Lainey our long-cherished routine of visiting our local polling site, my old primary school, P.S. 46, also known as the Edgar Allan Poe School. During this annual event (which had become a kind of pilgrimage), Lainey always re-explained to me the extraordinary blessings of democracy, which (she insisted) should be cherished by all Jews, especially those (like us) whose not-so-ancient forbears had lived within paled settlements with limited rights, granted by some goyishe ruler who did not despise Jews entirely. It was from Lainey that I learned how to vote Democrat "up and down the ticket" and to take special heed of candidates whose last names sounded Jewish.

Activating Emotions

Squirrel Evans

I knew that bastard had no place in Three Corners. I knew that very first day, him never denying what he'd done or even apologizing, never once trying to understand our ways. He thought he was too good for us, driving a red convertible like some movie star and living like a king in Haven House, home of our glorious commanders who'd shaped our boys to serve their country with dignity and pride. Instead of such noble men, we had this piece of crap, this unpatriotic bastard who'd all but promised to vote a commie for president—which would have sullied our reputation and caused our fine town to fall on hard times. No, no, no. I couldn't let that happen. We had ourselves a fine town. And Gavin and me had it particularly good—him with his gas stations and stores, and me with my mail route and selling stuff. We couldn't let that bastard Barry Roth ruin all that. The way I figured, I had no choice but to rain some lead around his head and watch him haul ass back to New York.

I had my duty. I had my God-given rights. I had my squirrel gun.

Jacqueline

Stupid me. Sometimes I'm just too stupid to walk this earth. Sometimes I think my mother and Mavis and Alice left me because I was just too stupid to be. But that nice older man, Gerald, the one with all the questions about Alice and the museum, he didn't seem to think I was stupid. Before going back to New York, he asked if he could tell Barry about the pretty spot by the river. It seems Barry was looking for just such a spot where he could read or write outdoors with no one to bother him, so I said sure, show him the place. And then one day, some weeks later, when Barry was in the diner, having himself some pie and coffee, he thanked me for telling about the big flat rock by the river ... and I suppose someone heard us talkin', because it got back to Squirrel, like everything did.

Billy Acers

It's crazy ironic but Gavin had been so damn nervous about talking or texting on the phone, he insisted on meeting Squirrel again at the Red, White, and Brew for a private face-to-face. Crazy ironic because they were the only customers at the time and I was able to gather the gist of their plan.

Brenda Lissome

Learning what Gavin was up to, I wouldn't have minded a bit if he got caught and went to prison—leaving me the house and the businesses. At least then I'd be rich by myself and could maybe divorce Gavin and marry Billy.

I thought it might be nice if Billy and me had a baby, but then I thought: if I was a rich woman, maybe I could do even better than Billy.... Truth be told, my ass was sore and splintery from all the times he took me in the toolsheds ... though I did laugh the first time he said how much he liked having me over a barrel. Still, bottom line, I liked Jacqueline better than either of them men, so I told her what Billy had overheard Gavin say to Squirrel at the Red, White, and Brew.

Barry Roth

Lainey was right: now that I was discovering love, I felt ready to write again. But I needed to know more about Emily. I sensed that knowing would feed loving ... would feed writing.

At her place or Haven House—but mostly on the big flat rock by the river—we discussed our separate pasts and the possibility of a shared future. She was murky about what she wanted. She felt strangely in the dark about her own life and did not think she could make smart choices about the future until she was enlightened. One day, having joined me on the flat rock in the shade of the dogwoods, I asked her to tell me again about her childhood.

"What do you want to know?"

"Everything."

"That's a big ask.... Where should I start?"

"Anywhere. Just talk."

"That's harder than you think.... Give me some cues."

"Okay. Tell me about your parents.... Tell me about their tailoring.... Tell me about Alice.... Tell me about Haven House.... Tell me about your Sunday breakfasts.... Tell me your Easter egg story."

Emily Schnyder

I loved telling Barry my stories. He wanted to know everything and he never hurried me. If anything, he sometimes asked me to repeat things ... go deeper ... explain my thoughts using different words.

I trusted him. Even so, I asked why he was doing this.

"Because I care about you and want to know you better. And I think you know more than you're telling. I think you're keeping secrets from yourself."

"I would tell you if I knew."

"But you can't. You buried your secrets so well and deep, you have no idea where they're buried."

Blank Ballots

Alice Bouchet

Four years earlier, on Election Day, I cast a blank ballot for the first time in my life. I could not vote for that reality show fool ... so I didn't vote at all. I didn't take sides. I didn't take a stand. I pretended to vote but submitted a blank ballot. I thought this would be a good compromise, but it wasn't.

My inability to take a stand wore on me over the next three years. With the terrible fool preparing to run for reelection, I did not want to repeat my cowardly voting. And the stakes had grown higher: the terrible fool had proved himself a racist bigot and traitor—and Three Corners' very survival was now tied to its branding as our nation's most conservative town. My oppositional vote on Election Day might salve my personal conscience, but it might also destroy the town's economy and blacken my family legacy. And that's the bigger reason I went to New York—not for its culinary delights, exotic entertainments, and large pool of romantic possibilities, but to avoid facing the demands of my birthright.

***

Regarding Allen, I think I always knew what would happen, but I needed to let it play out so I could believe the choice had been his—that it was his failure to grab the golden apple, not mine. Eventually I realized it didn't matter which of us failed—the result was the same—and it got me thinking about my life all over again. Where did I really want to live? Who or what did I love most?

When Gerald returned with his report about Freedom Hall (Allen had already left—so sadly, it broke my heart), I freshly saw my right to vote and my responsibility to the museum as a pair of sputtering torches only I could fix.

Taking Aim

Jacqueline
One day, some years back, Squirrel said I was damn transparent and I punched him good because I happened to be near a mirror and could see that he was lying or pulling my leg. I must have hit a tender spot because he whimpered some and made me apologize—after telling me what the word could also mean.... And so, three days before Election Day, when he said he was taking his new gun to do some snipe hunting, I had a good idea what he was really up to because he was so damn *transparent*.

Gavin Lissome
I made it real clear there'd be no extra value in killing, and if he did kill him, I would deny any association with the tragic event. I wanted Barry to spend Election Day anywhere he liked—except Three Corners.

Squirrel Evans
With my new rifle and zoom scope I knew I could nick him safely at forty yards ... but Gavin said attempting even a slight flesh wound would be too chancy.
I left my house carrying my rifle, wearing my hunting cap, weighing my options.

Jacqueline
I knew Squirrel was planning to do Gavin's evil bidding. I

knew he must have some blackness in his heart to consider such a thing. I knew it was my job to try and save him.

I'm no saint, as everyone knows, but Squirrel was my man and if I ever hoped to be a bride, I had to keep him alive and free. So I went that day an hour before I knew Barry would arrive at the nice flat rock and I settled myself behind a stand of birch, maybe thirty yards from Barry ... maybe sixty yards opposite another stand of birch, where I knew Squirrel would set to take his shot.

Squirrel Evans

When I thought how much consternation that bastard was causing, I was sorely tempted to send him to an early grave. But I saw the repercussions of my deed like a string of sad events: being arrested ... sitting behind bars ... eating meals off battered tin plates ... Jacqueline growing old and gray, unloved and childless, still serving pie and coffee at the diner....

And there I was, crouched low in a stand of shady birch, holding my rifle, my finger on the trigger, when suddenly, everything I stood to lose—Jacqueline, my job, my town—pained my heart so hard I raised my rifle, sighted the tree just past Barry's head, and squeezed the trigger.

Jacqueline

My Daddy had a gun and taught me to shoot before he taught me to gear shift. Somehow, when he passed, I could not find that ol' gun and missed shooting it. Squirrel would have given me no end of grief if I had wanted to buy me a new gun, which is why I bought him a brand-new squirrel gun for his birthday—and asked for his old one, which he gave me, though somewhat reluctantly, maybe because he knew I was a great shot. Those were my thoughts when I saw Barry looking so peaceful-like on that nice flat rock and imagined Emily beside him, like a pair of innocent fawns. I couldn't let anything happen to either of them, so when I saw Squirrel raise his rifle and begin to sight, I sighted real fast and squeezed: *BAM!*

Barry Roth
I heard two bangs ... a flinty zing ... a thwack like shattered wood ... a scream ... and in that instant I remembered my father's famous exit strategy: "Time to get out of Dodge!"

Emily Schnyder
Of course, he ran ... but he wasn't "frightened out of his mind" or "crazed with fear," as he later described. He couldn't have been. He never sought shelter. He never hid in the shadows. He came for me.

Barry Roth
I could have fled to Freedom Hall (I had the key) or run into First Baptist Church (it was open) or sheltered inside Haven House, but for the first time in my scaredy-cat life I acted with selfless courage and ran—faster than I thought possible—all the way to Emily's house.

Emily Schnyder
I'd been in the sunroom, reading, when I saw him bounding up the porch steps. We reached the front door at the same time. He was sweaty, exhausted, breathing heavily. I brought

him inside, into the kitchen, and gave him a glass of water.

He wouldn't sit. He spoke between gulps.

"Someone shot at me ... maybe two people.... I grabbed my book ... kept my head down ... just ran."

When his breathing evened, he sat down at the kitchen table and we talked.

"I'm not going to be a target," he said. "And I'm not going to put you at risk."

"But why?"

"Why what?"

"Why would anyone shoot at you?"

"Not sure. Maybe to influence my vote ... maybe to stop me from voting."

"But why guns? I don't like that they used guns. That's ... desperate."

I didn't say anything else. Barry looked like he was thinking.

"Look," he said with sudden conviction, "the museum is closed today, tomorrow, and Tuesday for Election Day. Let's go. Right now."

His decisiveness excited me.

"Go? Where? How can we go?"

My whiny voice wasn't meant as a strong challenge. I wanted him to convince me.

"The timing is perfect," he said. "Allen returned yesterday. He said he'd be back to work on Wednesday. He and Jacqueline can hold down the fort."

"But for how long?"

"Not our problem. We need to go."

"But where?"

"Home."

That stopped me. "I am home."

He looked at me with beggar's eyes.

"My home," he said. "New York. Just for a while. Until we think things through."

I was silent. Stunned. It was too much. Too sudden. All I could do was shake my head, signaling *no*.

All was silent. Our whole world was just the two of us in that kitchen.

"You're right," he said, now sounding quite calm. "It's not the right time to go to New York. There's someplace you need to go first. Trust me."

My Heart, the Anvil

Alice Bouchet

I wrote a letter—a real letter, written with a fine pen on fine paper—then placed it in an ivory-colored envelope and sealed it. But I could not bring myself to address it and drop it in a public mailbox. That seemed too impersonal. Gerald deserved better. Far better.

Gerald Ellison

I lived in Chartwell Towers, a quietly elegant building, despite its brash, gold-lettered awning and liveried doormen who greeted residents and visitors alike with a simple "Sir" or "Madam."

"A letter for you, Sir."

With that, he retrieved an ivory-colored envelope from a silver platter and handed it to me: *Mr. Gerald Ellison, Apartment 14H.*

I thanked him. Without checking what else I might have received that day in my mailbox, I took the East-bank elevator upstairs to my fourteenth-floor apartment.

Upon entering, I placed the envelope on the dining room table with the intention of reading it as soon as I had kicked off my shoes, eased into my shearling slippers, and poured myself a cognac.

With those preliminaries accomplished, I lifted the envelope to assess its heft. It was light—no more than a single sheet of paper—and written (based on the envelope's inscription) in an elegant, fountain-penned hand. I assumed it was from Alice. I hadn't heard from her in several days. With a silver letter opener (shaped like a Turkish scimitar) I slashed the envelope, hungry for her words.

Dear Gerald,

As the daughter and granddaughter of military commanders, I know the hurt of receiving a brutal order. But I also know that it is sometimes necessary. According to Sun Tzu, an officer's vacillation and fussiness will sap the confidence of even the most loyal soldier. And so, forgive my bluntness, but I am leaving New York—and this is why:

You are wonderful, and I am not. You are generous and engaging, intellectually and emotionally open, and I am not. I wish I were more like you—or, at least, a better version of myself—but I am not.

I have lately discovered some things about myself and none of these discoveries makes me proud. The essential thing I've learned is that for all my apparent bravado I am at my core (or very nearly at my core) a coward. This came as a shock as I'd always assumed I owned at least a share of my family's famed bravery. But lately discovering that there are all kinds of bravery—and perhaps none so important as bravery in love—I am rethinking my long-held assumption.

Sad to say, it seems I have a problem with loving that stems from a cowardice of ego: I'm afraid to attach personally; afraid to absorb intimately. Sharing personally seems not to be my thing. Sun Tzu wrote: "If you know the enemy and know yourself, you need not fear the result of a hundred battles." I'd read that line a thousand times, always focusing on the words "know the enemy" without paying any attention to the words "know yourself," which is why, I believe, I have lost all my battles with love—and possibly the war.

I am leaving New York today. I thought I would like to be here for Election Day, but for personal and civic reasons I need to return to Three Corners. I don't know how long I'll be there. I don't know if I'll ever come back.

You have been a wonderful friend. Perhaps we'll meet again. I just don't know. Please send me your bill for the report. Given the new circumstances, I think it's only fair. I have reviewed the report twice. It's very thorough, as I knew it would be.

Thank you. For everything.

Alice Bouchet

Gerald Ellison

Each word a hammer blow—my heart, the anvil.

During that thundering torture, I learned more about myself than I had in twenty years. I saw—with brutal clarity—that I'd been counting on her affection, even praying for it; that I'd prized her intelligence and innocence like some rare and precious mineral. That she seemed to like me only made the situation worse.

I shredded the letter and incinerated the shreds, destroying all evidence of what might have been.

Alice Bouchet

I'd been vague with Gerald, writing that I had to return to Three Corners *for personal and civic reasons*. But I was no longer vague in my own mind, in my own heart. For I saw, in retrospect, that New York had been an impossible challenge for Allen—and still he had come for me. So now it was time for me to return the favor: to lay it on the line with my dear sweetheart, once and for all, on the shared home turf of our beloved town. And while there, being brave in love, I knew I must do one more thing I'd never done before: live up to my family legacy of brave leadership by voting my conscience.

Allen Briggs

It's like everything was the same and everything was different. The same because all the houses and streets were just like I left them—different because Alice wasn't there.

I didn't think Three Corners could go on without her—at least, not like it was. It was her town. She'd meant so much to Three Corners, and to me personally.

Destination Fated

Emily Schnyder
I didn't know where we were going. I didn't know what to expect. And yet, there was an inevitability about the destination, as if I'd been there before, in my dreams.

Barry Roth
"Why are we going to Newark Airport?" she asked.
"New York has three major airports. If you're going to Jersey or Manhattan, Newark is the most convenient."
"Is Jersey the same as New Jersey?"
"Yes. We're picking up a rental car at the airport and driving to Saddle Brook."

***

The flight was uneventful and quiet—but not relaxing. Emily pretended to read the inflight magazine and check her phone while I pretended to read a novel. Each of us was aware of the other's agitation.

While collecting our baggage and renting a car, we exchanged only the barest and most practical words.

Emily Schnyder
We approached our destination in relative silence. As there was no advance signage, I had only vague hints ... memories of memories ... to suggest what I would see.

Barry Roth

Saddle Brook seemed like a nice town but we found ourselves on a forlorn street (seedy homes, weedy lawns) that came to an ironic dead end.

Emily Schnyder

It was like a scene from one of my dreams … or maybe something once seen and long forgotten:

Looming ahead were two brick columns, each topped by a large, wrought-iron Star of David. The two columns were connected by an iron fence of black palings that prohibited traffic. There was no fence or obstruction outside the two columns—just an open expanse of burial plots, gravestones, and sepulchers.

Barry Roth

When I'd begun to suspect Emily's background, I'd contacted Alice. Perhaps because we had insinuated ourselves in each other's life, she'd been reasonably forthright, telling me about the cemetery and the Schnyder family plot and exactly where to find it. When I probed further (emphasizing how close Emily and I had become), she explained why she'd withheld so many secrets for so many years.

Emily Schnyder

Before arriving, Barry had contacted someone from the cemetery's main office who had sent him a map marked with X's and yellow highlight. With the unfolded map in hand, he led the way in silence.

On one of the main roads was another brick column, not as large and imposing as at the main entrance, but inlayed with a bronze plaque:

> WORKMAN'S CIRCLE
> BRANCH 219
> CEMETERY COMMITTEE
> SAMUEL SCHNYDER , PRES.
> GEORGE SEMEL, SEC.
> Z. LIPENHOLZ
> MORRIS RUSSAK
> ISAAC FREED
> KARL LEFKOWITZ

Barry Roth

I stood beside her while she examined the plaque. She stared quite a while before speaking.

"He's my grandfather."

"I know."

"How long have you known?" she asked.

"About two weeks."

"You could have told me."

"I thought you'd want to see for yourself."

Pause.

"You spoke to Alice?" she asked.

"Several times."

"How is she?"

"Not that well," I said, shaking my head. "New York hasn't entirely agreed with her. She might be coming home."

"She say anything about me?"

"A great deal…. She loves you."

"I know."

Pause.

"She tried her best," I said. "She had to make some hard decisions."

"I can imagine."

"It was hard for her too."

"You mean raising me?"

"No. She loved that part. Being a sort of mother for ten years was the best experience of her life. She said that."

"Then what was hard?"

"Your parents entrusted her with many secrets, which they spelled out in their terms of guardianship and in their will. Alice understood what your parents wanted for you and agreed to their wishes."

"Then why was it hard for her? She was doing her duty. I'd think she'd be good at that—she's done it all her life."

"It was hard because your parents accorded her some discretion."

"What does that mean?"

"According to the will, Alice could have shared your parents' secrets any time after your twenty-first birthday."

"When I left Haven House and returned to my own home?"

"Exactly."

"But she didn't."

"I know."

"She could have told me ten years ago."

"Yes."

"Then why didn't she?"

"She didn't think you were ready."

"She said that?"

"Yes."

"And what made me ready now? ... You?"

"I played a part, but it was you. You were ready."

There was a long, uncomfortable pause. I thought she might be angry.

"My parents are buried here?"

"Yes—and your grandparents ... some aunts and uncles too."

"You know the grave numbers?"

"They're all marked on the map."

"Show me. I want to see them all."

Barry Roth

We passed gravestones by the hundreds whose inscriptions were hauntingly similar: *Forever in Our Hearts ... In Loving memory ... In Memoriam ... Devoted ... Beloved ...*

I followed the plot numbers on the map until we came to row G, plots 23 and 24. The double tombstone was handsome but not unusual. We might easily have walked past had it not been for the plots' freshly trimmed grass and beautiful border of fall flowers.

Emily stood before the double grave with sentry-like attention before reading aloud her parents' names and the dates of their births and death. She then drew a sudden breath and convulsed in tears. I stepped aside to give her some privacy but she snatched my hand and drew me close that I might bear witness.

"I'm Jewish," she said, wiping her eyes with her free hand. "Like, one hundred percent Jewish?"

"Mayn yiddishe maydele."

"I can guess what that means."

With that, she raised our clasped hands to her lips and kissed the back of my hand. She then dropped my hand and stood very still, thinking her private thoughts, which she ended with these words:

"I'm surprised by the fancy gardening. So unlike them."

I smiled. I wondered if I should tell her.

"You can thank Alice," I said, quickly deciding that secrets were a thing of the past.

"She did this?"

"Some years ago, she asked the cemetery to send her a current photo of the gravesite. She thought it looked forlorn and undistinguished but wasn't sure if she should interfere. She wasn't sure what you would want."

"But she went ahead."

"She did. She endowed the cemetery with a trust to ensure the Planting and Perpetual Care of your parents' graves."

Emily shivered, then collapsed into my arms.

***

Before we left, she asked, "What's with all the little rocks on top of the gravestones?"

I said, "They're meant to soothe unquiet souls."

She looked uncomfortable, so I added, "Basically it's to show that the deceased have not been forgotten."

She gathered a few small rocks and carefully placed them on top of her parents' gravestone.

"Do you know a special Jewish prayer?" she asked.

"No. I know very little Yiddish and even less Hebrew."

"Wait—they're *two* different languages?"

"Yup."

"Jesus!"

I laughed. "Yeah … that's not gonna work."

She laughed too, then closed her eyes and said her own silent prayer.

Efficient Fate

Emily Schnyder

"What's next?" I asked.

"Sometimes fate makes it easy."

"What does that mean?"

"Sometimes things fall into place and make decisions easier."

"For instance?"

"I heard from Alice. She's left New York and returned to Three Corners. She said she could easily find a place to live until our lease arrangement is up—unless I was willing to end our swap agreement."

"She knows we both left Three Corners."

"Of course."

"She knows we went to the cemetery to visit my parents."

"She does."

"She knows we're heading to New York."

"She'll assume that."

"What say you?"

"I say, *Ever onward!*"

Lainey Roth

I learned later that Barry had fibbed, saying he'd just landed in Newark.

"What a lovely surprise!" I said. "When can you visit?"

"I need to check my apartment first. I'm sure Alice left it spotless, but I'd like to resettle in a bit."

"Let me know if you need help. I'm happy to come over."
"That's okay. We'll be fine."
Pause.
"*We'll* be fine?"
"I have a friend with me."
Pause.
"A female friend?"
"Yes."
A gift from God! My Barry is coming home—and he's bringing a girl!
"What's her name?"
"Emily."
"Lovely! What's her last name?"
"That's enough of the name game, Lainey."
Okay, life isn't perfect. Maybe her last name is Abdullah or Clooney or Martinez. Whatever, I'm sure she's wonderful.

Morris Fine

Lainey told me that her son Barry was in town and that I should return to my own place for a few days—maybe longer. I was hurt, but didn't say so. I wanted to meet Barry. I wanted to know him and wanted him to know me. Why couldn't Lainey see that?

Lainey Roth

Morris was a dear. Lately he'd been so consistently considerate, I thought it might be a permanent change in his nature. Well, maybe nature can't really be changed—but habits can, I supposed. Anyway, when I mentioned that Barry was in town, his mood seemed dour, so I banished him temporarily. Really, I wanted to have Barry all to myself. Emily too.

Nurse Jacqueline

Jacqueline
I heard *zing* ... *thwack* ... a scream ... and thought: *Lord, what have I done?*
I couldn't take it back. I knew that. *But what to do?*
I wanted to run ... from Three Corners ... from the scream ...

Squirrel Evans
I heard ... *zing* ... *thwack* ... then the birch beside me exploded, bark flying like shrapnel—*my eyes!*

Jacqueline
I couldn't leave him. It didn't matter what I'd done. He was my man, my life, my future. *I'm comin', Squirrel!*

Squirrel Evans
"I'm hit! I've been shot."
"Let me see."
"I can't ... my eyes!"
Pause.
"Now, you listen. You ain't been shot. I shot the damn tree next to you. You just got somethin' in your eye."

Gavin Lissome
I knew what Squirrel had done and what Jacqueline was doing for Squirrel, and it got me thinking about me and

Brenda. For sure, Jacqueline had been wrong to shoot so close to Squirrel and in such a hurry. She might have taken out his eye or even killed him. As it was, a piece of splintered bark had tore into Squirrel's right eye and Jacqueline had to drive him—in Squirrel's own pickup, which he'd never let her drive before—all the way to St. Louis to see a specialist. Anyway, he didn't lose the eye but had to wear a special patch for a month. After that, his injured eye was generally okay, except when it came to reading. Reading gave him a bad headache, which made sorting the mail a big problem. I think that's when Squirrel found out what he really had in Jacqueline. All those years of her helping him sort the mail came in handy. For two months after the accident—if that's what you want to call it—she sorted the mail and accompanied him on his delivery rounds, Squirrel giving her pointers and such, so they were able to deliver the weekday mail without a single mistake.

Had Jacqueline not been there to help, the mayor might have had to call in someone from Marion—or even farther. And, let's be honest, once a new person gets to doing your job, you never feel like it's entirely yours anymore. So Squirrel knew that Jacqueline had saved his job, and likely his eye too. In fact, that's what the doctor said to them both when she drove Squirrel back to St. Louis for a check-up: that he couldn't have done a better job, dressing and caring for Squirrel's wound. That made Jacqueline mighty proud. In fact, she felt so good about helping him, and so competent driving his truck all the way back home, she suggested that she should also help him with the *Courier*, which Squirrel had neglected to publish during the two months his eye was recovering.

Seeing Jacqueline and Squirrel pull together like a pair of happy oxen made me think of me and Brenda. Now, I have something to say—and it's the sorest thing I ever admitted: I knew Brenda had messed around with Billy Acers, bartender of the Red, White, and Brew. I knew, but it didn't really bother me ... until I saw how close and happy Jacqueline and Squirrel had become. Then I saw what I was missing and I started looking at Brenda like I used to—like the pretty girl I took to St. Louis for the live theater show and champagne dinner. Thing is, I didn't know what to do about my revived feelings. But one inspired day, I visited Golden Orchard and bought the biggest bouquet of fresh flowers I could carry. When I arrived home, Brenda was watching TV and I just handed her the flowers and told her what I'd been thinking. She shut the TV and gave me her full attention.

Brenda Lissome

Someone famous once said "Timing is everything" and I think that person was a genius. Just look at me and Gavin. For a really long time we were like two ships passing on the street and then one day Gavin seemed to remember who I am and all of a sudden he's all attentive and romantic like when we were younger. I liked it. And I knew he wasn't playing me, like he did when he wanted someone's business or a favor. I could tell he was acting genuine.

And he never let on about Billy—though I knew he knew. He knew everything, and what he didn't know, Squirrel did—and Squirrel told him everything. But Gavin didn't make me squirm or lie. He behaved like a real gentleman. He just wanted to know what I was thinking, which I thought was just wonderful. I didn't think it could get much better. But then he suggested that we walk to the school together on Election Day and cast our votes as a couple. And afterwards, when he was finished shaking hands and taking pictures, we took a leisurely stroll towards our house, the nicest house in Three Corners (except, maybe, for Haven House) and he asked if I would like to have a baby someday. I told him I'd have to think real hard about it—but inside I was smiling ear to ear.

Electric Expectancy

Allen Briggs

I received another New York postcard from Alice. But this one was different. Her handwriting was the same but tiny this time, like it was scaled down, like she'd had a lot to say but felt cramped for space. I suppose she could have written a regular letter or sent an email—or even called me on the phone.

Whatever her reasons for sending a postcard, I was pretty sure guilt played a part. But I didn't care. I forgave her. Past was past and Alice was coming home. She said she and Barry had voided their agreement and she was returning to Three Corners ... to Haven House ... to the museum ... to me. Yeah, she said that, and I have the proof. It was the only postcard she sent from New York that I kept.

Alice Bouchet

I arrived home on the morning of Election Day. School was closed, the museum was closed, but the town was very much alive, as if some electric expectancy hung in the air.

My beautiful home, my haven, was spotlessly perfect—just as I'd left it. I wasn't sure whom to thank—Barry, Allen ... perhaps both.

When I sat to have my morning coffee, I saw a rose (one of my own, picked from my very own garden) standing in a freshly filled vase. The lone rose seemed proud of its boldness, as if making a declaration only another lone rose might understand.

Allen Briggs

Alice called me at exactly nine a.m.

"What time you planning to vote?" she asked.

Just like that. No how-do-you-do ... no reference to New York ... just right down to business.

"I have a busy day," I said.

"What's on your plate?"

"Oh, I have this, that, and the other thing."

"I figured as much. But when would you like to vote?"

"When would you like to vote?"

"What I'd like to do is saunter down Main Street and arrive just as the clock strikes High Noon."

"You planning a showdown?" I asked.

"Something like that. Care to join me?"

Alice Bouchet

I knew I loved Allen and I knew he loved me. We had the stuff of love in our hearts, even if we lacked the gumption and good sense to express it. But New York had changed us both—taught us things about ourselves—reminded us who we really are and what each of us really wanted.

I was certainly happy I'd made the trip. I'd met Lainey and knew we'd be friends 'til the end of days. And I'd met Gerald (a brilliant, darling gentleman), who'd helped me see the future of my museum—and thus, the future of Three Corners.

I'd loved New York, but I was glad to be home. And if I never eat another bite of Cuban-Chinese, my tongue will forever savor its fantastic fusion flavors. And if I never hear another shimmy-shaking note of salsa, I will forever remember the Sounds of Brazil and the thrill of Gerald's fingers on the back of my naked shoulders as we danced in the shadows.

It had all been so lovely. It just wasn't for me and I think I knew that, even then. Sadly, I'd needed to see and feel New York through Allen's eyes to confirm my intuition ... which is why I'd lured him away from Three Corners (away from his every comfort and happy familiarity) and dropped him into the city's maelstrom, even when I knew for almost certain that he would founder.... Oh, Allen, I'm so sorry!

Allen Briggs

It wasn't until I was home again (and saw everywhere the facts of the life we'd shared) that I knew for deep certain what Alice meant to me. Haven House ... Freedom Hall ... the diner ... the school ... the Post Office—this was our life, together.

Alice Bouchet

I asked him to pick me up at 11:30. I'd never said that before, *pick me up,* like it was a date, which it was—in my mind.

Allen Briggs

She was waiting for me on the front veranda, almost directly behind the Honor Stone, wearing a new dress. It was different, like something a younger woman might wear to a fancy cocktail party. She must have bought it in New York. I hated it.

"You like it?" she asked, twirling like some ballerina.

Thank God, no one was watching.

"It's beautiful."

She came down the steps and stood close enough to whisper:
"Thank you for the rose."
"I plucked it from your garden," I whispered back.
"I know that."
Pause.
"I also plucked the rose I gave you on prom night."
"Yes," she whispered. "I've always known that."

Alice Bouchet

I'm pretty sure I'd been born friendly and outgoing, but being a Bouchet—and the Commander's daughter—I'd not been encouraged to mix with people, unless they were special friends of the family, held important positions, or were the children of the town's leaders, like the mayor or principal. By the time I was a teen, I knew people talked about me and pointed, and not always in a nice way.

***

My walk down Main Street was calculated to catch people's attention, especially Allen's. I was used to walking slightly ahead of him; by walking beside him—in sync, step for step—I hoped to signal a change in our relationship.

Allen Briggs

There was something different about her walk that day. Whether she'd slowed down or I'd speeded up, I felt—for the first time—like we were on an equal footing.

Strange thought: When she used to walk slightly ahead of me, I was used to seeing her hand hanging at her side, and while I knew it was a strong and capable hand, it sometimes struck me as a useless appendage, hanging there all by itself, doing nothing. That day, as we marched down Main Street together, I wondered what would happen if I touched her hand and held it.

Alice Bouchet

People were walking on both sides of the street, looking our way and smiling. A few called out "Hi there!" or "Good to have you back!"

With so much bonhomie in the air, I sensed Allen might try to take my hand, but with him waving with his left and saluting with his right, both his hands were busy.

Allen Briggs

It wasn't easy. What with keeping pace and greeting folks coming and going, I felt like a marching tin soldier. I just wanted some time alone with Alice ... or just not so many people watching ... just in case I reached for her hand.

Alice Bouchet

Pastor Pitchford, Reverend Morgan, and Father Steele passed like an ecumenical parade. Behind them strolled two good friends, the mayor and doctor (one of whom was suspected of being gay, though opinions differed as to which). They were followed by Three Corners' three beauties—Melissa, Regan, and Darla—in outfits they might have saved for Easter Sunday.

I never liked those girls for the many cruel ways they'd disrespected Jacqueline and Emily, but on this day I gave them all a wide smile. You see, I was in a good mood, made happy by my stylish new dress (chosen by Lainey) … my hip new haircut (a going-away present from Lainey) … the promise of my new relationship with Allen … the prospect of redesigning and expanding Freedom Hall … and the thrilling expectation of voting my personal principles for the first time.

Allen Briggs

I knew the dress was new and daring, but there was something else and I couldn't put my finger on it until a strong breeze blew our way and I saw her hair respond in a single, undulating wave, like a murmuration of starlings—something else Alice had taught me. I liked her new hair. The dress was growing on me.

Alice Bouchet

Despite my good mood, there was a dull pain in that part of my heart where I stored my feelings for Emily: so much like a young sister when I first met her … so much like a daughter when she lived ten years with me in Haven House. Her absence was a painful void.

Allen Briggs

Holidays were a big thing in our town. Fourth of July was big. Christmas and Easter were big too. But nothing brought us all together like Election Day. I mean, everyone had a house and a backyard … and the town had three churches … but we had only one polling site—and that was the lobby of Courier Day, where we'd all gone to school. On Election Day we all came together, congratulating ourselves for being a group of united, civically responsible Americans.

Alice Bouchet

That year, casting my vote was more freeing than any other act I can remember. It didn't matter that my vote was anonymous. Going against the deep grain of my town's collective conscience returned me to my true individualistic self. It gave me back my confidence, reinvigorated my truest personal principles. When the votes were counted, I knew at least one—mine—would challenge the perfect unanimity of Three Corners' conservative claim.

Allen Briggs

I hadn't thought much about how I would vote. I mean, I knew what I would do, it just hurt my head to think about it. Thing is, I faced a personal quandary. Four years earlier I knew our candidate was bat-shit crazy ... but our museum was still new and flourishing and I didn't want to be the one to jinx it by ruining our town's perfect voting record, so I submitted a blank ballot ... which is what I thought Alice must have done too, but we never did discuss it. Still, it left a bad taste in my mouth. Not because of how we had voted, but because we hadn't felt close enough to share our feelings.

Alice Bouchet

I pushed my ballot into the strongbox like I was throwing down a gauntlet, then looked about to see who might pick up my challenge. But there was no response, no protest. Just my gathered fellow townspeople, smiling and respectful.

I needed to get away. I couldn't bear their optimistic camaraderie.

"Come back with me," I said to Allen, as soon as we were outside the school doors. "I'll make us an early dinner. We have lots to catch up on."

Allen Briggs

"Sounds lovely," I said. "Thank you."

We walked side by side, our synced pace already feeling more natural. I imagined her hand dangling between us, but I let it be.

"Do you want to know how I voted?" I asked.

"You don't have to tell me," she said, without turning to face me. "You don't have to tell anyone."

"I know that. It's sacredly private, which is why I want to share it with you: I voted Democrat for the first time in my life…. And you?"

We had just reached the steps of Haven House. I'd trimmed the bushes a few days earlier, so the Honor Stone showed proudly.

"Glad to hear it," she said, turning to face me. "Politics makes strange bedfellows."

That stopped me in my tracks.

I caught her expression and she seemed as shocked as I was, maybe more.

Alice Bouchet

A slip of the tongue. But I wouldn't take it back and I sure as heck wasn't going to explain. Instead, I turned on the faucet. Over the sound of rushing water I said, "It felt wonderful to vote my conscience."

Allen did not refer to my slip. He protected me, as he always did. Maybe himself too.

"I thought I'd be nervous," he said, picking up the dropped thread. "Like something dramatic would happen if I voted

Democrat. But nothing happened. The sky didn't fall."

I shut the water and turned to face him.

"Were you actually nervous?"

"I was ... but not as nervous as when I asked your father if I could take you to the prom. That was the most nervous I've ever been."

"But you did it."

"I did."

"And you voted your conscience today."

"I did."

"Me too."

Pause.

"I think it's important to face the things that frighten us," I said.

"I agree," he said. "And I like this honest talking."

"Me too," I said. "I'm taking cues from you."

"From me?"

"You've taught me a lot. Especially this year."

"I didn't think I could ever teach you anything, Alice."

"Well, you have—and I'm grateful."

Pause.

He said, "Since we're being so honest, I have a question."

"Fire away," I said, feeling nervous, vulnerable ... hopeful.

"Alright," he said, straightening his shoulders. "You here to stay?"

This was it. The moment I'd waited for all my life.

Allen Briggs

"Look out the window," she said, indicating the bay window that faced Main Street. "See Barry's red car? He asked me to return it to the dealer. But I'm not going to."

"Why not?" I asked, excited by her daring.

"I like it. I'm going to keep it."

"Just like that?"

"Yup. I bought it from Barry. Now it's my car. Or, I should say—our car. I have a set of keys for you."

She picked up a set of keys that had been on the table and handed them to me. For the first time in my life I met her gaze firmly, lovingly, and with my large strong hand clasped hers, keys and all.

Flickering Illuminations

Emily Schnyder

My reaction to New York was different than Allen's or Alice's. Aside from the fact that we three are very different persons, I looked at the city as my possible new home.

Having arrived the day before Election Day, Barry suggested we stay local, keeping to the Lower East Side, taking it slowly.

Barry Roth

Emily needed to know what Alice had told me. She needed to know who her parents were and why they died as they did. I felt she should know all this before she met my mother and we all went to vote together.

Emily Schnyder

We passed the Tenement Museum, Katz's Deli, and a hundred more reminders that the Lower East Side was once the epicenter of America's Jewish immigrant culture. According to Barry, most American Jews could trace their heritage to this small neighborhood—only five hundred acres, about the same size as Three Corners. On another day I would have peppered him with a hundred questions, but on this day I was preoccupied:

"Tell me about my parents."

Barry Roth

Almost every factual thing I knew about Emily's parents

I'd learned from Alice. Emily had shared with me what she knew (or remembered, or thought she remembered), but those were mostly shadowy recollections, nightmarish loops, emotional associations—all intensely suggestive and highly subjective.

At the time, I hadn't yet seen any pertinent documents—no Schnyder immigration records or birth certificates; no will or codicils; no Workman Circle membership or cemetery contract. I had only Alice's limited testimony (based on her remembered conversations with Emily's parents), her recollection of the will (as it pertained to her), and her tenuous understanding of those players—major and minor—who'd been involved in the suspicious death and cover-up of five persons in Marion and Three Corners nearly twenty years earlier.

Emily Schnyder

We were sitting in the lower level of Tijuana Picnic, one of Barry's favorite neighborhood restaurants. It looked and felt like a Mariachi grotto. Before we ordered, the waiter brought us a basket of black chips and a three-legged stone bowl filled with a chunky green paste. Barry explained all I needed to know about guacamole and tortilla. I ate a few guac-laden chips and then said, smiling, "Okay, let's get the ball rolling. Tell me about my parents."

My good cheer was fake. So was my appetite for the chips and dip. But I needed to keep my fingers and face busy lest Barry see the signs of my frantic nerves.

Barry Roth

I began with Alice's earliest recollections of accompanying her own mother to the Schnyder home and tailor shop. Though her mother had told her that the house had been owned by tailors for many years, Alice had no recollection of ever meeting Emily's grandparents.

Emily Schnyder

I'd never considered how many times my parents might have spoken to Alice or how much they might have revealed. It must have been quite a lot because Barry knew many things I didn't. For instance, he knew my paternal great-grandparents had emigrated from Ukraine and been processed at Ellis Island around 1900. He knew my great-grandfather had been confident of being admitted because he and his family had been healthy and he'd had a good trade. Barry also knew this inciting fact: When my great-grandfather boldly wrote *TAILOR* on his application for citizenship, the clerk emitted a loud groan and said, "New York already has a thousand Jewish tailors. What else can you do?"

According to Barry (who had it from Alice), my great-grandfather was unprepared for what he felt was a desperate situation. He had fully intended to provide for his family (a wife, two children—another on the way) by practicing the ancient Schnyder tradition of tailoring.

Feeling suddenly bereft of purpose and plan, my great-grandfather pleaded desperately with the American officials, claiming he'd been the head of a legendary family of tailors, famous for making the uniforms worn by the cadets who serve Czar Nicholas II.

Barry Roth

Though short on details, Alice had made the all-important

point that Emily's great-grandfather was referred to someone who knew someone who made arrangements for Mr. Schnyder and his family to move to Three Corners in order to accept the important job of making and maintaining uniforms for the cadets and officers of the George Long Military Institute.

Emily Schnyder

Even with a spotty script, Barry was a steady and reliable narrator. I, however, was a mess of a listener. All the while he spoke, revealing long-suppressed facts of my backstory, I was distracted by the flickering illuminations in my brain.

Barry Roth

I thought it best to build on that first major scene: Alice as a young woman, talking business with the parents, each sitting at a wide work table dominated by a sewing machine and spindles ... bolts of fabric ... buttons ... satin stripes ... Emily in the shadows between them, playing with the pretty scraps.

Emily Schnyder

That's how I remember them: huddled at their desks or bent over coffee cups at the kitchen table ... doors locked ... blinds lowered on Sunday mornings.

Barry Roth

"Funny you mention that. Alice had been curious about the Sunday morning blinds and asked your parents about them."

"Really? What did they say?"

"Care to guess?"

Emily shrugged. "I guess they didn't want anyone to see them at home while everyone else was coming or going to church."

"That makes sense—but not quite right."

"They were determined to hold onto their Jewishness in secret?"

"Only partially true. Remember, they worked on Saturday, the Jewish sabbath, and took off Sunday—like everyone else."

"Then why were they so careful about the Sunday morning blinds?"

Emily Schnyder

The explanation made no sense. Or it made crazy sense, like my whole childhood. It seems my parents loved their lazy Sunday breakfasts but did not want anyone to know they ate bacon and eggs. Imagine that. The third generation of a living lie—an unsuspected Jewish ghetto in the heart of a conservative Christian town—but they didn't want anyone to know they ate bacon!

"But no one knew we were Jews. Why would anyone care what we ate?"

"Your parents could not bear to be thought of as bad Jews."

"But they weren't thought of as Jews at all."

"Better that than bad Jews."

I didn't understand. Then again, I'd only been a Jew for about ten minutes.

Barry Roth

We discussed how the closed blinds insulated her family.

"But I went to church dances ... bake sales ... even chorus."

"Your parents weren't opposed to secular activities."

"Just the religious ones."

"Exactly."

"But they were impossible to separate," she said.

"I'm sure."

"So, what was their rule of thumb?"

"They didn't have one. They took it one case at a time."

"Oy. That must have been crazy hard," she said.

Emily Schnyder

According to what Alice had told Barry who told me, I was very young when my parents last observed a major Jewish holiday behind drawn blinds and dimmed lights, as if we three were a secret cabal.

"I remember whispered prayers ... silver winecups ... candles. But it's all so vague. Why don't I remember more? What's wrong with me?"

I didn't want to cry but the tears came anyway.

"There's nothing wrong with you."

"Then why don't I remember more?"

Barry Roth

"Your parents were very careful. Besides, it all came to an end around your tenth birthday."

"That's when I met Alice."

"Your parents were uncomfortable with your friendship."

"How do you know?"

"Alice told me."

"What were they afraid of?"

"It seemed a bit much to them. You were just ten and she was twenty. They wondered why she should take such an interest in you."

"That doesn't seem fair."

"Well, there's more to it."

"Tell me."

"By the time you two were getting acquainted, Alice was in charge of the college's uniforms. That made her responsible for the bulk of your parents' tailoring business."

"Wasn't it good that she took an interest in me?"

"Eventually, they saw it that way. But at first, they were worried you might say something … reveal something … that might hurt their business."

"I was only ten. What could I have possibly revealed?"

"That you and your family were Jewish."

"But I didn't know it at the time."

"You knew of their special *celebrations*."

"I suppose. But I didn't know we were Jewish. I just thought we were odd."

"Well, your parents did not want to take chances. They needed Alice's business to survive, so they made two decisions. One was to let her be your friend."

"And the other?"

"To stop observing the Jewish holidays."

"But why?"

"They wanted you to forget. What you knew was too dangerous—now that Alice was both your friend and their business broker."

Emily seemed stunned.

"So … Alice robbed me of my Jewish heritage."

"That's unfair."

"Why?"

"Your parents knew you were lonely and saw Alice as a special friend and mentor. Eventually, they came to really like and respect her. So much so, they drew up a will that named her as your guardian."

"I suppose there wasn't anyone else."

"That may have been true. Nevertheless, they really respected and trusted her."

"What did the will say?"

"I haven't seen it. But according to Alice, it stipulated that she would draw from your parents' savings to pay for the upkeep of their home and for your general well-being. The will also stipulated that on your twenty-first birthday you would assume financial responsibility for your home and resume living there."

"I knew all that. What don't I know?"

"The will instructed Alice to tell you about your Jewish heritage, which your parents spelled out in the will's longest codicil."

"She never did that."

"I know."

"She kept my Jewishness from me."

"That's true. But in fairness, the will did not stipulate *when* she should tell you."

"What possible reason could she have had for waiting?"

"I'm not sure, but I can guess."

"Go ahead. I want to hear."

"Okay. Consider this: By your own admission, you've always been an odd duck. When your parents died, you were an orphaned odd duck whose life had been entrusted to Alice Bouchet—something of an odd duck herself—except she was also the queen of Three Corners and you were going to live with her in her castle."

"Not much of a castle, but go on."

"Alright. During your decade in Haven House, the Long Military Institute began to fail. By your last year, the tailoring business was pretty much kaput. Alice and some local tailors addressed the occasional job."

"So sad. I can't help think my parents' deaths ruined the college."

"That's your guilt talking."

"I know."

I wanted to touch her hand and soothe her—but I needed to finish.

"So, you turn twenty-one and Alice shows you the door."

"That's what it felt like."

"I'm sure. But she had no choice—according to the will."

"Still—"

"Still, you had to return to your childhood home. Only, by then your life had completely changed. Your parents were gone. Their business was gone. You had to reinvent yourself while living alone—in a town that was never friendly to you. Can you see why Alice didn't mention you're Jewish?"

A long pause.

I was worried about her. How much could she take? And we still hadn't addressed the elephant in the room.

"We've got to talk about the eggs."

The Eggs

Emily Schnyder
When I first heard he'd tried to wrest the sword from the Honor Stone and bronco-bust our most sacred totem, I thought he must be crazy. But the next day, when I read the interview in which he revealed himself as someone daringly different, I thought, *Maybe he's my kind of crazy.*

As it turned out, we are well suited. Barry gets me and I get him. So I was shocked when out of nowhere he started talking about eggs.

Barry Roth
"Things aren't always what they seem. Changes in light, time, point of view ... can all influence how we see things."

"You talking eggs or life?"

"Both. In your case I think they're strangely related."

I must have hit a nerve. She stood up, looked about, then sat back down.

"What are you saying?"

"Look, everyone's perspective is uniquely skewed. But new points of view can improve understanding."

"My perspective is skewed?"

"Let's just say your family had a very unique perspective."

"They weren't weird, if that's what you're saying. They were good parents."

Again, she started to cry. I was happy we were alone in the grotto.

"Emily, your grandparents and parents were strangers in a strange land. Understandably, they were distrustful, so they kept secrets—even from you. And you were just a child."

Emily Schnyder

"I'm not sure what you're saying," I said.

"What I'm saying is that it's all connected."

"What's all connected?"

"All your darkest moments seem to involve eggs—which relate to your parents' death—which still haunts you with a terrible guilt."

Barry Roth

She just didn't see it. It was like asking her to see black stitching in a black garment in a blacked-out room.

I had to build a case, example by example, and make the connections starkly obvious. I started with the earliest example I remembered.

"You painted an Easter egg against your parents' wishes. Only, because you'd never done it before—having been raised outside the Easter tradition—you didn't know to use a hardboiled egg. When your teacher held up your beautifully painted egg for everyone to see, she inadvertently crushed it. The exploding ooze and laughter horrified you."

"I was humiliated…. It was one of the worse moments of my life."

"I know. I'm so sorry."

Pause.

"Do you remember other strange moments dealing with eggs?" I asked.

"No. Not off the top of my head."

"Well, I do."

She just shrugged, looking sad.

"Do you remember our Passover seder?"

"I think so. Sure."

"Do you remember discussing the symbolism of dipping the egg in the saltwater, commemorating the tears of our ancestors during their desert Exodus?"

"I don't think so. Maybe."

"You bobbled the hardboiled egg and freaked out when you dropped it—expecting it to break."

"I don't recall."

There was a pause. I didn't want to push her.

"Do you remember stopping at the fresh egg stand on the way to Marion?"

"I remember a nice old couple selling handmade trivets and baskets."

"You don't remember staring at the open boxes of eggs, unable to decide which to buy?"

"No. I don't remember that."

"Do you remember driving home in silence and when we arrived, you simply said, 'Let's go to my place. I'll make brunch.'"

"Sorry. Doesn't ring a bell."

"Do you remember showing me around your home? You were proud of all the changes you'd made."

"Yeah. I sorta remember that."

"Do you remember the brunch? Do you remember what happened?"

She shrugged. She didn't ask what happened.

"You offered to make omelets. You asked if I like bacon."

Another shrug.

"Do you remember your mother's blue mixing bowl?"
"It was a wedding present. It's beautiful."
"Do you remember what happened to it?"

Cause of Death: Unknown

Emily Schnyder

For ten years, guilt and fear prevented me from returning alone to my childhood home. As my twenty-first birthday approached, Alice increased my readiness training with hours of reconnaissance runs, practice sorties, and battle-tested Sun Tzu strategies.

"You're ready as you'll ever be," she said three days before my birthday.

"I don't feel ready."

"Trust yourself. Trust your training."

Three days later, in the early evening, Alice accompanied me to within a block of my old home. She gave me a motherly hug, then kissed the top of my head as if anointing me.

"See you tomorrow."

I assumed she'd return to Haven House, where she'd be alone for the first time in ten years.

***

I stood a while on my front porch, facing my front door, wavering between courage and cowardice. Finally, having cleared my mind (if only for an instant), I forged ahead.

Once inside (avoiding the kitchen and bathroom), I timidly climbed the creaky stairs and on reaching the wooden landing leapt into my old room, dove onto my childhood bed, and cowered there under a tent of blankets, recollecting (through the long, impenetrable hours of the black night) what it had been like to sit on the hard stairs as a twelve-year-old, paralyzed by my parents' desperate howls.

Barry Roth

"It wasn't your fault."
"I didn't help them."
"There was nothing you could do."
Silence.
"I mean—really, factually—it wasn't your fault. You weren't responsible for your parents' deaths. But I know who was."

Emily Schnyder

My brain fluttered like a shaken snow globe.
"Who?"

Barry Roth

"It's complicated."
"Spill it. Just say the damn name."
"You need more narrative. More context."
"No! I have my rights. It's my story!"
"You just want me to spill?"
"Spill it!"
"Fine. Gavin Lissome."

Emily Schnyder

I never expected it. At the same time, it made perfect sense. In fact, as I considered it just then, it seemed the only name possible.

Barry Roth

I did my best to piece together a narrative that began at the beginning and moved ahead sequentially, relying on what I'd learned from Alice and Allen, Jacqueline and Squirrel, and everyone else I'd come to know during my time in Three Corners.

Sometimes I relied on specific narrative markers and cues to stay on track, to continue making the story credible and compelling: "Gavin Lissome was the richest man in town. He owned the gas station, the grocery store ... another gas station in Marion ... and probably more."

"I know. I was born and raised there, remember?"

"Bear with me, please."

"Okay. Go on."

"Because he was the richest man in town, he was very influential. He made friends with everyone he thought important—and when that wasn't possible, or desirable, he did favors for people so they'd be in his debt."

"So, everyone owed him."

"Pretty much."

"But I never thought he was a bad man."

"I never said he was."

"And yet, he killed my parents."

"Whoa, that's a big leap."

"Well, that's what you said. So, did he or didn't he?"

"Let me finish telling the story, then you decide."

Emily Schnyder

Barry took his sweet time, laying out the story in its proper order, perhaps thinking of a novel he'd like to write. But all I wanted was the climax, the truth: some target for my grief and pain.

***

Most of what Barry knew he'd learned from Jacqueline, who knew something saucy about everyone in town from helping Squirrel sort and deliver the morning mail … waitressing at the diner … and through her friendship with Brenda Lissome. Brenda got her gossip from her husband Gavin, but her best scuttlebutt had come from her boyfriend, Billy Acers, bartender of the Red, White, and Brew, who'd overhear the town's sins, plots, and confessions, especially when the place was uncrowded and he'd lower the whirring fan and interfering music so as to better eavesdrop.

***

Eventually, Barry got to the heart of the matter: Gavin's role in the death of my parents. Ironically, this information came mostly from Alice, who might have been left in the dark had Gavin not applied to the Town Council for a large loan to purchase a pair of new tanks to replace the ones that had corroded and ruptured, loosing thousands of gallons of gasoline … which eventually contaminated the egg farm in Marion.

Emily Schnyder
"How did I never hear about this?"
"They buried the lead. In fact, they buried the whole story."
"Who's *they*?"
"Everyone involved."
"Everyone who? Everyone Gavin asked for help? Everyone who owed him a favor?"

"It wasn't always a favor. Those who knew saw a personal advantage in killing the story."

"Why? Because my parents were Jewish?"

"That had nothing to do with it. No one knew your parents were Jewish—except Alice."

"Then why bury the story?"

"Because Gavin's wealth was tied up in the town's success. If he went down, the town might seriously suffer."

"So, my parents' death is—a nonstory? Like it never happened?"

"I suppose."

"And yet, it's a fact that they died ... and didn't just die ... they were killed. And Gavin was chiefly responsible."

"Alice thinks at least three other people died from what was likely egg poisoning."

"Around the same time?"

"Yes."

"Who else?"

"I think another couple in Marion ... and Mavis Wilson."

"Didn't she work at the diner?"

"She and her husband owned the diner."

"I remember. They helped Jacqueline after her father died."

"That's right, and some years later, they hired her to work in the diner. Mavis was like a mother to her. Apparently, her real mother had run off with some army stranger when she was quite young."

"So, Mavis—Jacqueline's sort of stepmother—also died of poisoned eggs?"

I could see her mind running with the coincidence.

"That's the idea," I said. "There were at least five similar deaths, but no connection was ever proved."

"How can five similar deaths not be investigated? Weren't there accusations? Charges?"

"There were at least five coroner's reports, but in each case the cause of death was noted as heart attack, old age—or just *Unknown*."

"That's it?"

"No one requested an autopsy, so the coroner just rubber-stamped each case and filed it away."

"Not even a fine?"

"Gavin insisted on a clean slate. Even a small fine would have indicated a degree of culpability. Anyway, that's what Alice said."

"Still, how the hell did he skate so entirely?"

"Three Corners is a small town. One mayor, one sheriff, one doctor—and they all sit on the Town Council."

"Still—?"

"Alice thinks Gavin sensed his potential liability and acted quickly to dig out the old tanks … clean the spill … fill in the hole … cement it over … and install two brand new tanks nearby."

"But the oil had already spilled."

"Yes."

"So the damage was done."

"Yes."

"What about the doctor and the coroner? Where were their ethics in all this?"

"Interestingly—in the case of your parents—they had strict instructions to bury the bodies with all due haste. It's a Jewish thing."

"So, they were just following orders."

"I suppose. But they did their best to prepare your parents' bodies according to specific instructions. Alice made arrangements to have the caskets shipped to Saddle Brook, New Jersey."

Emily looked so sad.

"They were buried so far away I couldn't visit. Alice wouldn't say why."

"Did you ask?"

"I did, but she wouldn't say.... I really wanted to visit them. I was so lonely."

"I'm sorry."

She dabbed her eyes with a shredded tissue.

"I remember the funeral—sort of."

"Alice said it was a quiet service held in her backyard."

"No one was there."

"Well, some people were there."

Her eyes filled with heavy tears.

"Not one girl from school … none of our neighbors … none of my teachers—not even my art teacher, and I thought she really liked me."

She started crying again. This time it really got to me.

"But Alice and the college chaplain were there," I said. "And also Allen and Jacqueline."

Her crying subsided; she wiped her eyes and residual sniffles.

"Is that right? I don't remember. I should send a note to Allen and Jacqueline, thanking them."

"Emily, it's been twenty years."

Country Mouse, City Mouse

Lainey Roth

I remember my mother's father, my *zayde,* referring to his neighborhood tailor as his *schnyder,* so when Barry let on that that Emily's name was *Schneider* (as I imagined it), I couldn't help hoping she was Jewish.

Worse (I just couldn't help myself), I began seriously considering whether I should soon gift Barry and Emily my large and beautiful apartment or wait to see if they might actually prefer to live together in Barry's small apartment on the Lower East Side.

I gave no consideration to moving in with Morris. His apartment was large but crammed full of awards and totems commemorating his years spent saving endangered Jews. I respected his legacy, but I sure as hell didn't want to live with it.

The next day was Election Day, and while it was a momentous opportunity to defeat the current president, a terrible lying tyrant, my mind was focused mostly on Emily and her parents—my future *machatunim.*

Emily Schnyder

I'd still been reeling from the screeching and rocking of my first subway ride when Barry and I arrived at the front of his childhood home on East Seventy-Third Street, a magnificent fourteen-story apartment building with a honey-colored façade and wide brick terraces, accented with elaborate, wrought-iron railings.

We'd arrived a few minutes early and were waiting for his mother (whom Barry referred to as *Lainey*, which I still found shocking), and then she was suddenly there, walking toward us through a shallow courtyard, wearing an *ensemble* so impressively perfect (suit, scarf, sunglasses), I thought she looked like Eva Peron ... or a movie star ... like no woman I'd ever met, certainly nothing like my mother, as I remembered her.

Barry Roth

Lainey opened her arms wide and Emily fairly leapt into her embrace. After a few seconds, they separated.

"She's beautiful," Lainey proclaimed. "Come," she said, taking Emily's hand, "let's go vote."

Emily Schnyder

I was shocked when she took my hand and continued to hold it. Alice never held my hand. My mother might have, but I don't remember.

***

A quarter mile from the polling site one could feel the charged atmosphere. Lainey called the day a "once-in-a-lifetime event." Barry called it a "generational election." Both agreed it would decide the future of American democracy.

I was just glad to be away from Three Corners. I pictured Alice walking down Main Street to the polling center at Courier Day. I had a feeling Allen would be with her and that they would not be submitting blank ballots.

I imagined Jacqueline walking arm-in-arm with Squirrel, protective of her man and his bandaged eye. I never liked Squirrel—I know he never liked me—but Jacqueline would always have a warm place in my heart.

I pictured Brenda and Gavin standing together outside the school, Gavin shaking hands with everyone who mattered. Oddly, the vision offered no clarifying sense of how I really felt about him. The only thing I knew for sure was that New York was already beginning to feel like home and Barry was my best friend and partner.

Barry Roth

It seemed perfectly right—and very fortunate—that Emily should be with us on that historic day. In truth, neither Lainey nor I were particularly altruistic or even politically active. We made a show of our Election Day routine, having ritualized our participation so people would see us—and we would see ourselves—at our noble best. I said as much to Emily, who responded, "I figured that, but it's still a hell of a lot better than submitting a cowardly blank ballot."

Lainey Roth

Every once in a while I like to host a dinner party. The extensive planning makes me feel like I deserve an esteemed place in the long line of my ancestral mothers—*balabustas* all.

"Lainey, I adore you—but you are a terrible fraud."

We'd had this conversation many times. Barry knew I'd hire a cleaning lady and have the entire party catered—except for the serving of coffee and desserts, which was my opportunity to grandly display my presentation skills. He did not mind any of this. He only disputed my claim to being a balabusta.

"Honey, in this case, I'm doing all this for you."

"How so?"

"I want Emily to know what a capable Jewish mother I am—and what we might both expect from her."

Barry Roth

I needed hours alone with Lainey to tell her about my time in Three Corners and my relationship with Emily.

"Do you love her?"

Just like Lainey to cut to the chase.

I answered vaguely, something about personal issues and things to work out.

"But do you love her?"

"Did you love Bert?"

Lainey smiled. "Fair question. I thought we could work out our issues, but no, I didn't love him—not really."

Emily Schnyder

I knew I loved Barry. Everything about him fascinated me. He was smart and endlessly interesting. He had a good heart, and I knew he would make a great husband and father. I said all this to Lainey, who'd asked me to lunch.

"How can you be so sure?" she asked, a slight smile betraying her happiness.

"Because he gets me ... and I get him. It's a first for us both."

"You know, he dated a lot of women."

"I know. But he never talks about them. They must have bored him. Anyway, they're all gone."

"But how do you know you're a good match?"

"We talk about everything. We talk until we fall asleep. We talk in our sleep. We wake up talking."

Lainey laughed. "Talking is a great start, but marriage takes a great deal of resolve and commitment."

"We know that. We're both strong."

"How strong?"

"We're like a pair of thorny capers, a plant native to Jerusalem and famous for its endurance. Cut down to its roots, it still survives."

Lainey smiled in a satisfied way and then chose another tack: "Do you worry that you're Country Mouse and he's City Mouse?"

"We've talked about that. We may have to compromise."

"What does that mean?" she asked, looking suddenly nervous.

"It may mean Brooklyn or Queens."

Lainey Roth

I remembered my nightmare: Barry marrying an Israeli beauty and raising a brood of olive-skinned darlings who had to be reminded who I was whenever I visited their hilly West Bank settlement.

I didn't want my grandchildren calling me *Lainey*. I wanted to be called *Grandma*. And I wanted them to run and hug me when I visited, which I hoped would be often.

Brooklyn or Queens would be fine. In fact, they had logistical advantages, as I could continue living in my beautiful, beloved apartment and visit them when I liked.

A few weeks later I asked Morris to move back in with me. He was good company; I gave him that.

Barry Roth

What a year. Lainey had answered an unsolicited letter from some lady in the Midwest and so many lives were changed forever. That's the beauty of life, as I see it: the randomness ... the chance opportunities ... the surprise influences ... the unlikely meetings and partnerships—and the opportunity to make art out of it all.

Of course, we didn't know how it would all play out, but Emily and I pledged to be honest and true—and to never, ever, submit a blank ballot.

The End

About the Author

Steven Jay Griffel is the author of five previous novels that are part of his David Grossman Series. His book, *Forty Years Later*, became an Amazon #1 Bestseller.

Made in the USA
Middletown, DE
29 November 2022

16335848R00201